TROPICAL DEPRESSION

TROPICAL
DEPRESSION

a novel of suspense

Jeffry P. Lindsay

DONALD I. FINE, INC.
New York

Copyright © 1994 by Jeffry P. Lindsay

Library of Congress Catalogue Card Number: 93-074486
ISBN: 1-55611-401-X

Manufactured in the United States of America

10 9 8 7 6 5 4 3 2 1

Designed by Irving Perkins Associates, Inc.

This novel is a work of fiction. Names, characters, places, and incidents are either the product of the author's imagination or are used fictitiously. Any resemblance to actual events, locales, organizations or persons, living or dead, is entirely coincidental and beyond the intent of either the author or publisher.

This book is dedicated, with love, to the five women in my life:

> *To Lillian, who made it probable;*
> *To Doris, who made it possible;*
> *To Susan, who made it conceivable;*
> *To Hilary, who made it inevitable;*
> *and to Hannah, who made it enjoyable.*

All my gratitude and love for making my life worth living and my book worth reading.

CHAPTER
ONE

He was standing on the dock at City Marina as I came in. He still stood there beside the ice machine as I eased into my slip, tied up, and wound up business with the day's charter.

I'd been fishing that day with a guy in his forties who ran a machine shop in Rochester and couldn't talk about anything except the Buffalo Bills. It had been an okay charter—very good, in fact, if you just wanted a chance to get away from the wife and talk about football the way this guy did. We'd hit into a few permits on the flats south of Woman Key. We got one good jump out of a tarpon, a big one. My guy had been so flabbergasted by the size and majesty of the fish he'd forgotten to bow to it and the line had snapped. That happens maybe four times out of five, but he didn't seem to mind. He said seeing something like that jump made the whole trip worth every penny. I wished I had that kind of outlook.

My charter was still in a good mood when he climbed off the boat, with his ears newly pink from the tropical sun. I glanced up the dock.

Roscoe just stood there, in a shadow made by the slant of the afternoon sun, over by the dockmaster's shack, nursing a Coke and watching me tie off the spring lines, hose down the boat and the fishing gear, and filet a couple of three-to-four-pound mutton snappers we'd brought in from the cut on the near side of Ballast Key. By the time my charter had climbed into his rented Buick and

headed for Duval Street and air-conditioning, I was getting curious
—and a little mad.

It didn't seem like a very nice way to act. I hadn't seen Roscoe
McAuley for almost eighteen months. Seventeen months, two
weeks and four days was the actual count. Anyway, he hadn't
changed much: he was just a hair over six feet tall and not an ounce
over 185. He was black, skin the color of shoe leather, with soft
brown eyes you wanted to trust even when you knew better. He ~
sported a thin mustache and a whiff of very expensive cologne. He
looked about as much like Kirk Douglas as a man could and still be
black.

Roscoe was a headquarters cop. What he was good at—and he
was *very* good at it—was police paperwork and politics. He had
risen far and fast in the LAPD without learning anything about
how it was on the street, out there alone in a cruiser. He would
probably go a lot further. He had a political streak in him that let
him play all the right games on an instinctive level, and he was so
smooth and sharp you could shave with his resumé.

Roscoe had been the one to try to talk me out of leaving. He
had always been good at sincerity and making you feel like duty was
a real thing, something you should care about and work hard at.
He'd had a lot to say on the subject; it hadn't been enough. I had
taken my back pay and come back to Key West.

During the first bad days of trying to think up some reason not
to swallow a bullet I had thought of this place, how I'd come here
as a kid and learned about boats and fishing. It was the only good
memory I could come up with that didn't involve Jennifer and
Melly, so I had come. I thought coming here would take me away
from all the bad memories, but of course I was wrong about that.
We all carry around inside us more than a lifetime of bad memories
and we can never outrun them. We can only change the scenery.

I thought I had done that, and then here came a big hunk of the
old scenery in the shape of Roscoe McAuley. He still just stood
there, watching me. I finished stowing the clean-up gear and
walked up toward the dockmaster's. I pushed past Roscoe without
saying anything and went in.

The air-conditioning hit me. I don't mean that figuratively.
Walking into the shack was like getting whacked on the forehead
with a two-by-four. It was over ninety outside, and close to one

hundred percent humidity, but inside the shack it was a bone-dry sixty-five degrees and the contrast had a weight to it that made your temples throb. It was like having an ice-cold waterbed dropped on you from a great height, and for a few seconds I just stood there panting and feeling my forehead shrink. Between the temperature and the darkness of the room after the heat and blinding sunlight of the flats, I couldn't move. If somebody had wanted my wallet they could have walked up and taken it from me. But they would have been pretty disappointed in my wallet.

"Billy!" came the hoarse gargle from the cluttered corner where the cash register sat in the middle of a blinding stack of shiny-wrapped candy, fishing gear, waterproof suntan lotion, floating key rings, chewing gum, sunglasses, Slim Jims, and crap.

Captain Art was on his stool in the center of the glitz heap. This was not a surprise; Captain Art lived on the stool and I had never seen him leave it during business hours. He was over sixty, over three hundred pounds, and could have been poster boy for the Skin Cancer Foundation. His dark, leathery tan, built up by a life in the outdoors, was mottled with dozens of pink blotches. If you hung his hide on the wall it would look like an enormous off-color dalmatian from a three-year-old's coloring book.

I stepped over. "Hey, Art," I said. "Any messages?"

"No messages," he said. "No charter fer tomorrow, either."

He was looking at me funny, maybe a little hurt. "What?" I asked him.

"You telling me everything, Billy?"

"No, Art," I said, "want to hear my third-grade report card? What's up?"

He shook his head, a little sad, and gave a great loose-lunged cough. He cleared his throat and spat something the size and shape of a mouse brain into the standing ashtray beside him. It made a clang like a round-bell. "You got trouble out there, Billy. He's just been standing there since right after one o'clock. What's the deal? I got a right to know if I got trouble on my dock."

"Old acquaintance, Art. He's a cop. Won't be any trouble."

Art cocked his massive wobbly head to one side and looked at me, like Jabba the Hutt imitating a parakeet. I could hear his breath rattling in and out. "Don't try and shit me. I never been wrong about something like this, Billy. I smell some trouble on that dude."

"Cop smell," I told him. "I'll get rid of him."

The phone rang, but Art looked at me for a full two seconds longer before he moved a huge, wobbling arm to answer it. "Shitwad," he mumbled. He managed to get the phone up to his face around three or four extra chins and I went for the door, grabbing a bottle of mineral water from the cooler.

I had almost gotten used to the meat-locker cold of Art's shack. So when I stepped back out onto the dock again the heat rose up from the pavement and smacked me hard. When I could breathe again I screwed the top off the bottle of water and looked to my right.

Roscoe was still standing there, hugging a pool of shade by the ice machine. His eyes were aimed down the dock now, to the channel under the bridge where one of the big party boats was coming in. I stood beside him and sipped the mineral water. Without taking his eyes off the big boat, he nodded at me.

"Hey, Billy," he said softly. "You look good. Dark." He gave his head a half-shake. "Sharp clothes, too."

Like most fishing guides who work in the blistering Florida sun all day, every day, I was wearing a pair of tattered khaki shorts and an off-white, long-sleeved shirt. The shirt was about four years old, stained with blood and other fishy effluvia. I'd gotten it at Banana Republic because it had a lot of pockets, never knowing then it would end up as my fishing guide uniform.

"You always did have a good eye for clothes, Roscoe. But that suit is a bit much for Key West. It must be murder," I said. He looked away for a few seconds and I studied him.

Always a sharp dresser, Roscoe was wearing a dark gray double-breasted number with a continental cut that must have set him back twelve hundred dollars. I could have been wrong about the price. The only place I'd ever seen one like it was on the movie moguls I'd busted—and on guys working their way into the upper levels of the LAPD, where Roscoe was inserting himself lately. I'd heard he'd even done some classes at the California Law Enforcement Command College, that dark-suited stepping-stone to Captain and beyond. They taught you all kinds of things about police command there, like choosing fabric.

Myself, I'd never had much use for that kind of suit. Of course, I'd never made Detective either, and maybe those two facts were not totally unrelated.

Roscoe shrugged. "You haven't seen me in a year and a half and you want to talk about my clothes?"

"No. I don't want to talk at all. But I told the dockmaster I'd get rid of you." Just seeing him was rubbing salt in some wounds that still felt fresh, and I didn't feel like being polite.

He nodded again, like he was expecting my bad attitude.

"You're going to have to talk to me to get rid of me, Billy." He spoke very softly, with an undertone of sad deliberation that reminded me of the last talk we'd had in L.A., before I left. It was not something I wanted to think about.

"Whatever you want to talk about, I'm not interested in, Roscoe. I'm gone. I'm out of it. I live here now. I take people fishing. I don't want anything more to do with you, and people like you. That's why I left."

I turned half away and looked down the dock to where the party boat was tying up now. A gaggle of people who had been pale this morning and were now bright red rhumbaed down the ramp and onto the dock, chattering and fumbling with sports bags stuffed with unused sunscreen and spare T-shirts. About half of them seemed to be pointing video cameras at each other.

I was watching a leathery old woman in a tank top and khaki shorts lead the way off the boat when Roscoe's soft cough yanked me back.

"I know why you left, Billy," he said in that gentle voice. "Why do you think I came all this way?"

I turned on him. I was mad. "You don't know jack shit about anything, except what's in GQ and whose butt to kiss and I don't give a good goddamn why you came all this way, I just want to see you and your goddamned suit on the next flight out of here."

"Billy—" he started, but I wasn't done yet.

"No, goddamn it, I am all the way out of it, out of anything you could possibly know about, care about or understand. Now why don't you get out of here and find an air-conditioned waiting room somewhere before your two-hundred-dollar-an-ounce cologne sweats off and you smell like a cop again."

I turned away. He had taken it pretty well, but I guess I should have expected that. He was a determined guy and would be willing to wait me out. Well, I was pretty determined nowadays, too. At least as far as forgetting Los Angeles was concerned.

Down the dock the leathery broad waved off the young mate and started fileting a big pile of grunts and lane snappers all by herself. The mate looked like the kind of eager idiot who thinks getting a job on a head boat is a legitimate way to make a living. Probably thought it would be a big help in picking up girls. I didn't blame the old woman for trying to get rid of the mate. I was sixty-five feet away and the way he hovered and oozed his cheap, tip-hungry smile still made me want to brush my teeth.

"I'm sorry about your loss, Billy. You know that." He said it with a funny twist to the words I couldn't quite figure out. "But I'd like to tell you a little story." Roscoe was still standing in the shade behind me, still using his soft, sad voice, like I had just asked after his mother's health instead of telling him to go to hell. He didn't wait for me to encourage him; like I said, Roscoe was smart.

"I guess you heard about the riots we had back in May," he started off. "You musta been pretty glad you weren't still out there in harness." He chuckled, just a half a laugh that might have been a cough. "They even had *me* in blues, out on the street. It was very bad, Billy. Mostly because we didn't have any idea about what was happening, or—" He paused a little too long and I heard him take a ragged breath. "Anyway, there was this kid."

He stopped talking and concentrated on breathing for a minute. I sipped my water. I was pretty sure this was one of his management seminar techniques for making me feel involved in the conversation. It's like the way CHiPs always call you by your first name when they're writing you up. I guess they want you to feel involved in your speeding ticket.

I played along. "What kid, Roscoe?"

He still didn't answer. I turned and looked at him. He gave me a goofy half-smile and a half-shake of the head. "Just a kid," he said. "Sixteen years old. Still dumb enough to think people are basically good. Dumb enough to think he could make a difference, you know? A lot like you, Billy."

"Suck my butt, Roscoe."

"I mean it, Billy. Your biggest problem as a cop was, you still felt for people. Tried to really help 'em instead of just doing your job as a cop." He gave another of his asthmatic half-chuckles. "Seven years on the force and you still a rookie in your heart."

"Guess I learned better, Roscoe."

I could hear him sigh. "Guess you did. But you didn't learn enough, Billy. Not if you think you can run away from it like this."

Down at the head boat the leathery old gal put her filets into a couple of those thin plastic bags they hand out and then just marched away. The smarmy mate watched her go and said something close to the ear of a stocky blonde girl standing by the ramp. She smiled politely. A dark-haired guy came off the boat and put an arm around the blonde and they walked off together. The mate watched, then went back on the boat. There was nothing left to look at down the dock, not even that damned geeky mate. I turned to Roscoe.

"Is that what this is about, Roscoe? That why you came all this way? To tell me about myself?"

I could see real rage in those soft brown eyes and just for a second I thought he might let all the years of smooth control drop away and hit me, call me motherfucker—just for a second. Then he gave me a little smile. "No, Billy. That ain't what this is about. My nickel running out?"

"Yeah," I said, "it's running out. I got a three-pound mutton snapper I have to take home and eat before it turns to bait from sitting in the sun. I've been in the sun and salt water all day myself and I need a shower. I have two ice-cold bottles of St. Pauli waiting in the fridge and a ballgame coming on in two hours. I got a life, Roscoe. It might not be much, but it's got nothing to do with you, or L.A., or cops anywhere. I don't care about any of that shit. I don't care if the Dodgers never win the pennant again, and I don't care about you, except I got to get rid of you. So if I have to hear your story to do that, give me the story. Then just get out of here."

He cocked his head at me, eyes gleaming, for all the world like a very dangerous robin. Then, head still tilted to the side, he shook his head slowly in wonder. "You never used to be mean like this, Billy. You letting two bottles of beer waiting turn you mean?"

"No," I said, "it's the shower. If I don't get my shower soon I'm going to burst into tears."

"Well, then," he said, with that strange half-smile he'd picked up since the last time I saw him, "can't keep a man from his shower."

Roscoe took a deep breath and looked away, over to the parking lot. He blew out his breath and shook his head again.

"There was this kid," he said finally. "And he thought he could make a difference." He stopped talking again, but not for as long this time. "You got to understand how this went down, Billy. First off, we knew something might be coming and we were as ready as we could get. But we weren't ready for this. We weren't allowed to be ready. Deep in their honky Presbyterian hearts, the commissioner and the chief and all senior staff were thinking it couldn't happen like this ever again. Because all that terrible shit with the Nee-grows is twenty-five years ago. Why, they even got some very promising Nee-grows moving up on their own staff."

"I heard," I said. "Congratulations."

He let it slide. " 'Sides, the black community hasn't been able to get all together on something in almost as long. So what we were ready for and what we got were not even in the same ballpark."

He sighed heavily. "It was just so fast. They announced the King verdict and suddenly the town was on fire. There was no sense to it. Far as I know, there were no Koreans on the jury, but suddenly it was the Korean shopkeepers were getting it the hardest.

"So the Koreans are on their roofs with all these automatic weapons ready to pop the first black face they see, even if it has a badge."

He spent some time breathing again, looking down and trying to figure out if there was something he could do with his hands. There wasn't; he shook his head and went on.

"What I can't understand is how we handled it so bad. You know the department, Billy. Good cops, most of 'em. Damned good."

"Tell that to Rodney King," I told him, and took a long pull on my mineral water. It was a cheap shot, and Roscoe's smile said as much.

"You never work midnights, Billy? You never hear about the kind of pumped-up halfwits get dumped on that shift? All the losers and discipline problems the PBA and the ACLU won't let us fire?"

I didn't say anything. I knew it as well as he did. A lot of cops who shouldn't be cops were stuck on the late shift where they were out of sight and, in theory, out of harm's way. A lot of good cops were on that shift, too. I'd worn the uniform long enough to know you couldn't tell by watching thirty seconds of videotape whether the Rodney King beating was done by the bad cops or by good ones gone temporarily nuts. Sometimes I had trouble telling the difference anyway.

"Get on with it," I said.

He nodded like he'd won the point. Maybe he had.

"I know you wondering, whether you want to admit it or not. So I'll tell you, I don't have any idea how it got so bad so fast. Chain of command didn't just break down—it was never in place. Almost like it was deliberately sabotaged." He stopped and shook his head. He looked puzzled, a little hurt, like a man betrayed by something he cared about and was sure of.

"Was it?" I asked him. He just looked at me for a moment and for the first time he was a cop looking at an outsider. I'd never been on the receiving end of that look before. It made me nervous. "Come on," I said. "If it makes you happy I'll say you're right, okay? I *am* curious. I read about it and I don't see how it could have happened like that. What went wrong?"

"Billy," he said, "I don't know what happened. Far as I can tell, nobody knows what happened. But it makes no sense for somebody to try to fuck things up like that. Anyhow, they didn't need to. Morale has been real bad, everybody keeping their heads real low. Maybe when we came up against something definite like that it should have snapped us out of it. You know, action instead of thinking. Maybe it should have brought us back onto our feet again. It didn't. It knocked us on our asses. We folded, Billy. We just cut and run. The first few hours, when we might've turned it around, we were getting mixed signals or no signals. Nobody took charge. So we just kept pulling back and pulling back and all of a sudden we were back too far to get in again and do anything and we got four days of anything goes. This area about the size of Rhode Island, and it's total anarchy.

"But then something started happening in there." He paused here and looked away toward US 1. There was a steady stream of traffic going by. There always was. A Conch Train turned the corner and went past. I sipped my water and waited for Roscoe to go on. The people on the Conch Train seemed to think they were having fun. I didn't correct them.

"I'm kinda proud of this part," Roscoe said at last. Something about the way he said it jerked my head back around and I looked at him hard. But his face was still closed, except for that half-smile. "With no police presence in the area at all, and I mean *none,* you'd expect they'd all just go totally loco in there, burn everything, loot everything, shoot, rape, slash and shit on the kitchen table."

"Isn't that what happened?" I said, and now he swiveled to look hard at me.

"No, it's not," he said. "That ain't what happened at all. That's just what TV said happened. But nothing is TV-simple. They just gotta make it look like it is or they can't explain it in thirty-second sound bites. What really happened was that the majority of people in the area started coming together. I mean, even in the worst areas of Watts, ninety-some percent of folks hate like hell what's going on around them. You know that. But they never seem to realize they got the bad guys outnumbered. There's always been something missing, some little spark or—you know, a little grain of sand for the pearl to grow on. They never had anything like that. Then this happened and there was this kid.

"This kid. This sixteen-year-old black kid. He organizes this group so when there's attacks, looters, shooters, whatever, he shows up with a group and does a nonviolent confrontation thing until the outlaws back down. Black kids like him, some Korean kids, some Chicanos. And they're all working together. They out-policing the police. Making a difference in a way that looks like it's going to last. You know, a new community coalition.

"And then somebody shot him."

Roscoe took a deep breath. It sounded a little bit ragged. I looked hard at him but could see nothing behind the deep hurt in his eyes.

"It was an assassination, Billy. With a high-powered rifle from a rooftop. Somebody went to big trouble to get a shot and they shot down this kid. And I can't find out why."

"Why not?"

Funny smile again. "Not much evidence for starters. And this isn't exactly what I do, you know. But mostly the pressure's coming down from upstairs not to stir things up, for political reasons. The city is getting back to normal, they say—like that was good. They say the kid was just another looter at worst, or at best somebody in the wrong place at the wrong time who got popped by a nervous Korean shopkeeper."

There was something that sounded almost like pain in his voice now, and he started talking faster, more deliberately, like a lawyer who thinks he's already lost the case but has to pull out all the stops for the jury anyway.

"I say no way. No way in *hell,* Billy. They shot him too good, and with the wrong kind of weapon. Koreans mostly have assault rifles or shotguns—they don't know what they're doing with these weapons. They just want something that sprays lead. This boy was dropped with one clean shot from a hunting rifle. This was murder, Billy. Somebody didn't like what this kid was doing, and they hunted him down and they killed him. Somebody murdered this kid and I want them." He must have heard his own voice shaking and stopped for a moment, taking a breath and giving me an apologetic smile before he went on.

"But they won't even let me go after it. Not even me . . . And they won't put anybody good on it. They're trying to sweep it under the rug, make it go away, make sure nobody remembers, that nobody sees clearly who that boy was and what he tried to do, and that's—"

He stopped here, like asking me the real question was too hard. He'd come three thousand miles to ask me a favor and now he couldn't do it. Pride kicks in at funny times.

So he was quiet for a long time. So was I. I figured there had to be more to it than that. But there was no more. Roscoe stayed quiet. When I looked at him again he just gave me that strange half-smile. It looked bitter now.

My bottle of mineral water wasn't quite empty, but the half inch on the bottom was warmer than spit and suddenly less appealing. I put the bottle on top of the ice machine.

"Why, Roscoe?" I asked him, trying to look at him hard enough to get behind the mask his face had become. "Why did you come all this way? Why not just write this one off like every cop in the world writes off a couple every day? Why me?"

"The politics on this one are bad, man. Nobody in the department is allowed to touch it. They don't want nothing stirred up. But it's important, and it'll take a good cop to hang it on somebody. You still a good cop under there, Billy. You don't quit," he said, and he said it so seriously, so completely straight, that for a minute I believed him, believed he was talking about some other Billy Knight who never quit and always got his man. That's how good Roscoe was, even when he wasn't working at it.

I shook my head. "There's lots of good cops in L.A. Some of 'em are black, and they can go where I can't on something like this. I'm not that good."

"Yes, you are," he said. "You were that good. You were about the best street cop I ever saw. 'Sides, I need somebody on the outside who knows what the inside looks like and can't be waved off by the chairwarmers."

"Roscoe, you are a chairwarmer."

"Billy, I know you are the man to do this like I know my own name."

He was using that smooth management technique on me again. It made me mad.

"Why didn't you save yourself all this trouble and just call me, Roscoe?"

"Guess I was afraid you'd hang up on me."

"I'm hanging up anyway," I said. I half-turned away, but there was nothing to look at. After a minute I turned back and looked at Roscoe. He was just watching me with those sad brown eyes. He looked like a teacher whose favorite student had just let him down in a big way.

"You have changed, Billy. Gone inside and closed the door. I guess maybe you're not the man I needed you to be."

"You got that right. I'm not a cop anymore. I'm not. I'm not a private detective. I'm not a Wackenhut or a school crossing guard. I'm a fishing guide. You're not interested in fishing, just leave me the hell alone. You want to go fishing, great, give me a call. I get four hundred fifty dollars a day. Bring your kid."

I turned and started away. Before I got three steps away, two things stopped me dead. The first was a sudden sick feeling that I knew what Roscoe was about to say.

The second thing was when he said it.

"I can't bring my boy, Billy," he said. "That kid we were talking about—?"

"No," I said. It was a stupid thing to say, but it was all I could think of.

"Yeah," he said, in that terrible soft voice again. "My Hector was the boy. The one got shot. He's dead, Billy," said Roscoe, going on long past what was necessary. "My Hector is dead."

I turned slowly and watched that sad little half-smile trying to work its way onto his face one last time. It didn't make it. Roscoe turned away and walked off down the dock. I tried to think of something to say. I tried to make my feet move, either toward Roscoe or back to my boat. I failed at both things. Instead I just stood there in the terrible five o'clock heat and watched Roscoe walk to a metallic blue rental car, get in, and drive away.

CHAPTER
TWO

I don't know exactly how long I stood there beside the ice machine. I finally heard Art tapping on the window and I jerked my head around. He was peering through the glass, moving his mouth at me. I realized I had been standing there too long, that I didn't look right just standing there.

I noticed my reflection. Billy Knight, living ghost. Nobody would ever call me handsome. Intriguing maybe, with my slightly lopsided face, the faint trace of a scar down the left side, eyes blue and the right eye slightly bigger, sun-bleached dark blonde hair, broad, heavy shoulders, standing just under six feet tall. I could see hollows in my cheeks and under my eyes that didn't used to be there.

But beyond that, beyond the superficialities of how a cop might describe me on an APB, there was something wrong with the way I looked. There was some haunted thing looking out from just behind my eyes, and Roscoe had brought it out of its cave. It had been watching me for months now, slowly settling back inside, and I had been stupid enough to think it was going away forever. Now I knew better; it was just hibernating. When Roscoe pushed the right buttons, it rolled over in its sleep and said Spring is here, and poked its nose out again.

And there it was, looking out at me from inside, looking at my reflection and seeing only bones, worm food, a tiny chuckle in the great, dirty, shaggy dog story of life. That's how it attacks; it gives you Real Perspective. It makes you realize that the only real purpose we have in this world is to provide fertilizer for plants. Everything leading up to getting dropped into a hole in the ground is just another routine step in manufacturing the world's best self-replicating plant food.

Oh, I had Real Perspective, all right. At three A.M. on any of those hundreds of sleepless nights it kicked in and gave me a patronizing peek at how things were. It patted my shoulder with a friendly, manly touch and whispered suggestions about my gun, and the only defense I had found against it was to pretend. Just pretend everything was normal and that to continue to walk around every day served a purpose. What purpose? We'll get to that later. For now, just pretend the purpose is there and maybe you can fool that thing behind your eyes into going back to sleep. Just act normal.

Except I didn't even know what normal was anymore.

It was something I'd been conscious of a lot the last year, for the first time in my life. Maybe most people never think about it, and from the time I was a kid until last year I didn't either. I always assumed that whatever I was doing, however I looked doing it, that was normal, and that was it.

Things had changed. Since that day eighteen months ago I felt like an imposter, somebody hiding in my own body. I'd been very careful not to stick out, not to act in any way that would make me look different, not to give people any reason to ask me any questions. One thing I liked about taking strangers fishing was that the talk tended to be pretty specifically about fish. It left personal things out of it. If somebody got too curious about me I could always just point to a fish.

That's how I wanted it. It had taken a lot of work to get functional again, and I didn't want to risk losing the careful equilibrium I had built up. I wasn't sure I could do it again.

For the first few months I'd watched a lot of TV. I'd even managed to sit through parts of a couple of talk shows—sometimes as much as five minutes at a time. According to most of the talk shows it wasn't good to avoid my feelings. It was healthy and natural and honest to talk things out. It was self-destructive to bottle things up. What the hell: It wasn't quite as self-destructive as swallowing a

9-millimeter steel-jacketed slug, and that ought to count for something.

Art was knocking on the window again. I realized how worried he must be to get up off his seat and come all the way across the room.

I made myself step back into the vicious freezing cold of Art's shack.

"The hell's the matter, Billy? Been standing there like that for— Christ, I dunno. Hell's the matter?"

"Nothing, Art. I was just thinking."

He shook his massive head. Three chins crashed into each other. "Fucking cop, huh. Told you he 'uz trouble. Smelt it on him." He put a finger the size of a kielbasa up beside his nose. "This don't miss much. Could tell he 'uz trouble."

"No trouble, Art."

"Thirty-five years in this goddamn town," he told me. "Think I can't smell trouble?"

"There's no trouble, for Christ's sake, Art," I yelled at him. The sound of my voice was too high and much too loud, so I gave him a big, loopy smile so he could see for himself there was no trouble. "I'm going home." I turned for the door, staggering slightly as some trick of the cold locked my knee up for half a step. I shook it off and made it to the door.

"Dickhead," I heard Art mumble behind me.

Outside, I walked to the other side of the shack, where my bicycle was chained to a piling. I undid the lock, flung the chain into the battered basket, and headed out onto the street and across US 1. I had a car, but I hadn't started it up for six months. I wasn't even sure it would still start.

There's a special word for anybody who drives a car in Key West: tourist. Real Conchs have battered bicycles with large, American seats and those high handlebars that every kid in the country lusted after in 1966. With the high handlebars it's a lot easier to stay upright under Key West conditions.

Most of the bikes have a half-smashed basket on the front, and generally a half-smashed rider holding onto the handlebars. But even if you're sober, the way you ride a Conch bike is the same, easy enough for any drunk. You lean half-forward, drape one forearm over the handlebars, and slouch over in a kind of boneless way while your legs move on the pedals as if you were going downhill and you're just keeping up with the spinning wheel; you're not really pedalling at all, just letting gravity pull you along.

It works out pretty well on an island that's completely flat and only a few miles long and a few miles across. Gas is expensive, and unless you're hauling lumber, cars are a waste of time and money and take up too much room. Besides, nobody is really in a hurry here. Tourists are here for a break from the hectic rodent marathon. Residents generally don't have anything too pressing; at worst, they're keeping a tourist waiting a few minutes—which is actually one of the real pleasures of living here, so nobody minds.

I generally managed to get across US 1 without serious injury, but it always amazed me. If the road wasn't so straight nobody would make it all the way to Duval Street. Nobody is really driving as they come through here. They're hanging onto the wheel often enough, but they are either wrestling kids or gaping out the window. In a lot of ways people feel like they've come to a foreign country, so I guess they assume a red light means something else here.

I was as bad as any tourist right now. I couldn't get that last picture of Roscoe out of my mind, as he tried that pained half-smile one last time and turned for his rental car. So I ended up partway across the street before I realized I was in traffic, going against the light. I made it back to the curb without losing a wheel or a leg, but just barely. A thoughtful guy with a blonde crewcut leaned out the window and very loudly told me what my head was full of and what he figured I liked to put in my mouth. It wasn't very original; I barely heard him.

When the light finally changed I missed it and had to wait through another cycle. I felt trapped. Roscoe had found me and in just a half-hour stripped away all my carefully built-up defenses. He was right; I was still a cop underneath. I still cared.

A red convertible filled with college kids went by. The horn honked and a beer bottle spun from the backseat and smashed at my feet. Small pellets of glass pattered off my hat, and one stung my cheek. My left leg was wet with warm beer that smelled like the urinal at Sloppy Joe's. It woke me up, and when the light changed a few seconds later I wheeled across and headed for home.

My home that year was about halfway across the island, across the

street from a small canal that emptied into the marsh above House-
boat Row. The house was a small, squat cinderblock cottage built
in the 1960s. The yard was overgrown when I moved in and hadn't
gotten any better.

Inside the low coral rock wall around the lot there were enor-
mously tall patches of weeds sharing space with the blotches of
hardscrabble dirt where nothing could ever grow. A huge key lime
tree leaned over the back door and dropped fruit on the cat who
lived in the crawl space under the house.

The house had once been painted Florida pink, a strange bastard
color halfway between tan and the hot blush of a Puerto Rican
whore's toreador stretch pants. The paint was fading now. Chunks
of it had flaked off to show a pastel green undercoat. I dropped my
bike on the poured-cement front step and kicked the front door
open.

The house had two small bedrooms, a living-dining room, a
bathroom about the size of a coat closet, and the kitchen. At the
moment the house was dim, and hot enough to melt plastic. I
switched on the big Friedrich window unit and a throaty roar of
arctic air pushed me towards the kitchen.

The kitchen had a pass-through about five feet wide with one
louvred shutter on the left side. The other shutter, for the right
side, had been gone when I moved in. I stood in the kitchen doorway, with the pass-through on my left, and looked at the refrigerator. It was older than me and streaked with rust.

I thought about Roscoe and what he had said. I thought about
getting out one of the bottles of St. Pauli Girl beer. Then I thought
maybe I should take a shower first. I couldn't decide and felt my
shoulder muscles getting tighter as I just stood there, unable to
make a simple decision.

What I should do, I knew, was just grab a beer. It was right
there, ten feet away. Just step over, open the door, grab a beer. But
then—I couldn't really take a beer into the shower. Maybe I should
take a shower first. Get clean, sit down, *then* have the beer. Except
then the beer wouldn't taste as good. So have the beer first. Except—

It was too much. Both decisions suddenly seemed to have enormous consequences. I just had to choose, one way or the other, and

I couldn't. I could feel the tension in my shoulders spreading, the muscles starting to knot, and before I knew it I was shaking from the strain. It was all coming back to me. Roscoe's visit had brought it all back.

CHAPTER
THREE

March 18. It was not a date I was likely to forget. The day had started badly. The freeways were full of mean drunks and Type A personalities with too much engine in their car and not enough sense of their own mortality.

The air that day was a solid yellow-brown, a poisonous, barely breathable ooze unlike anything I've ever seen anywhere else. Sure, other cities have pollution. New York has a dark brown cloud cover that can rip out your throat when the wind is right; Mexico City has a vicious fog so thick you can feel the weight of it and watch it peel the paint off your car. But L.A. has something special. It clings to your clothes, drifts gently into your pores in that dry desert air, and gives you blinding pains in your throat and head that make you want to drive up onto the Santa Monica Freeway and look for somebody to run off the road. The pollution in L.A. is special. After you've lived there awhile you realize that the gauzy, yellow-brown air really stands for the whole city in a unique way. Like everything else about L.A., the smog is often pretty to look at, completely intangible, and ultimately poisonous. But hey—it sure makes for great sunsets, huh?

Great sunsets and lousy mornings. On my way in to roll call that yellow morning it was already over ninety and the smog was pounding its way in and making my temples throb. My eyes were stinging, there was a sharp rasp in my chest, and jolts of pain shot

20

around my skull if I tried to use my head for anything except pointing my eyes.

I had plenty to think about and it all hurt. Jennifer and I had just finished another of our early-morning screaming matches. She had this nutty idea that just because she married me she ought to see me every now and then. She said I had this two-year-old daughter who thought the mailman was her daddy.

A cliché like Cops and Divorce can be a tremendous pain in the ass when you're living through it. You can't find much comfort in the fact that you're falling in with the statistical norm. I was fighting it with both hands, but we were edging closer and closer to divorce. It seemed like every morning when I left for work and every night when I came home there was another yelling session. Each time we shouted we said things we shouldn't. Each awful thing we said was a little worse than the one before, a little harder to gloss over, apologize for, rationalize. I felt like we were both passengers on some kind of wild amusement-park ride. The guy running it was drunk, the ride was spinning out of control, and nobody could do any more than ride it out and hope we all landed okay.

Except lately it was looking like we weren't going to land at all.

We'd said some truly hurtful things this morning. Most of them centered on my shortcomings as a father and a human being. It was getting tougher to explain myself—even to me. I loved my wife and my daughter, loved them so much it hurt sometimes. But I worked long hours. I had to. I was a cop. I had been a cop for a long time before I got married, and I expected to be a cop for a long time to come. It was the only way I had been able to work things out for myself, to balance what I believed with who I was and how I lived. It worked for me.

And on the darker side, I loved the faintly queasy thrill of it, of never knowing when a bullet or a knife might be aimed at my back. I loved waiting for danger, meeting it, beating it. I loved the high-stakes crap game of putting my life on the line, gambling it to keep the rest of the world safe.

It was not just the thrill of danger, but danger that *meant* something. Resisting it mattered, helped in a small way to make things better—or at least kept things from getting much worse more quickly. I guess that's what Roscoe meant when he said I was still a rookie in my heart. Most cops lose their idealism pretty quickly; I never did. I liked doing something that was both important and dangerous. I never felt so alive as when I was answering a call that might mean my death. That's why I resisted promotion, fought to stay on the street. I loved seeing results, and I loved the danger.

I could see where that might not make sense to someone like Jennifer. She was a resolutely Good Person. She was tough, strong, but she hadn't seen what I had and so she still believed in the basic goodness of human beings.

I never tried to disillusion her. That sweet inner core of hers was my anchor to the fake Real World that most people live in. I came home from work in my world and gladly stepped into the loving order of hers. I could leave it all at work: the whores ripped up by their pimp's knives because they blew their money on crack, the shit-bums who drowned because they were so wracked by wine and TB they couldn't even roll up onto the sidewalk when it rained, the day-old babies fished out of dumpsters in several pieces—all the grisly, nightmare pieces of reality that swept me along every time I went on duty. I could walk away from it and into sanity in a way that most cops can't, and it was only because of Jennifer. She kept that bright, wonderful, silly version of How Things Are alive and well, and I let her, grateful that it could include me, somebody who knew better.

I could see now that was a mistake.

I lived in both worlds, understood both sides. She never did, never could understand what it meant to be a cop. She thought of it as a career, the kind of thing you could change if it wasn't working out. Everything I tried to tell her about how it really was just made her all the more convinced that it wasn't working out, that the sooner she got me out of it and into something sane, like selling real estate, the better for all of us.

And so now Jennifer's Real World was getting ugly, too, and I had no place to hide from it except in my work, and of course that just made it all worse on both ends, until the whirlpool got so overpowering I didn't know where I was anymore.

Days like this one weren't helping much. After two and a half hours of paperwork I had a court appearance. In court I learned that I was just this side of Adolf Hitler and only twelve years of demented Republican power-brokering and the consequent dismantling of the Bill of Rights kept me from a long-overdue prison sentence for my crimes. That took me through to lunch time.

I started back to the station thinking I'd had a rough morning. I wasn't even halfway to my car before it got a lot worse.

I had just turned the corner on the top floor of the parking garage when my beeper started yipping at me. It was a long way down to the telephones, and almost as long to the far end of the garage where my car was parked. I sprinted for my car.

My head was pounding from the smog by the time I got the door opened. I slid onto the front seat, snatched up the radio, and called in.

Maybe you've never heard police radio traffic. There's a very rigid structure to it. There's an order, a rhythm, and a way things are done.

Let's put it this way: If there had been a nuclear attack on Universal Studios I would expect Central to tell me in a calm, unemotional voice using the correct call codes. If Long Beach Harbor were under attack by Japanese war planes, Central would tell me where to go and what to do in a flat tone, with clear dispatch numbers.

So when the dispatcher stuttered at me and couldn't seem to think of the right thing to say, that set off all the little alarms. I got a Code Three 10–19, which didn't make too much sense: Emergency, return to station. When I asked for a repeat, I got a 10–23, stand by, and a hiss of dead air.

A long moment later my radio crackled again and gave me a 911–B for a 10–35, followed by an address on Boyd Street: Contact the officer there for a confidential message.

I didn't get it at all. "Central, is this Code Three?" I asked.

Nothing. Then, "Lincoln Tango Two-oh, Ten–Twenty-three," again.

More nothing. I was already rolling. Boyd Street was five minutes away. As I turned onto Los Angeles Street I tried again. "Central—"

I was cut off by the dispatcher. "Lincoln Tango Two-oh, that is a Code Three. We have a Two-oh-seven in progress."

I hit the siren and stepped on the gas. Two-oh-seven is kidnapping, and like all cops, I hated it like poison. I didn't know why they wanted me for it, but they'd have a reason.

And they did. They did have a reason. Oh boy, did they have a reason. One of the all-time great reasons.

Boyd Street is in a depressed downtown area. It's full of flophouses, sweatshops, and Korean toy warehouses. The address I had took me to a flop near Sixth Street, only a few blocks from the Greyhound station on Fifth Street, known as the Nickel, the center of downtown L.A.'s Skid Row. It's the kind of area that's so scummy you want to burn your shoes after you step on the sidewalk.

There was quite a party going by the time I got there. There were two paramedic trucks standing by, six patrol cars, another four unmarkeds, a fire truck, and the big truck I knew belonged to the bomb squad. It was all I could do to find a parking place. I finally pulled onto the sidewalk two doors down, in front of a rolling steel door. As I got out, a Korean man stuck his head out the door I was blocking, looked at me, and spat carefully about four and a half inches from the toe of my left shoe.

On the rooftops all around, through a poisonous yellow L.A. haze, I could see that the SWAT team was already deployed. They lay or kneeled motionless in their positions, already sited in and hoping for a quick shot.

The SWAT guys always want to shoot fast. Not because they think they're so good, although most of them do. Not because they want any glory or excitement or because they are ravening beasts consumed by bloodlust. They want to shoot to get the job done and go home. They want to sit in their easy chairs with a can of beer and watch game shows. The dullest, most unimaginative guys in the world are the hired killers. Maybe they have to be.

Below the SWAT team on the sidewalk, on both sides of the street, a line of blue uniforms straggled across the street in an arc in front of the place, behind their cars or whatever other impromptu cover they could find. They all had weapons out, too, but very few of them were as nerveless about it as the SWAT team. So far I didn't see any press.

The place everybody was paying attention to was one of the old flops that are all around the area. For twenty bucks you got a week in a room with no door and a mattress so flimsy you could feel the fleas moving inside it. You generally find a family of eight or ten in each room, working in the sweatshops and saving up for a green card. This place was called the Rossmore, according to the faded spidery red letters above the door.

My precinct commanding officer was already striding toward me. His name was Captain Spaulding, and nobody kidded him about it. He had a flat nose and a big mustache. He was a hard guy, even for a downtown cop. About fifty years old, he'd run the PAL boxing program for fifteen years and would still go three rounds with anybody stupid enough to offer. In his younger days some wise guys had coshed him and thrown him in the trunk of a Cadillac. Captain Spaulding punched his way out of the trunk, bending the sheet metal into a piece of abstract art, and killed two of the wise guys with blows from his bare hands. The other one ran for his life.

"Billy," he said, and that was a bad sign. Like a high-school football coach, Captain Spaulding never used first names. I could see beads of sweat rolling into his thick black mustache. The day was hot and smelled like hell was leaking up through the pavement.

"Captain?" I was starting to feel a cold trickle of sweat myself. Since this morning, when I got the working-over in court, reality had been about fifteen degrees off. Now, seeing the captain's face, it turned a little further, and even though I had no idea what he was about to tell me, I knew now it wouldn't be on my wish list for Christmas.

"Billy," he repeated, and put a hand on my shoulder. I could feel his stone-hard fingers through my jacket. He jerked his head at the Rossmore. "Your wife and kid are in there."

Just like that. That was the captain's style.

I blinked. I didn't know if I was going to throw up or laugh. What he had said was so wildly improbable I couldn't take it at face value. There had to be something else, some strange metaphor he was trying to make.

"Excuse me, sir?"

He nodded and looked even grimmer, never breaking eye contact with me. "They came down to the station to see you. You were in court and they left." He ground his teeth. "We're not real sure of what happened. We think the perps were hanging around outside the station. Maybe they figured they'd grab a cop. Maybe figured your wife and kid would work better."

I found myself shaking my head, as if I could keep it from being true. "What do they want?"

"They want a trade. Your wife and daughter for a buddy of theirs."

I heard myself breathing. I was panting, on the verge of fainting from hyperventilation. Everything was flip-flopping between horrible slow motion and fast-forward. I felt like Wile E. Coyote. I opened my mouth; Captain Spaulding was already shaking his head.

"We can't do it, Billy. The guy they want is gone. We had to let him go about two hours ago. Two feds showed up with extradition papers and we had to ship him back east on a homicide charge."

The last sentence dropped several octaves down as things slowed down again. I'd heard people describe the LSD experience, and that's what this felt like. Spaulding's words were terrible slow globs and his face looked like a Cubist painting. I couldn't remember how to breathe.

Captain Spaulding slapped my face. It hurt a lot. Normal time returned.

"You okay, Billy?"

"No, sir," I said. "I'm not okay at all." I concentrated on getting some air in and felt it steady me. I turned to look at the flop. "I'm going in there."

His fingers gripped me tight enough to break the skin. "No you're not, son. Listen to me. Lesley Bishop is already on the line with these guys. She says she's getting somewhere and I'm going to let her run with it for now. Lieutenant Mendez has his SWAT guys all lined up and you know they're good. We can do this, Billy, you know that. We can take care of this with our own people and do it right. We take care of our own."

It was true. Lesley Bishop was our negotiator and she really believed she could sell shit to a dog. The SWAT guys were top-notch too—the whole crisis team was. Most often the precinct cops are better at these situations than the feds or anybody else that might get thrown in.

There are two simple reasons for that. First, the precinct knows its own turf. Second, its people get more practice. There are more snatches, stand-offs, blow-ups and fuck-ups every day in every precinct in L.A. than the FBI's local office handles in a year.

That also explained why there was nobody from the press here yet. If the TV cameras showed up, so would the FBI; and about two dozen more county, state, and federal agencies. Captain Spaulding was keeping it quiet. He'd even made sure the call I got wouldn't tip anybody monitoring that something newsworthy was going down. By keeping the press away he kept control. It was my wife and my daughter, and I was one of Spaulding's men. Every guy on the watch would drop whatever he had going and come help if it was necessary. Like the captain said, we take care of our own.

One side of me could appreciate that. The other side wanted to grab a twelve-gauge and kick down the door.

Of course, Spaulding knew that. That's why he was meeting me personally, clamping his steel-spring hand on my elbow, leading me back to his improvised command center, and sitting me down in the front seat of his car. "This is going to work out fine, Billy," he said. "It's going very well."

"Very well," agreed Lesley Bishop. She had a cellular phone beside her and one of those electronic travel alarms. She used the phone to talk to the perps and the clock to time herself, so when she said she'd call back in five minutes, she'd watch the clock, wait carefully for ten minutes to pass, and call back. It was her favorite negotiating technique.

"Where are we, Lesley?" Captain Spaulding asked her, clearly for my benefit.

She smiled. She was obviously pleased with herself, but that didn't mean much. She usually was. "Right on target, Captain. Nothing oddball about any of this, straight out of the book. They want their buddy released, half a million bucks, and a chopper to LAX. We have to have a jet waiting to take them all to Mexico." Her smile got bigger. "I got them going on the money. I told them we could do it but that much took time." She nodded at me. "It's one of my tricks. I get them thinking just about the money. That gets their greed going and they start mentally counting the haul. They forget about everything else."

I just looked at her. She looked briefly puzzled that I didn't congratulate her on her brilliance, then looked very startled as she realized why. "Oh!" she said. The smile returned. "Your wife and daughter are fine. One of them says he has a daughter the same age. He's playing with her."

Her travel alarm beeped and she turned away to pick up the telephone.

Captain Spaulding leaned over me and re-inserted his fingers into my flesh. I was starting to feel like I'd have to have them surgically removed. "Okay, Billy? We got two guys in there and it's all under control. Our reading is, they're just gangbangers who went a little further than usual. These guys are not that good. We can take them. We can do this one. Lookit—" He pointed at the Rossmore. "Second floor. They got a corner room." He chuckled. "That's what I mean, these guys are D-U-M-B. They got two windows at right angles. See? So SWAT can get about eight shots into both of them in under two seconds." He kneaded my shoulder. I managed not to scream in pain. "We're going to take them, Billy. As soon as I get the word from Mendez, I'll give him the go. We can do this. You just take it easy. Your family will be fine, Billy. You stay put."

He turned away. I stayed on the seat; the habit of discipline is strong, and anyway, I wasn't sure what my legs would do if I tried to stand.

The radio spat. "Mendez."

Spaulding spoke back, staring up at the Rossmore. "Spaulding."

"Blue ready. Red ready."

"Stand by," said Spaulding and put down the radio. He turned to me. "They're in place. Clear shots on both guys. We worked it out ahead so even if the perps can monitor they can't know what we're doing."

"Captain," I said, and flinched away as those terrible fingers came for my shoulder again.

"Relax, son. I'm taking extra special care here. Nothing can go wrong. Just take it easy." He leaned closer. I could see his teeth. Two of the front ones were slightly whiter than the others, obvious caps. "I got an observer circling the rooftops. He's checking it all out, looking into every corner of the room from every angle. He's not even going to use the radio, he's coming right back to report to me in person."

He gave a squeeze. His fingers put pressure on the exact same spot he'd been squeezing since I got there. I almost moaned. "You see, son? It's all thought out. This is a family matter, and I'm not leaving anything to chance."

I heard the soft patter of sneakers. Levine, a young cop I hardly knew, slid up beside Captain Spaulding. A pair of very good binoculars hung from around his neck. Levine was lean and intense and still idealistic and about as streetwise as a Shriners parade. He was the kind of cop who put in five years on the force and then left for law school.

"Captain," he said softly, looking at me nervously.

"What've you got, Levine?" Spaulding said. The tone of his voice snapped Levine's head back around to look at the captain.

"Sir. I checked them out from every angle." He glanced at me again, out of the corner of his eye. "Red has a MAC Ten. He's by the window. Uh, the hostages are fine, sir. The woman is in the corner. Blue is sitting on the floor with the kid. He's got something in his lap, uh—"

"What kind of something?" the captain demanded.

"Uh—" Levine started, then broke off to collect himself. He didn't want to look vague in front of Captain Spaulding. That would show up on his rating and screw up his chance at law school. "It's a Walkman, sir. I could see the wire coming out the top."

Spaulding nodded. "These guys always have to have music. Okay." He turned to pick up the radio. "Spaulding," he said. There was an answering crackle. "Mendez," the bored voice answered.

Something was bothering me, and as I heard Spaulding say, "Ten–Twenty-three," it hit me. I turned to Levine.

"How sure are you that was a Walkman?"

He glanced nervously over at Captain Spaulding. "I'm sure," he said.

"Did you see headphones?"

"N–no—he was holding one in his right hand, I think—"

"You think? But you didn't see for sure?"

He licked his upper lip. "Headphones had to be there. I saw the Walkman."

Spaulding's radio squacked. "Ready blue," it said.

"What did the Walkman look like?" I said, coming to my feet now.

Levine was backing away a half-step at a time. "Just—you know. A Walkman. A black plastic box. Red wires coming out the top—"

The radio squacked again. "Ready red," it said.

I lunged for Spaulding's arm. "Captain, wait—" I started, but he was saying, "Do it!"

I was already running for the building. The shots came exactly together and sounded like only one shot. Like I say, those guys are good. I was through the front door and halfway up the steps when the explosion came.

It wasn't all that big. Probably just a couple of sticks of dynamite wired to a thumb switch. Push the button down and it turns on; take your thumb off and boom. It's called a dead man's switch, since it turns on only when the man holding it is dead. It's easily wired to any charge, big or small.

This one was pretty small. It was barely big enough to throw me backwards down the stairs and out into the street on my head. Just big enough to take out most of that corner of the building and all the windows in the building next door.

Plenty big enough, of course, to kill everybody in that small corner room of the Rossmore.

CHAPTER FOUR

I woke up in the quietest room I've ever been in. Everything was white. I had a bad taste in my mouth and I couldn't hear anything except an annoying hum. My head hurt. I was lying down in some kind of bed. There was a stiff, crusty feeling on my left cheek. I raised a hand to touch it and felt bandages. My hand fell away all by itself and I was asleep before it hit the bed.

I woke up again. I still heard the hum, but I could hear other noises in the background now. A man in a three-piece suit was leaning over me. I decided he wasn't a doctor. He didn't look like a doctor. He looked like a hyena. That probably meant he was a lawyer.

He held up a sheaf of papers and moved his mouth in an exaggerated, overcareful way, like he was talking to a retarded foreigner. "Can you just sign here, please?" he said.

Yup: a lawyer. I closed my eyes.

I woke up again. This time it was a doctor. He was a mean-looking old man with a bow tie, a beard, and a nasty glint in his eye. He wore a white coat. He was holding up my left eyelid with a hard thumb and shining a bright light into my eye.

"Cut it out," I yelled. Or at least, I thought I yelled it. What came out was a kind of muffled, raspy whine.

"Good. You're awake," the doctor said. He snapped off the light. "I think you're going to live." He sounded like that offended him.

31

I wasn't sure I wanted to live. I wasn't even sure what it meant. I closed my eyes.

I woke up again. Captain Spaulding was sitting in the chair beside my bed.

"Billy," he said, and stopped. The hum was gone now. I could hear fine, although everything still sounded like it was coming from the next room.

"Billy," Captain Spaulding said again. I closed my eyes, but this time I didn't go to sleep. This time I couldn't. Seeing Spaulding there, hearing him calling me Billy—

It had happened. It had really happened.

They let me go home the next day. The house was neat, a little too neat. It had been cleaned up by someone who expected to be away for a while.

They had given me the note Jennifer came down to the station to leave for me. It said she'd had about enough and she was taking our daughter away for a few weeks. They would stay with her brother in Paso Robles and call in a few days. She hoped we might be able to work things out, but she wasn't holding her breath.

That night was the first time I tasted my gun. It tasted pretty good.

But I didn't pull the trigger. I don't know why. Maybe I was just being stubborn. Jennifer always said I was too stubborn. Maybe it was the fact that I couldn't seem to summon up the energy and motor skills to do anything but turn on the TV and fall into the easy chair.

And maybe it was curiosity. Some funny things had been going on and I guess I wanted to know how it was going to come out. That hyena-faced lawyer was on the phone to me a dozen times over the next few days and came to see me in person four times, since I kept hanging up on him. He'd come to my house, where I was just sitting in a chair with the TV on. I had special condolence leave. Hyena would knock and when I didn't answer he'd kind of oil in the door and wave his stack of papers and wheedle for me to sign. It turned out he worked for the city. I was supposed to sign a half-dozen forms that said I didn't hold the city responsible for the deaths of my family.

I didn't sign. Even when Captain Spaulding showed up at my

house and asked me in person, as a personal favor to him, I wouldn't sign.

I was not holding out for anything, not planning to sue, not trying to prove anything. I just didn't feel very much like signing anything. I really didn't feel capable of anything that complicated. I would look at the heap of forms requiring my signature, and my eyes would drift away. I couldn't concentrate on anything long enough to sign. All I could think about was all the really good reasons to swallow a slug.

The City, meanwhile, was worried sick. Mind you, L.A. has two dozen excellent reasons for being worried sick every day of the year, but now they thought they had a new one.

When a cop was injured trying to save his wife and kid from a bomb blast caused by what might have been overzealous aggressiveness on the part of the cop's commanding officer, the City figured it had a PR problem. The media agreed.

Nobody knew where the gangbangers had learned how to rig a bomb with a dead man's switch, and I guess we'll never find out. But a few of the reporters figured somebody should have known. And the City decided I was stonewalling, refusing to sign because I was gathering my dark forces to sue the shit out of them.

So about two weeks after the Rossmore's surprise remodeling, a different lawyer came to see me. He was much more refined than the hyena. He looked like an Episcopalian bishop. He wore the nicest suit I have ever seen in my life and carried a $3,000 briefcase.

He told me that the City still hoped to avoid any kind of difficulty over the matter and if I was simply willing to sign a release, a quitclaim, a statement, and a waiver, the City would, while certainly not acknowledging any culpability, nonetheless be willing to make a final payment in appreciation of my cooperation in letting this whole painful matter come to a quiet close. The bishop said he was authorized to go as high as a half-million dollars on the condition that I sign a couple of standard forms, which he happened to have with him in his $3,000 briefcase.

When I still didn't answer, he gave me a small sympathetic smile and left the forms on the table. He put the check on top of them.

If I'd been firing on all cylinders, and if I'd been in any shape to give a damn, I would have realized that all this attention meant the City was scared to death I would sue. There'd been an awful lot of suits against the city the past two years, and they'd been paying out damages in the millions on a semiregular basis.

A half-million bucks looked like a pretty good bargain compared to a long and drawn-out lawsuit that would certainly create a wave of negative publicity and probably end up costing $5 or $10 million anyway. Especially since as part of the bargain they got a statement signed by me—written by them, of course—clearly stating that I forgave them completely for everything they had never even done.

It was a couple of months before I put all that together, though. For the first few weeks it was all I could do to get up in the morning and reach for the coffee instead of my weapon.

About ten days after the bishop left his stack of papers I had a spasm of neatness. It was three A.M. I was watching an old sci-fi movie. I'd seen it before. But the sudden sight of giant ants terrorizing Los Angeles had a funny effect on me. It made me see myself from one step away, in just the same way seeing the giant ants on familiar streets made me see the City in a funny way.

I was suddenly filled with a strange energy for the first time since I'd come home. The place was filthy. I jumped up and loaded dirty dishes into the dishwasher. I threw all my laundry into the washing machine. I took a shower and shaved. I swept the floor. And in clearing off the stacks of mostly unread newspapers from the dining table, I found the stack of papers from the bishop.

The papers were unfinished business. I couldn't throw them away; more would come and that would make more clutter. The neatest solution, clearly, was to sign them and mail them immediately.

I circled the room at high speed, looking for a pen. I had to stop to organize the magazine rack by my easy chair. I got the spines lined up and put the older issues in the recycle stack by the back door. That reminded me of the empty bottles in the kitchen and I moved them to the recycle box for containers.

Back in the living room, I saw the stack of papers again, and again circled the room looking for a pen. I found one by the stereo and paused to alphabetize the tapes. When they were straight I hurried back to the papers. I signed them. I stuffed them into the envelope provided. I made out a deposit slip and signed the check. I put it into an envelope and had to go look for a stamp. I went by the bedroom and noticed the sheets needed changing. I stripped the bed and took the dirty sheets to the washing machine. The first load was done and I moved it to the dryer. I put the sheets in the washer and headed back for the living room.

I saw the envelopes sitting neatly on the table and slapped my forehead: a stamp, of course. I found one in a small drawer of the telephone table. But there were several directories there that were more than a year out of date. I carried them to the recycle box and decided I should move the box out to the curb. I did, and noticed that the yard was a mess.

I turned on the spotlights, got a rake, and managed to pile up several large heaps of leaves, dead grass, and so on. I went back into the house to get garbage bags and saw the envelopes again. I remembered the stamp, now in my shirt pocket. I put it on the envelope and took both envelopes out the front door. There was a mailbox on the corner, and no time like the present.

But as I reached the sidewalk in front of the house I noticed a stack of newspapers I had never gotten around to picking up. I grabbed them and took them to the recycle box. I carefully leaned the two envelopes against the recycle box so I would remember where they were. I took the plastic bags off the newspapers, sorted the newspapers by date and stacked them in the recycle box. I took the bins to the curb.

I got back from the curb and saw the heaps of refuse in the yard. I walked back into the house for garbage bags and noticed the dryer had stopped. I put the sheets into the dryer and took the dried laundry out to sort it.

I carried the stuff to my bedroom and dumped it on the bed. On top of the heap was a tiny pink sock.

I picked it up. It must have been left in the dryer. It was just one small, pink sock. It had been my daughter's.

I fell on the floor beside the bed as if somebody had bashed all my bones in with a mallet and I lay there, holding the sock. I just lay there and cried for over a half hour. After a while no more tears would come; I'd dried up my tear ducts. I lay there for another twenty minutes making raw, ratchety sounds until I just ran out of energy. Then I just lay there for another half hour. Finally I got up and slumped wearily down the hall. I got my pistol.

This was the second time I tasted the barrel. There was such a pain in my heart that I didn't even have the strength to pull the

trigger. I would have loved to, but all the energy was drained out of
me and into that small, pink sock. I sat there in my easy chair with
the gun in my mouth and watched the sun come up.

I was still sitting when Charlie Shea, my partner that year,
showed up to see how I was doing.

Charlie took the pistol out of my hand and made coffee. He even
got me to drink some. Charlie was very persuasive. He was a lousy
cop but a very nice guy.

I drank a cup of coffee with Charlie while he talked about precinct gossip, the Dodgers, and the latest from Putz Pelham. Putz
had been undercover, looking into kiddie porn. He'd gotten carried away and screwed about two dozen "actresses." Now he was
scared to death he'd caught something and was dying. Charlie
thought that was pretty funny.

Charlie never said a word about the forms I was supposed to sign,
although I was pretty sure he got some heavy pressure to talk to me
about it. But he was a good enough cop to know what it means to
be a partner, so he just talked about nothing for a while.

Outside, the recycling truck came. I heard them collect my stuff
and I thought about the forms and the check I had left in with the
old newspapers. But I was tired. I sipped my coffee. That seemed to
make Charlie happy.

It was after that morning I started to find my feet again. I don't
know if it was the release of finally crying, or the realization of how
close to the edge I had been, or even Charlie Shea's soft and pointless talk. Maybe it was the combination, perfectly timed. In any
case, I was starting to come back.

I still gargled my gun from time to time. I would work up my
nerve to go out somewhere—the grocery store, even a movie—and
something would remind me of Jennifer or Melissa. I would see a
box of a particular brand of cereal and my hand would start to
shake. I would go past a swingset where Melissa had played, or the
place where Jennifer had her hair done, and my whole body would
feel numb. I'd be filled with that pointless energy again, and often
as not, I'd end up fondling the barrel of my weapon and looking
down into the chamber, thinking about inhaling.

The walls of the house began to close in on me. It was Jennifer's
house, after all. We'd figured out together what we could afford and
she had searched until she found this place. It was small, but it was

in Venice. Jennifer said that meant the air was better, which was important with kids to think about. The schools were good here, too, and if it wasn't really safe to walk the street at night—well, it wasn't really safe anywhere, was it?

Now I found it impossibly small. Everywhere I turned I found some small reminder of my dead family. I couldn't stay in the house, but I couldn't go out too long, either.

Everything was a reminder to me. I slowly started to realize that if I was going to live I had to get out of L.A.

Even that thought caused panic in me. I had no idea how to start doing that.

Luckily, I was still having episodes of manic energy. Fugues, I think they are called. In one of them I sat down with a calculator and a stack of real estate ads. Comparable houses in my area had increased in value tremendously in the last three years. With what I could get for this one, I would be pretty close to rich. I could go anywhere, do anything, live the kind of life every man wants to live.

Whoopee.

In another of my fits of manic energy, I mailed in my resignation from the LAPD and put my house on the market. Soon after that Roscoe McAuley came to see me.

I know why they picked Roscoe to come talk to me. I don't know why they thought it would do any good.

Roscoe got the job because he was slicker than anybody else in the precinct that year. I knew him as well as anybody did—but nobody really knew him. We'd been at the Academy together. A few years back he'd gone on some ride-arounds with me because Captain Spaulding thought that was the best way for Roscoe to learn the turf. The captain hoped some street smarts might rub off on Roscoe, but if they did nobody noticed.

I guess it made more of an impression than I thought at the time. Roscoe had remembered and come all the way across the continent to see me when his own kid got killed.

Anyway, Roscoe had a long talk with me. He said I still had a future with the force and I was throwing it all away. I told him I knew I was throwing it away. I told him I was throwing it away because it was garbage and that's what you did with garbage, you threw it away. He looked at me with those Command College brown eyes and said he could understand that I felt that way now, but in case I changed my mind I might want to leave a door open.

I told him thank you but I had other plans. And it came to me, right as I said it, that it was true. I did have other plans. I was going to move back to Key West and go fishing every day.

I guess I thought of Key West because I had lived there at another troubled time in my life and found some peace of mind there.

When I was fourteen my parents divorced. I went to live with an uncle when the infighting got dirty. I had stayed for almost a year. My Uncle Mack had taught me about fishing, and every summer after that I spent in Uncle Mack's battered Whaler, learning the waters and habits of the fish. When Uncle Mack died I knew enough people to get a job as a mate on one of the charter boats, and I'd put in enough time to make getting my captain's ticket pretty easy if I ever wanted to.

Now I wanted to. Now I wanted to run to that forgiving sea and rock in the comfort of the slow salt waves. I wanted to wake up every morning in a place where I'd been happy once and fish with strangers, never seeing a face that might remind me of what had been.

In a frenzy of decision I got the house sold, held a massive garage sale to get rid of the furniture and household stuff, packed away a few things important enough to keep into a small self-storage box, and left. In a brand-new Ford Explorer I drove slowly across the country by back roads, stopping frequently, and arrived in Key West in late summer, a time when the town is taking a nap and the jacaranda trees are littering insanely bright flowers in the streets.

I found my little falling-down cottage and leased it for a year, with an option to buy. I bought my battered bicycle and nosed around for a few weeks until I found the *Windshadow,* a sixteen-foot guide skiff.

And here I was. I thought I was safe and sound and tucked away from all the crazy-making people and places. Free from memories, a new man.

Until Roscoe McAuley showed up and brought it all back, to fall on my unprotected head like a piano dropped from the fourteenth floor.

I didn't want to go back there. I couldn't. I didn't want to do anything that would remind me of that terrible place. I wanted to stay here in the sun and worry about nothing more complicated than where my next charter was coming from. Maybe that wasn't a whole lot to do with my life, but it worked for me. It had kept me from squeezing the trigger. I could still taste the barrel but I had not squeezed the trigger, and if I went back there, back where it happened, I might want another taste and this time I might not be as strong.

I realized I had been standing in the kitchen without moving for some time. I didn't know how long, but the shadow slanting in the window was longer now. My first thought was of Roscoe, of how he had looked as he climbed into his rental car. Maybe he felt the same way now. Maybe the thought of going back to L.A. where somebody had killed his kid, too, froze him up and made him want to slump onto a shady bus bench and let it all pass by. Maybe he was thinking of me now, a little jealous that he didn't have a place to hide like I did.

Except I wasn't sure I had a hiding place anymore, either. Roscoe had found me, and he had brought ghosts with him.

The beer wasn't appealing anymore. I took a shower.

CHAPTER
FIVE

Mallory Square faces the sunset. A lot of places do, even in Key West. But through some loony magic you can only find here Mallory Square has become the capital of sunset.

It's not much to look at in daylight. It's no more than a parking lot with a deepwater dock on the far end. Cruise ships have started tying up there in the last few years. There are desiccated cigarette butts stomped flat and patches of ancient gum with all the sticky pounded out of them. There are oil stains and empty beer cans and weeds growing up in the corners.

The area closest to the water is concrete and slightly raised. Originally built as a wharf, it now provides a natural stage about twenty feet wide. Every night the stage fills with street performers and tourists and as the sun goes down they celebrate.

Maybe Key West, or what Key West has turned into lately, doesn't need much excuse to celebrate. Maybe the party would happen even if the sun didn't go down. It's still called sunset and it's still the biggest single draw in town. There are theaters, museums, shops, restaurants and bars, T-shirt emporiums, biplane rides, strip joints, and whorehouses on the island. People come to see the sunset.

Even in Los Angeles we'd heard of Sunset at Mallory. I thought maybe Roscoe would go there. He might want to see it since he'd come all this way anyhow. He might figure the place would be so full of people nobody would notice him. Anyway, it seemed like a good place to look for him.

By the time I got to Mallory the carnival was going full blast. Considering the savage mood all that carefully packaged gaiety was putting me in, I couldn't imagine what it was doing to Roscoe. If Roscoe *was* here—I only had a half-hunch to go on, a little rabbit of an idea that poked its head up and then disappeared. Since there was nothing else to tell me where Roscoe might be, I followed the rabbit. Sometimes these ideas are right, for whatever subconscious reason.

Sometimes they're wrong, too. I let the crowd push me all the way through the open-air nuthouse one time; past the fire-eater, the jugglers, and the cookie lady, all the way down to the far end of the dock where a guy in a kilt stood torturing a bagpipe. Then I worked my way back again, back towards the big stucco wall that keeps the peasants away from the pool at the Ocean Key House. I saw no sign of Roscoe. There was no reason I should have, just this feeling I'd had as I stood there in the shower and realized I had to try to find him.

Finding somebody in Key West isn't easy. There are too many hotels and they aren't generally crazy about giving out too much information. By the time I could call around to the likely ones Roscoe might be gone. Other than that, I wasn't sure where to look. If you can spare the time, the best way to find somebody is probably to stand on the corner in front of Sloppy Joe's, and sooner or later whoever you're looking for will pass by.

I didn't have the time. I didn't really know why, but I was in a hurry. Somehow I felt like my problem was linked to Roscoe's. There were two dead kids, his and mine. I was feeling an urgent need to find Roscoe fast, almost as if finding him might bring the kids back from death. It wasn't rational, I know, but it had gotten hold of me. I could feel my hands quiver with the need to find Roscoe and talk to him.

I still didn't have any idea what I would say if I found him. All I had was a bad taste in my mouth at the way our talk had ended. I wanted to make him see that I'd help him if I could but there was nothing I could do. No hard feelings.

But mostly the encounter had left me on the edge of paralysis again, on the shore of that dark sea where I'd floated for seven

months, and the thought of swimming there again filled me with a
nervous energy that was almost desperate. I couldn't go back there.
I'd never get out a second time. Maybe if I could find Roscoe, talk
to him, I could get rid of this feeling of dread that was rising up in
my throat.

Just to be sure, I worked my way back through the crowd one
last time. I saw a busload of fat Germans taking pictures of a guy
balancing a loaded shopping cart on his nose. I saw another busload
of Japanese tourists taking pictures of each other. I saw the leathery
old woman I'd seen getting off the head boat this afternoon. She
was eating a cookie the size of her head and watching the slack wire
act with a grim expression.

I didn't see Roscoe. I ended up back at the dark end of the dock,
beside the bagpiper again. Suddenly, just as inexplicably as it took
me over, the sense of urgency drained out of me. I sat on the sea-
wall and looked out to Tank Island, hanging my feet over and just
listening to the piper's psychotic squeal. I felt so bad he started to
sound good to me. I sat there and listened to him shriek through
his four standard tunes a dozen times.

There were not a lot of donations dropped into his hat, but
maybe money wasn't the main reason he did this every night.
Maybe he felt some kind of deep pride in his heritage or his music
and felt that it had to be heard. Maybe just standing there night
after night and watching the sunset while he made his blood-cur-
dling din was enough reward and he didn't even think about
money.

And maybe if I clapped my hands three times Tinkerbell would
be okay and the national budget would balance.

I sat there for a long time. The sun went down, just like it always
does. The people cheered, flung their money at the entertainment,
and everybody went away happy. It got dark.

Most of the tourists would take their bulging billfolds up Duval
Street, stopping at random intervals to spend money. Judging from
the stores along Duval, everybody who came here went home with
at least two hundred new T-shirts and one king-sized hangover.

A lot of the hangovers would get started in Sloppy Joe's. Nobody
cared that the drinks cost too much, the floor was sticky, it was so
crowded you couldn't squeeze in without exhaling and there was
no air-conditioning. It was loud, it was centrally located, it was

famous. So the Germans and Japanese and Scandinavians, the schoolteachers from Jersey and the seed dealers from Iowa, all stopped for a drink, bought a T-shirt, and moved on.

I sometimes thought it would be neater all around if there were just some big machine that grabbed the tourists at the outskirts of our little island, held them up by an ankle, shook out their money, and then sent them home. The money would be evenly divided, without all the fuss and bother of pretending to sell them something they wanted, and the streets would be clean and quiet again, the way it had been when I was a kid here.

I sat on the concrete lip of the Mallory dock. The nervous energy that had driven me down here in the first place was long gone. I couldn't think of anyplace to go. I couldn't think of any reason to do anything. Even if I thought of something, I wasn't sure I'd be able to get up to do it. A tarpon rolled a few feet out. Mallory Square was quiet now. It was strange after the frantic screaming glitz that had been flopping and bellowing on the concrete only a few minutes ago. The party had moved on without me. In my fragile state, that seemed profound. It seemed like a perfect metaphor for my whole life. And I wasn't even drunk.

Self-pity is like masturbation. It's fun for a while, but sooner or later you realize how silly you look. I finally managed to stand up. I had no real thoughts about where to go or what to do, but if I stayed here any longer I might want to buy a bottle of Mad Dog and sing "You Are My Sunshine."

I rode my bicycle slowly up Whitehead Street to avoid the throng a block away on Duval. The street was quiet at this hour. The crowds had moved on from around Hemingway House. A cluster of black men sat on a porch and looked at me without expression. I crossed US 1 and, on an impulse, rode by the Blue Marlin motel. It was a small, clean motel with refrigerators in the rooms and in summer months it had the lowest prices. It was just the sort of place a cop might stay. I didn't see a metallic blue car in the lot, but that might not mean anything.

I dropped my bicycle in the breezeway outside the office and went in. The night clerk was a guy of about fifty. He was balding but he had carefully brushed the side hair over the bald spot and given it a dye job. It looked like the sofa in a disco lounge. He looked at me over the top of a copy of The *Advocate*. "Help you?" he asked dubiously.

"What room is Roscoe McAuley in, please?" I gave him my best business smile and let him look me over carefully for signs of a concealed nuclear weapon. He finally decided I might not be a terrorist, sighed heavily, and flipped open a book. "How is that spelled?" I gave it to him and he scanned the book for a moment, flipping a few pages and following his index finger down the columns on four pages before asking, "When did you say he registered?"

"Today. Maybe yesterday." And maybe not at all, I thought.

"We have no McAuley registered," he said in a very final tone of voice, and lifted his newspaper again.

I thought about saying thanks, but it seemed like a waste of breath. Besides, I didn't want to shatter his image of the rest of the world. I walked out of the little office and picked up my bicycle.

And then I was stuck, because I didn't know where to point it. I could keep trying the hotels. I could go home and call around to the two or three dozen other hotels where Roscoe might be, and they might or might not tell me if he was there.

But what it came down to was that I didn't know where to start looking for Roscoe, and wasn't sure why I should or what to say if I found him. I suddenly felt like a thirty-year-old man sitting on a bicycle in the dark. Maybe it was a good thing I never made Detective.

I pedaled home.

After the bright light of the sunset at Mallory, the night seemed dark and quiet. It was a warm night and the feel of it on my skin was soft. It made me edgy. I went past the rows of houses. Most of them had one small light by the front door, usually yellow, and a purple glow inside from the television. This was another sure sign I was in a resident's neighborhood; only people who lived here watched TV.

The streets here in the residential area were dark and nearly deserted. Most of the people who lived here year-round knew better than to go out after dark. For one thing, you might run into some drunken optician from Wisconsin who wanted nothing more than to follow you home and drink you dry and then throw up on your couch. For another, our island paradise had been catching up with the rest of the world, and over the last few years crack had come to Key West. That meant that the number of burglaries, robberies, and muggings were doubling every six months. Unless you stayed on Duval Street you ran the risk of becoming a statistic.

In fact, as I turned in at the corner of my street, I thought I saw a figure slip over the wall around my house. I wasn't positive, but I wasn't taking any chances, either; not when I might otherwise stumble over somebody who would gladly remove my liver with his bare hands if he could get over half a dollar for it, fast.

With the thought of a little bit of action I felt alive again. The sour taste was gone from the back of my throat and I could feel the blood pounding through my veins.

I took a deep, steadying breath and slipped off my bicycle. I put it quietly on the grass alongside the road and moved into the shadow of a huge oleander that grew up from the corner of my coral rock wall. I waited for my eyes to adjust to the darker yard. Then I moved across the wall as quietly as I could, slinking to the cover of my key lime tree.

From the lime tree I could see the side and back of the house. Sure enough, at the corner of the house, moving jerkily up to the window, there was a small figure. It—he?—appeared to be straining upward on tiptoe to look in the side window, which made him a lot shorter than the six-foot-high clearance of the windowsill. A kid, probably, strung out and wanting to see if anybody was home.

I moved closer. As I did, the intruder grasped the windowsill and started straining upwards in a clumsy chin-up. His toes were about six inches off the ground when I hit him hard, hooking a fist just above the belt into his kidney. He husked out, "Ekkk," very distinctly, and dropped to the ground.

I quickly grabbed his right arm and twisted it around behind his back. He rasped a little moan as I applied pressure, forcing his face down into the dirt.

"Can I help you with something?" I asked politely.

"Awwg, bloody fucking hell—!" I heard, slightly muffled from the mouthful of sandy soil he must have been chewing on. The accent was familiar, even with the voice muffled. I let go of the arm and, reaching under, grabbed a handful of shirtfront and hauled upwards. Sure enough, I pulled a familiar face straight up and held it a few inches from my own.

"Hello, Nicky," I said. "Lose your way?"

"Christ on a fucking bun!" he gagged at me. "You bloody fucking near killed me, mate! Jesus' tits, my fucking noggin is totally bashed in!" He spat a small amount of dirty sand.

"Sorry," I said. "Thought you were a prowler, Nicky." I set him down and brushed him off. Truth is, he was so light it would be easy to forget I was holding him a foot off the ground.

Nicky Cameron was my neighbor. He was an Australian by birth and had landed in Key West by some mysterious process similar to Brownian motion that leaves so many strange, dissimilar people on our island.

Nicky stood just about five feet even and weighed a full ninety pounds soaking wet with a beer in each hand. He was mostly bald, with a few scraggly brown tendrils of hair occasionally flopping over into his face. The face was dominated by two huge brown eyes. In between them was a foot-long nose that hooked slightly to one side, and a chin so far back from his face that it looked like a second Adam's apple.

How he had come by it in Australia I never found out, but somehow Nicky was stuffed with every existing scrap of New Age lore. He knew all about astrology, crystals, shiatsu, channeling, aroma and color therapy, Atlantis, astral projection, herbal medicine, and reincarnation. He ran a shop not far from Mallory Square that sold crystals, New Age music, posters, and other stuff you would otherwise have to go to California to buy.

Nick tended to mind everybody else's business, but I liked him. He was a pretty good neighbor, and those are hard to come by.

"Bloody fucking hell," he mumbled, rubbing his neck and spasmodically twisting his head to one side.

"Sorry, Nicky," I said.

"Put the Neighborhood Fucking Watch back ten years, mate. Can't go 'round pulverizing fellas."

"Sorry, Nicky," I said again. But I knew there was really only one way to apologize, and surprisingly, I suddenly felt like company. "How about a beer?"

His leprechaun face lightened a little. "Too bloody right, a beer," he said. "Reckon you owe me a fucking brewery for that one, mate."

He shook himself like a terrier, said "Right," to himself half under his breath, and led me up to my front door. I unlocked it and he pushed past me, making a beeline for my ancient refrigerator. By the time I caught up with him he had one of the bottles of St. Pauli Girl open and one-third drained. He was staring dismally into the back of the refrigerator, shaking his head with very real pity. "Oh, mate," he said sadly.

Half-annoyed and half-amused, I stared past him into the refrigerator. I didn't see anything to object to, but then I didn't see much of anything at all.

Still, what there was was very neatly organized. I was a firm believer in Tupperware, and the largest shelf was neatly stacked with five containers. They all had labels: Two of them said CHILI—JULY 5. Another one was LASAGNA—MAY 23. The other two labels had somehow gotten smeared and were no longer legible. But I was sure that once I opened them I could probably figure out what was in them.

There was also a quart of Acidophilus milk, half-gone; a quarter stick of margarine, a lump of very questionable but neatly wrapped cheese, and a jar of jelly someone had given me for Christmas almost two years ago. It was all very well ordered and about as appetizing as a gravel driveway.

"What's wrong?" I asked Nicky. He turned those two high-powered lamps on me full blast.

"Billy, lad, old son," he moaned sadly, handing me the other beer. "This is fucking close to tragedy here."

"Why is that, Nicky?"

"The Frigidaire, Billy," he said, raising a finger into the air and then pointing it at me. "The Frigidaire is the window to a man's soul."

I looked at him, his eyes gleaming mournfully. Sometimes, when he went off on his monologues, it was hard to remember how much shorter than me he was. I sipped my beer. "That's the eyes, Nicky. The eyes are the windows to the soul."

He shook his head forcefully. "Never say it, mate. It's the fucking Frigidaire. If old Johnny Keats had one, we'd be off on it all day long, 'stead of those bloody awful Grecian urns." He stretched out the last word in his uniquely Australian way, *eeeeehhhhrrrrnns,* making the word into a long moan against all that was prissy and awful. " 'Course, 'Strahlians"—he meant his countrymen—"our lot have that all figured out. Look in the Frigidaire and you know a man's soul. And, mate—" He shook his head again. "Mate, your soul is on the shit-heap. Aside from the fact," he added sadly, waggling a finger at me, "that I will now have to run off to the Seven-Eleven and get more beer, and something decent to eat."

That reminded me of my mutton snapper, still sitting in the sink. "Uh, Nicky, I got a good piece of fish here—" I stopped since he was shaking his head again, eyes closed to shut out my nonsense.

"A piece of fish. He's got a piece of fish. Billy, old sport," he said, reaching up to put a hand on my shoulder, "a piece of fish is not something decent to eat."

"I like fish," I said.

"Yes," he said with kindly logic, "but you're a bloody loony. Where's your veggies, Billy? And some rice? To say nothing of all the proper and necessary nutrients found only in beer?"

"You're drinking my nutrients," I pointed out.

"That's mean and low," he said with rising indignation. "You half-killed me and now you grudge me one of your horrible, tiny, watered-down beers. No, Billy," and he held out his hand to me, palm up, "the only thing for it is for me to buzz down and grab some decent grub. Otherwise you're going to harm yourself, and I can't allow that." He shook a finger so I would know he was telling the truth. "You need looking after. So fork over, mate." And to my surprise I found myself handing him twenty bucks, even as I wondered what the hell it had been about his company I had thought I wanted tonight.

"Fry up the fish, Billy," he admonished as he capered out the door. He vanished, then stuck his head back in again. "You *have* got an onion, haven't you, mate?" he said, and then he was gone.

I turned back to the sink and rinsed off the fish. Every now and then I wondered why I actually liked Nicky, but I always ended up shrugging it off. I liked him. He was such an improbable guy. He seemed to move at about twice the speed of everybody else and was so full of manic rationality it was impossible to stay mad at him. He always had everybody's best interests at heart, and never stopped telling us all about it. Nobody could stay mad at Nicky, even after watching him eat.

He was one of those tiny people, clearly evolved from the ferret, who must eat twice their weight every day, and Nicky was not refined in his attack. He ate with both hands and a wide-open mouth, spraying crumbs in all directions. He had a lot to say on most subjects and could not sit without wanting to talk. That usually made for problems at the table. I spent most of my dining time with Nicky dodging crumbs, trying to keep them off my food as they flew out of his mouth and across the table, rocketing high in the air, bouncing off the saltshaker, careening everywhere.

Still, there was an incredible charm to the man. I had seen women twice his size fall helplessly into those gigantic, luminous eyes and follow quietly, without struggle, as he led them off to his battered cottage next door. I didn't think he could make an enemy if he wanted to.

I put the fish into a large baking dish and squeezed some key lime juice onto it. I'd let it soak in for a minute before I put it under the broiler. I smeared on a couple of pats of margarine. As an afterthought I sprinkled some cumin on top, then sliced on my last onion.

As I put the dish in the oven, the front door banged and Nicky was back with a paper bag under each arm. The bags looked bigger than Nicky. He roared into the kitchen and flung the bags onto my rickety kitchen table, already unloading them and opening two fresh beers before I could even open my mouth to speak. "Here we go. Not much to choose up there, bloody awful store, but thank you Jesus, they had two last six-packs of Foster's. Not that Foster's is my first choice, you understand, but it's the best we can hope for in this benighted cultural backwater. Cheers, mate," he said and drained off about half of the squat blue-labeled bottle. He slammed open the oven door, slammed it closed again. "Fish in? Lovely. Now piss off," he finished, shoving me out of my kitchen. He had things flying out of the bags and into pots and pans before I even made it to my chair.

I sat. I was suddenly exhausted, whether from Nicky's unbelievable take-charge energy or from the letdown of my total screw-up with Roscoe, I couldn't tell. I leaned back in my chair and held the beer bottle without drinking for a long moment. The racket from the kitchen was near the noise level of a Concorde taking off, plenty loud enough to bring complaints from the neighbors except that they, like me, were used to Nicky, totally charmed out of their natural hostility by his wide-eyed dazzling animation.

I let my mind drift. I still felt bad about Roscoe. I knew I should

have found him. This was my island and I knew pretty well where
he might go. But my first two guesses had been bad and I no longer
had the energy. I gave up. I never used to give up. Something had
changed in me; the thing that used to drive me was no more than a
torpid passenger now.

Screw it, I thought, closing my eyes. I didn't ask for this. Besides,
I had just proved I was useless at this kind of thing. I couldn't even
find Roscoe. I was just not thinking like a cop anymore, and in a
way that would have seemed lazy and cowardly a year ago, that
seemed to me to justify turning down Roscoe, refusing to go back
to my old world, refusing to look at all the memories of my old life
again.

I was not the guy I used to be. I hated Los Angeles and everything I could remember about it. I knew that going back there
would bring back all the things I had worked so hard to forget. I
could not go back there. I couldn't.

"Wake up, mate!" bellowed Nicky, standing about four inches
from my ear. I didn't quite hit the ceiling. "Grub's on! Hop to!"
And he was racing back to the kitchen with a manic cackle, a trail
of rice already catapulting from his mouth. I wiped a few grains
from my ear and followed him.

"Oh, fishy fishy fish," he beamed at me as I finally made it to the
table. He cut the fish and served two-thirds to himself, one-third to
me, slopping it onto plates already heaped with rice and a vegetable
medley containing broccoli, green beans, carrots and mushrooms,
all boiled into submission. "Dig in, Billy. Go on, laddie. Eat up, go
go go," he said, mouth already stuffed with two forkfuls of rice,
one of veggie, and one of fish. I dodged a flying broccoli flower and
sat.

"Well, Billy," he beamed at me. A grain of rice hit my forehead.
"Life is worth living after all, eh?"

He waggled an eyebrow, and then his face disappeared into the
plate. He wouldn't have seen or heard me if I disagreed, so I didn't.
I ate my fish.

CHAPTER
SIX

The next three weeks went by without any real incident. The thought of Roscoe slipped into my mind a few times. I'd bat at it and it would go away again. It just didn't seem to be anything to think about. There wasn't much point, anyway; I felt very bad for Roscoe because I'd been there, been through the hell of losing a child. But he'd counted on that, hoped I'd have an empathetic response, and that made his visit a little too cold-blooded and calculated for me. I was having enough trouble right where I was, doing nothing more complicated than going fishing. I didn't need to get back into the big game again.

I'd made a halfhearted try at running Roscoe down at the airport the morning after my dinner with Nicky. Fighting a foul little beer hangover—which Nicky never seemed to get, no matter how much he drank—I had pedaled over to the airport and looked around. But either Roscoe had gone out sometime the night before or he was still lying low somewhere.

Of course, they don't tell you much at the airlines. The overly made-up woman at the American Eagle counter was just barely willing to admit that they had a flight to Miami, and under threat of torture she finally conceded that it was possible for someone to make a connection there for Los Angeles. But that was it. Since it was more than I expected I wasn't all that disappointed. I figured Roscoe had flown out last night, after crapping out with me. I went home to an unwanted day off, feeling almost virtuous about my inability to track down any information at all.

It was August and it was hot. Business always slacked off in the heat of the summer, so much that most of the fishing guides left town. There were fewer charters, but there were even fewer captains around, so things evened out. I was averaging two or three charters a week and that kept me busy enough so I didn't have to think too much about anything. In fact, for a fishing guide just starting out, two or three charters a week is pretty good. I was tucking away a little money, building up a small reputation, and settling back into forgetting all about everything west of the Marquesas.

That second week in August I had four charters. It was a new record and I might have celebrated, except I didn't really feel like it, and anyway the fourth charter probably didn't count since it was only ninety minutes long. It was a record in its own way. It was the closest I had ever come to cutting up a customer and using him for chum.

The day started badly and got worse faster than the Florida weather. My charter, a pudgy, chinless guy from Manhattan named Pete, had showed up an hour late without apology. When we took off in my skiff the sun was already up. The tarpon had been hitting in the Marquesas for the last two weeks, but it was too late to go there now. By the time we made the thirty-mile trip the morning feed would be over and we'd have several hours of hot, dull work before the action picked up again. So I headed for Woman Key, which is much closer and has some pretty decent flats if you hit the tide right.

It's about a half-hour ride from the dock. Twenty minutes out Pete leaned back at me and signaled urgently. I throttled back and leaned forward to hear him better. Almost immediately I wished I hadn't.

"I don't pay for transit time, do I?" he asked aggressively. "Because I'm not going to."

I was still fairly new at this. I had to believe I hadn't heard him right. "What's that?"

"Tra-vel time," he said, drawing it out so even an idiot like me would understand. "Twenty-two minutes so far. I'm paying four hundred fifty bucks for a boat ride? I don't think so."

"It's a package, not an hourly rate," I said, showing him three teeth. "But if you'd rather fish right here, we can do that. Of course, then you're not getting your money's worth out of the guide, are you?"

He looked over the side of the boat. We were still in the Lakes, a series of flats and pools that run from Key West Harbor down to Ballast Key. At the moment we were idling over a stretch of un-healthy-looking weeds.

"They got fish here?" Pete demanded.

I shrugged. "Some grunts. A few eagle rays. Maybe a turtle."

"So where are we going? I want a tarpon."

I nodded at him like he had just made sense. "That's where we're going. To where the tarpon are."

He looked over the side again. An old Clorox bottle floated past. "Uh-huh. How far is it?"

"Another ten or fifteen minutes," I told him.

"So let's go," he said with authority, and turned back to face front again.

I pushed the throttle forward without saying anything. By the time we got to the flats on the south side of Woman Key, Pete was already fidgeting and looking at his watch. This is usually a bad sign.

Fishing, the way I do it, takes some patience. I like to fish proac-tively, like deer hunting. That means you stalk the fish carefully, because you have studied them and you know their habits and their hangouts. You pole up quietly, spot them, and cast directly, care-fully, to the place the fish will be just after your bait gets there: not too close or you spook them, not too far away or they go right by.

I had just finished explaining that the faint ripple one hundred yards away meant the tarpon were coming in and we had been poling quietly towards them for less than a minute when Pete mut-tered, "Oh, hell," and whipped a very clumsy cast straight ahead.

I was standing directly behind him, on the raised poling platform above the outboard, pushing the boat forward with my guide pole. I had to duck quickly as the crab on his hook whirred past my ear on his back-cast, snatched my hat off coming forward and whipped a good thirty feet ahead. His crab hit the water with a belly-flop smack, which knocked my hat loose from the hook. It went float-ing off to the right.

"What are you trying to do, Pete?" I said through carefully gritted teeth.

"This is supposed to be good fishing?" he accused. "You said fish. So where's the fucking fish?"

"Well, the fucking fish were up ahead. If you haven't terrified them into heading for Cuba with all that splashing, they might still be there."

"That supposed to be funny?" He glared at me. "How the fuck long am I supposed to wait? While you dick around with the pole like it's fucking Venice or something."

"How about if you wait until I tell you, then cast to something we can see? Is that too long?"

He looked sour and savage and turned away. He started to pump his reel furiously. "I'm not paying four hundred fifty bucks for a fucking boat ride," he grumbled. And since the reel was apparently too slow for him he gave a tremendous, two-handed backward yank on the rod. The tip slapped my ear and smashed onto the poling platform. Even as I turned slightly and watched the small silver loop of the rod tip snap off and roll onto the deck I felt the crab smack into my head just above the other ear.

"Some fucking guide," said Pete. "Can't find fish. Can't even duck in time." He snorted.

Some people belong on the dock. If they really have to go fishing they should do it standing on the end of a long pier, clutching a $6.98 Flintstones Model Zebco and a plastic bucket, swearing because the water is too far down for them to reach over and wipe the worm goo off their hands. They don't belong on a flat guide's skiff, sliding across the shallows on the edge of the great ocean. They don't even belong on a head boat, where there are more people in range of their half-deadly stupidity.

The problem is, flatfishing from a skiff got popular a few years back, the way fly-fishing got popular. And now all across America there are thousands upon thousands of garages with unused or once-used fly rods hanging next to the golf clubs and the badminton sets.

An increasing number of people have too much money and not enough sense to pound sand, as my grandfather used to say. So they take all that disposable income and spend it on things that looked really good on the cover of their sixty-dollar-a-year coffee-table magazines and then feel cheated when they don't look as good on them. They have spent their money on The Best, and it was a lot of money, and they think that is supposed to guarantee them a good time.

They think it's supposed to guarantee that they'll look just like the modern-day, upper-middle-class Norman Rockwell picture of themselves they have in their heads from the pictures on the coffee table and they feel cheated when it doesn't work out that way.

Nothing they do is fun, but it's all expensive so they try to persuade themselves that they really are having fun when they're not, or the game is rigged against them. They never figure out that a big bank balance is no guarantee of the good life. Somewhere along the way they read the fine print wrong, but they've already signed and they're stuck with the product.

So they end up just like Pete: rich, miserable, and dangerously stupid on a small boat.

I felt the blood trickling down the right side of my head from where the rod tip had slashed my ear. I felt the salt water rolling off a dull ache on the left side where the crab had smacked me at 100 miles per hour.

I stepped off the platform and moved forward to where Pete was sitting, snarling at me. I stared down at him for a moment, reviewing mentally the ways I knew to kill him, quickly or slowly, with my bare hands, or perhaps with the pliers, a few big shark hooks, a little bit of leader wire—I leaned down instead and pulled the rod out of his hands.

"This is a handmade rod," I told him. "It is worth more than the gold crown on your molars. When we get to the dock you will find an extra hundred and fifty dollars on your bill to cover repairing it."

"The fuck I will," he said.

"You are going to start fishing the right way, just like I tell you, or we're heading back."

"Fuck that noise, I paid in advance—four hundred fifty dollars, one day's fishing. Bait the fucking hook." He started trying to fumble a new rod out of its clamp.

I nodded at him, just like he'd really said something, and took his hand away, placing it in his lap and thinking how fragile the bones in the hand really are. I placed the broken rod back in the teak holder along the side of the boat and stepped back to the platform.

I put the pole in its clamps and tied it down. I turned to the control panel and started the engine.

"Hey! Won't that scare the fish away?"

I nodded at Pete and showed him some teeth. "I owe them that," I said, and shoved the throttle forward hard.

The acceleration caught Pete by surprise and he slid onto the floor. He scrambled back up onto the seat just as I made a wide turn and stopped to pick my hat out of the water. The stop threw Pete forward and back onto the floor. By the time he got back up again, white-knuckled on the gunwale, we were headed for the dock at full speed.

"What the fuck are you doing?" he screamed at me.

"Going home," I shouted over the noise of the engine. "Life is too short to spend any more of it with a dumb asshole like you."

All the abuse and screaming he'd tried before were just a warm-up. Now he really hit his stride. I'd never before heard some of the things he said, even in seven years as a cop. Maybe I'd underestimated Pete: some of it was impressive. I made a mental note to pass on some of the really choice ones to Art, who had a connoisseur's appreciation of good cussing.

But Pete was no artist; he lacked patience and stamina. In a few moments he was winding down, repeating himself, and he finally started to bottom out. "You stupid cock-sucking piece of shit! I paid for a full day! You can't fucking do this!"

"I'm only charging you for a half-day," I yelled back over the sound of the motor. "But when you add on the damage to the rod, it comes out the same."

"You dickhead shitbag butt-sucker!" he screamed.

Flats skiffs are delicate and light. Driving one across a moderate chop at full throttle can be tricky. Unfortunately it takes at least one hand on the wheel at all times, and that put me at a slight disadvantage. So I had to throttle way back again, until the boat was just barely moving forward, before I could lean forward and get my hands on Pete's shirtfront. I lifted upwards. The boat rocked slightly.

Pete was a fairly large guy, maybe six feet tall and basically skinny, but with a pretty good spare tire around the middle that brought his weight up to around one-ninety. He was also one of those guys who confuses belly size with strength, because he grabbed at my wrists and tried to yank my hands away. But the hands he clamped on mine just gave me better leverage. I pulled up and Pete rose eight inches off the seat. It scared him. He shut up.

"You can shut your mouth and ride back," I told him, trying not to let the strain of holding him up show in my voice. "Or you can open your mouth one more time and swim back. It's ten miles, but it's your choice."

I held him up for another second to help him make up his mind. For a moment he thought he was going to say something. He opened his mouth; I tensed my forearm and lifted an inch higher, moving him toward the side of the boat. He shut his mouth quickly. I put him down.

He was quiet all the way to the dock.

By the time I got the first line secured he was already halfway to his car. I guess he figured he was safe there, twenty feet off, because he turned around there to yell at me.

"You haven't heard the last of this, fuckbag!"

I smiled at him. "Yeah, I know. That would be too much to expect." I bent and turned on the hose to wash the boat down.

Pete turned even redder, furious at being ignored. He took a half-step towards me. "Motherfucker! I know guys can put you in the fucking *ground!*"

I couldn't think of anything really funny to say to that, so I just picked up the nozzle of the hose and pointed it in his direction. I squeezed the handle. A hard, very satisfying stream of water hit Pete square in the face. I wiggled my wrist, letting the stream play all over him for a few seconds, then cut it off and dropped it to the dock. "Have a nice day," I said.

He glared at me for a few seconds, then turned away and stomped off to his car, leaving a trail of angry wet footprints.

It was a small victory, and it didn't even really feel very good. Even Art didn't think it was funny.

"That shit's bad for business, Billy," he wheezed at me a few minutes later when I went in to his arctic shack to tell him about it. He shook a collection of chins mournfully back and forth. "You don't know who this guy's friends are."

"I don't want to know anybody who's a friend of that," I told him.

He shook his head some more. "You just don't know," he said.

"Guy came highly recommended. Now he'll go back and tell everybody what a rotten time he had here trying to catch a fish."

"Believe me, not this guy. He'll go back with a handful of fake pictures proving he caught five record tarpons. He'll show a testimonial from the mayor's office stating that he saved the fishing industry singlehanded. This guy is a bullshit artist, Art."

"You just don't know," he repeated. When Art got stubborn he was tough company. So I repeated a couple of Pete's more memorable words and phrases for him. It cheered him up, and for a minute or two we were actually having a good time.

I figured out later that by the time Pete was climbing into his car and dripping on the rented upholstery, and me and Art were chuckling over the whole thing, Roscoe had been dead for about three hours, three thousand miles away. By the time I was done laughing and on my way home, six quarts of Roscoe's blood had been hosed off the sidewalk and into the gutter. The lab trucks were just about done with the scene, although the yellow plastic tape would stay up a while longer.

Roscoe liked to keep a low profile. He didn't want anything splashy on his record. Nothing too gaudy like dying on the street in Hollywood.

Witnesses say Roscoe died with a kind of embarrassed look on his face. That figures.

CHAPTER
SEVEN

When I got home, Nicky was waiting for me on the front steps of my house.

"Mate," he said without any warm-up, "you're in the shithouse and you're in it deep."

"What's up, Nicky?" I asked. I was still a little burned up after dealing with Pete. I wished I'd thrown him in. I didn't feel like another Australian Oktoberfest at the moment.

Nicky handed me an envelope. "Telephone was ringing off the hook, Billy. It stopped. 'Bout an hour later, fella came 'round with this here."

I looked at the envelope. The little plastic window in the front had my name showing.

"It's a telegram, mate," said Nicky helpfully.

"Yeah. I figured that out," I told him. I sat beside him and ripped open the envelope. He peered over my shoulder as I read:

URGENT YOU CALL AT ONCE STOP

DT SGT BEASLEY

LAPD

213/3611549

So Ed Beasley had made Detective Sergeant. That was nice. He had been my partner for two and a half years a while back. We got along just fine until he got a case of ambition. But he was a good cop.

Unlike Roscoe, Ed knew the streets. As a young black kid growing up in L.A., he'd stepped over the line more than once before settling on becoming a cop, and he was one of the few people who knew from both sides the sick thrill of walking down an alley in the Nickel, not knowing if you'd find a wino puking or an ice head with a MAC 10.

Ed Beasley lived through some tough years on the street and he deserved to be Detective Sergeant. He could even be a lieutenant if that's what he wanted. I just couldn't figure out why he wanted to talk to me so urgently.

"I thought so," said Nicky, nodding. He was a slow reader, but he read everything he could get his hands on. Even my mail.

"You thought what?"

He clapped a sympathetic hand on my shoulder. "Yer lumbered, mate. They've got the wood on you good."

I looked at him, still irritated. His gigantic brown eyes radiated all-knowing good humor at me.

"What language is that, Nicky?"

He cackled. "Oh, you're in it good, mate. Your rising sign is in Aquarius. Until the new moon you got discord, loss of harmony, big problem with authority, which is where the coppers come in, see? Oh, and travel. You're taking a trip. It'll be awrful. At *least* until the new moon."

"Okay, Nicky." I'd had enough. I stood up, moving to the front door. "If you say so."

"Clear as mud, mate. Clear as mud. See if it ain't." He cackled again and moved off through the yard, back to his place. I never knew if he really believed all that stuff, but he sure could spout it.

I pushed into my house and put the telegram on the seat of my chair. I stared down at it. I didn't want to call anybody in Los Angeles. I didn't want to think about Los Angeles being there at all. All of it, the whole smog-drenched crap-heap of a city, led right to those two small graves along Sepulveda—but Ed Beasley was a decent guy, a good cop. He had been my partner, and unless you've been a cop yourself you can't really appreciate how much that means. It's a close relationship. It's for life.

I sat by the telephone and dialed.

I let it ring thirteen times. On the fourteenth ring, Ed picked it up himself.

"Beasley," he said. I knew him well enough to hear the strain and fatigue in his voice.

"It's Billy Knight, Ed," I said. "What's up?"

"Billy," he said, and I heard him take a deep breath. I could imagine him sipping from his cup of regular coffee—cream and two sugars—and reaching for the Kool that would be smouldering in the ashtray beside him. "Roscoe McAuley is dead."

I wished I had a cigarette. They are awful things and will kill you as sure as the sun will come up tomorrow and they disgust me, but there is nothing else I know of that you can do at a time like this that makes any sense.

A cigarette is a way of relating to a random universe, a wild and sickening cosmos that never seems logical and always attacks from odd angles in strange but very personal ways. Because smoking doesn't make any sense at all, somehow it's the only rational response to events that don't make sense, that sneak in under the belt and floor you, leaving you stunned and breathless.

I have never smoked and I hope I never will but when I heard Ed tell me Roscoe was dead, and thought of him sitting there with his Kool, I wished I had one, too.

"How did it happen?"

Down the long-distance line I could hear Ed blow out a cloud of mentholated smoke. "It's a funny thing, Billy. Roscoe was down in Hollywood. It's like two-thirty A.M., and he's crawling around in that shit. No place for a desk jockey like that. Nobody knows what he was doing there. So he's down on Cahuenga, near that twenty-four-hour newsstand."

I could see the place in my mind as clearly as if I stood there. "The World News."

"Right. And he comes stumbling out the alley, blood pumping out like from a fire hydrant. Somebody cut his throat, just about took his damn head off. He was holding it on with both hands when he hit the street. He died pretty quick. For a chairwarmer he musta been in pretty good shape, or he wouldn't of made it out the alley cut bad like that."

I took a deep breath. Behind the cold cop description Ed gave me I could sense his shock. We know it's wrong, but we think it anyway; cops are supposed to be immune. A stray bullet, sure. Going down in a face-to-face fight with the cocaine cowboys, or having a massive coronary just before retirement, we expect that. Cops are more aware of being mortal than most people. They expect to die more than most other people do.

But cops aren't supposed to have their heads hacked off in alleys. Especially a command cop like Roscoe. I knew the kind of shock waves Roscoe's brutal murder would be sending through the force. It might not seem fair, but a cop-killing gets a little extra effort, and a cop like Roscoe would get a little more than that.

"What have you got?"

Ed blew out smoke again. "Weird, Billy. Coroner says it was probably a straight razor."

It took me a minute to register that. "A *what?*"

"Yeah. I know. I didn't know they still made 'em. My daddy had one he'd put in his boot on Saturday night, but shit, Billy, ghetto kids nowadays got Uzis. Who the fuck uses a straight razor?"

I couldn't think of anybody. It also occurred to me that it wasn't my job to think of anybody. "Why did you call me, Ed?"

I heard him slurp a little coffee. "Just wondered what you knew, Billy," he said a little too casually. "Your name is in his appointment calendar. He flew back there to see you. Now he's dead. I wondered what you two talked about, that's all."

"His kid."

"Uh-huh." I could hear the routine cop suspicion settling into his voice. I was on the outside now, even to my old partner. I was in a drug zone, and a cop in an expensive suit had been brutally murdered after visiting me.

"For God's sake, Ed, you must have something besides me."

"Well, you know how it is, Billy. You guys just stood around and talked about his kid, huh?"

"That's right."

He blew out more smoke. "He flew all the way across the country, three thousand miles, to talk to you? About his kid?"

"He was very broken up about it, Ed. Had some crazy idea that I could help him find out who whacked out his kid."

"What'd you tell him?"

I came close to biting my tongue. "Ed, you sound like you take that idea seriously."

"That means you said no, huh?"

"Stop it, Ed. That shit is crazy. What was I supposed to do?"

"I worked with you for two and a half years, man. I know what you can do, just like Roscoe knew it."

"I'm retired. I take people fishing. Give me a break, I can't do anything you couldn't do a hell of a lot better."

There was a long pause while Ed sipped, then blew out a lungful of smoke before he finally said, "Roscoe thought you could."

I said a bad word. Ed didn't say anything, so I said it again and hung up. I stood up and paced the room, stomach churning.

Maybe Donahue was right. Maybe we can't run from our problems. If we do, maybe they run after us and catch up sooner or later. Maybe all the talk shows are right, all the pop psychology and easy, comfortable clichés. Maybe we really need to Face Negative Feelings and Be Okay with them. It didn't seem to matter too much right now.

It mattered a lot less to Roscoe. He'd come to me with a problem and I'd told him to go to hell. Now he was dead in a messy, public way. His last thought was probably how much he hated going like that, in the street, his suit and carefully knotted silk tie ruined by all that sloppy blood.

His problem had caught up with him. When he couldn't get me to help he tried to do it himself. He knew he wouldn't be any good at it, but he had to try. After all, he was a cop. He was a pampered, street-stupid headquarters cop, but he was a cop and that meant something. It didn't mean much to the person who had tried to saw his head off with a minstrel-show weapon, but to Roscoe it meant he had to deal with the problem. He knew from the start he couldn't do it, but he had to try.

So he tried it himself and sure enough, he couldn't handle whatever it was. Instead it handled him; casually, contemptuously, turning his carefully cultivated appearance into gutter garbage, a sad heap of guts in a $1200 suit.

Of course it was possible that his death was completely unconnected to his son's murder. It was possible—but not likely. Like the indoor cat that feels untouchable looking out the window but knows it will get its ass kicked if it goes outside, Roscoe knew he didn't belong on the street. Whatever drove him down an alley in Hollywood that late at night was important, and the only thing that important to Roscoe, important enough to risk a mark on his personnel file and to bring him all the way across the continent, was his son.

Ed Beasley was right. Whatever killed Roscoe was connected to his visit to me. I couldn't tell Ed any more than that, but I knew one more thing. Roscoe had found something. The pampered, indoor cat had found the bad coyote and it ate him. Roscoe was not tough, and he must have known that he was up against something that might get him. But big surprise; he'd tried anyway. He'd found something. And if Roscoe could find it, I was pretty sure I could find it.

And with that thought I realized something awful, something so sickening it actually made my face numb and my ears burn. As the thought formed I fell back in the chair, gasping for breath like a gill-netted fish.

I was going to go to Los Angeles. I was going to go back where I swore I would never go again and find out who had killed Roscoe and his son. In some really stupid and maybe self-destructive way, Roscoe's problem and mine had gotten twisted together. I couldn't stay here anymore. It wasn't safe. The beast had come out of the cave and found me and the only way to put it to rest for good was to go back and kill it where it was born.

I was going back to Los Angeles.

A half-hour later I was knocking on the door to Nicky's mouldering cottage. The door was glossy with a recent half-inch-thick coat of brown paint. The paint couldn't hide the fact that the door was full of dry rot. If I knocked too hard I had the feeling the door would crumble.

Almost before I finished knocking, Nicky was yanking open his door.

"Billy!" he bellowed. He eyed the brown paper bag under my arm. "Perishables? And I should feed the cat?"

I blinked. It seemed like the whole world was moving twice as fast as my best speed. "Yeah. How'd you—"

He was already shaking his head. "Mate, mate—din't I just finish telling you? Your rising sign, Billy. In Aquarius, lad. Think I make this shit up?"

"Yes," I said, with as much firmness as I could manage. I shoved the bag at him. "I'd really rather think you do. Table scraps are fine for the cat."

"And then what'll I have for breakfast?" He laughed, then stopped when he saw my face. "All right, Billy, take a deep breath, boyo. It'll be fine. Cat'll be fine. No worries, mate."

"Thanks, Nicky. There's beer in the fridge."

"Not for long, mate. Come back to us, Billy. Come back safe and soon."

Art was a little harder to manage.

"The fuck are you saying, Billy? Got two charters in the next four days."

"Cancel for me, Art. Give 'em to Tiny."

Art shook his head mournfully, just slowly enough to get his two outside chins rotating in opposite directions. "Tiny's a dickwad. Couldn't find a fish if it was blowing him. You're just getting started, Billy. Building up some momentum. Take off now yer gonna fuck it up."

"I can't help that. I have to do this, Art."

"I'm telling ya, you'll drop two, three grand you leave now."

"I have to."

"That kind of money, it can smooth over a whole lot of have to."

"Not this time. Keep an eye on my boat?"

Art spat at his ashtray. The tin tray rang like a gong. "Goddamn stupid son of a bitch. Serve you right the fucking boat sinks."

"Tiny can handle two charters."

"Tiny can't handle tying his own fucking shoes without tyin' 'em together and falling on his goddamned stupid ass. You leave now, Billy, goddamn it, you're not gonna work again until next year this time, that's a promise."

"I'm sorry, Art."

He slammed a fist on the glass countertop. There was weight to the move, but very little force. It made a flabby slapping sound, like dropping a large chunk of bacon on a butcher block. "Sorry don't mean shit, Billy! You got to take care of business! Is what I'm saying."

I'd had enough. I liked Art, and he was throwing enough work my way to make me grateful, but I was beginning to feel like I was facing a very large school principal.

"Art," I said, leaning in close enough to count the pores on his nose. "I am leaving. I have to. I'll call when I get back. Please keep an eye on my boat. Thank you." I looked him in the eye for a long beat. He looked back. He sighed heavily.

"Go," he said finally. "Go on, get outa here. Go."

"I'll see you, Art," I said. I turned for the door. The latch felt frosty as I pushed the door open. "Butthole," Art mumbled behind me. It seemed mild under the circumstances.

There wasn't much to pack. It all fit into one small suitcase. The suitcase fit into the battered basket on the front of my bicycle. I pedaled over to the airport, chained my bike to a signpost in front of the American Eagle building, and went in.

I just had time to make the feeder flight to Miami. The same overly made-up woman sold me a ticket, with a tight professional smile that said even if she remembered me from the last time when I came in to ask about Roscoe, she would never admit she noticed me now.

I shuffled out the gate, up the stairs into the airplane, and buckled up in a window seat at the back of the small jet.

Ten minutes later we were in the air.

CHAPTER
EIGHT

Miami International Airport has changed a lot since I saw it the first time when I was a kid. It used to be a sleepy place, the kind of airport you saw only on the way to somewhere else. It had been a large airport with a small spirit. It apologized for where it was and politely helped you get through to your destination. It was like being in a backward foreign country that had spent all its tax money to make one public building look modern, but instead it looked like an animal shelter in downtown Cleveland. It was homely, but kind.

But sophistication came. Miami had grown tremendously, not always in the right directions. So had the airport. The shyness was gone, and the politeness. Now it seemed false and brash, like a recycled set from "Miami Vice," and it was busier than Mexico City at rush hour, except the transportation wasn't as good. In fact, the transportation wasn't even as good as the San Diego Freeway at rush hour. The whole airport was carefully laid out so that no matter where you were going you had to walk at least twenty-five minutes to get there.

My flight from Key West arrived ten minutes late as the result of taking an eastward turn to avoid a bad thunderhead. It took me five minutes to find a screen listing arrivals and departures. Three people in airline uniform resolutely refused to help me. When I finally found the display terminal I was jostled seven times as I looked for my flight information. A kid spilled a Coke on my foot and then yelled. His mother glared at me.

I finally read my flight number. The plane to L.A. was leaving from a far-off terminal. I had ten minutes. I ran through four and a half miles of blind passages, sticky floors, and crowds thrashing by at a panicky gallop. I made my turn and pelted through seven construction zones, eighteen Latin American Shriners conventions, nine hostile cleaning crews, three metal detectors, two detachments of dope-sniffing dogs, and then outside for a final half-mile sprint in a rainstorm.

I made it to the gate as they were locking down the doors on the plane. Somehow I caught the gate attendants on an off-day. Instead of giving me a snotty explanation that I was too late, they actually smiled as they undogged and opened the door for me, wished me a pleasant flight in Spanish, and sent me on my way.

By the time I flopped into an aisle seat, gasping for breath, and shoved my bag under the nun in the seat in front of me, the plane was already moving backwards, headed for the runway. But this was Miami; after backing out and turning slowly into position, the plane simply stopped dead for fifteen minutes. The air-conditioning in the cabin went off. Within thirty seconds it was sweltering hot and the pocked Plexiglas windows were steaming over.

Within two minutes the cabin smelled like the Raiders' locker room at halftime.

The intercom beeped and clicked on. I could hear someone take a ragged breath. Then it clicked off again. The nun crossed herself.

And we sat there on the runway.

At the back of the plane a door opened and closed. A smell slid up the aisle. It reminded me of Boy Scout camping trips, when somebody peed on a pine log fire.

I thought about Roscoe. I had not really been his friend, but I was maybe the closest thing to a friend he had, because he trusted me for some reason. He was too ambitious, too aware of political risk, to have real friends in the LAPD. Friends slow you down; you might be held responsible for their mistakes and so you had two backs to watch instead of one.

But he remembered the time he spent in my car, and he came to me. The fact that he had come, even though I was still a political hot potato in LAPD, showed how important this had been to him.

The only other thing that had ever mattered to him was his family. I had spent around sixty hours cooped up in a patrol car with the guy, and the only time he seemed human was when he talked about his son.

That was before Melissa was born. If I'd had a kid at the time, maybe Roscoe and I would have been real friends. Maybe I would know why he had trusted me. And then maybe I would have gone to L.A. when he'd asked me. And maybe he'd be alive today.

I was glad it was not night. In the bright Miami sun coming into the cabin of the plane, the maybes were bad enough. In any case, I had to do this. I owed it. I didn't know if I owed it to Roscoe or to me, but I owed it.

The man in the middle seat next to me was fidgeting. He was huge, and he was sweating like only a big man can. The drops ran off the bald top of his head and into a neat fringe of dark blond hair. Then they would roll down the curve of his ear, onto his lobe, and fall onto his magazine with a tiny "plaf" sound. He turned the page of the magazine, carefully separating the damp pages. He let the magazine fall into his lap, limp. He stared at the seat in front of him, then at the intercom speaker above him, then took a deep breath. He loosened his red power tie and flexed his neck muscles spasmodically. He turned to me.

"Excuse me," he said, in a voice that sounded like it came from the bottom of a rusting old oil drum. "I'm getting very claustrophobic. Would you mind changing seats?"

I turned to face the man. Beyond him at the window seat I saw a profile like they used to put on coins. She was maybe thirty, with a shower of light brown ringlets falling away from her face and across her shoulders. Under the hair her neck looked impossibly delicate. I felt my heart kick and turn over in a way it hadn't for almost two years. "Sure," I said, quickly sliding into the aisle to let him out. "No problem."

The big guy lurched out after me and I slipped back into the middle seat. The woman at the window turned and gave me a brief smile, and then turned to look out the window again. It was only a small smile, a smile for a stranger. But even after she turned away I felt the smile sticking to me, making my face hot and my palms clammy. I wanted to bite her neck, spend a week chewing on her lips—

—and the bottom fell away as I realized what I was thinking. I couldn't do this. I couldn't feel this way. Like Los Angeles, this part of my life was over; it all ended at the Rossmore on March 18. I hadn't done more than think about a woman since that day. The thinking had left me shaking and guilty enough. If I were ever to do something beyond thought, like touch that creamy olive skin—I couldn't. In the deep three A.M. of my head and heart I was still married.

But here I was, going back to L.A., back to all the old ghosts. Maybe it was fitting that those other dead parts kick up, twitch into brief life, on that long plane ride back to my dead self. And yet—

I still didn't want to think about the feelings this woman was raising in me. If I had to go to L.A. I would, but I could not visit those sealed-off places in myself. I had put up heavy doors and locked them. To open those doors would let all the pain out again, and this woman was already fingering the padlocks. And yet—

Maybe I should just talk to her; odds are she'd be so dumb the feelings would die away again. Nobody can look like that and still be worth talking to. Every perfect profile I had ever met had nothing to say beyond advice on nail care. This profile was so far beyond the perfection of any other I had ever seen—how could anybody possibly live in there? She had to be what Nicky called a Twinkie; all delicious, bubbly dumbness in a transparent wrapping.

As a way to prove it to myself I looked at her hands. I have known guys who would chase a humpbacked sheep if she had large breasts, or great legs, or a firmly rounded butt. I have always been more attracted to a woman's hands. To me they reveal so much more about who she is than any other feature. Faces can be made up or controlled. Figures can be accidental, or contrived. And legs, after all, are just something to walk around on.

The hands alone are naked. They can tell you all you need to know about the person they're attached to. Long red nails and chubby knuckles? A bonbon eater, stay away. Stubby, chewed-off nails and twitching fingers? A nervous wreck, a bed-wetter, a neurotic. If you know what to look for, you'll never be surprised. Other features might be more seductive, but only the hands tell the truth.

This woman's hands looked strong. They were lined and the nails were neat; not painted, but glossy with health, trimmed to a useful length. Like that impossible neck, the hands were close to perfect.

I looked up at her profile again. She had turned away to look out the window, and in turning had caused a tendon to stand out on her neck. It ran in a graceful curve up from her shoulder and into the halo of her hair, accenting unnecessarily the unbearable delicacy of her neck. At the corner of her mouth I could see a very slight smile playing on her full lips.

I felt two steps back from the grave for the first time in eighteen months. I had to speak. If she was a Twinkie I needed to know, and fast, because otherwise—I couldn't say. I was not ready for otherwise. But I had to talk to her.

I took a deep breath and opened my mouth, with no idea of what sort of clumsy, stupid, fatuous dumbbell thing I was about to say to her. It didn't matter; just noise, anything to see that smile again.

"Thanks," rumbled the rusty voice of the big guy on my other side. "Thanks for switching seats. Every now and then I get like that. A little panicky. Just a little. I appreciate it. Usually it's just when we're not moving, you know? Something about just sitting there on the runway, I start to picture a big bull's-eye on top of the plane. I mean, if something went wrong, like another plane coming in on top of us or a fire or a"—he lowered his voice and almost whispered the word—"bomb, I mean we'd be stuck here. They don't want you to think about it, but hey, no way we could all get off this thing if it was burning. No way. Anyhow."

He stuck a large soft hand in front of my face. I stared at it stupidly for a long second, disoriented at being jerked back to such a strange place, to such an improbable monologue. He smiled and gave a little dip to his hand to let me know what he had in mind and, instead of strangling him for interrupting, I shook the hand.

"Jordan Loomis," he said. "I'm an actor. Going back home, back to L.A. Just wrapped ten days on the new Segall flick they're shooting here. Not a big part, but hey—I think it'll get noticed. It was pretty right for me. Kind of thing I do well, you know? Sort of second heavy is the technical term. You know, the guy who stands behind the featured villain and cracks his knuckles." He cracked his knuckles for me and gave me a mean little leer. Then he laughed. "Like that. Seen me before? I was in 'Evil Breeze' last year." He saw my stupid expression. "The miniseries. You didn't see it? In-credible. It got like a forty share. You don't watch TV? I don't blame you. Where you from?"

I stared at him. In spite of wanting to kill him for interrupting, I couldn't see any harm in the guy. He was even trying not to sweat on me. On the other hand, I could still see that old-coin profile out of the corner of my eye. She was turned to the window, obviously listening, a small smile teasing the side of her mouth. The smile was wonderful, but slightly wicked, like the smile of the Roman sena-tor's daughter when she sees the face of a sassy Christian as the lions come into the arena.

"Excuse me," I said to the actor. I turned towards the face at the window. "Pardon me, ma'am," I said to the woman, dropping my voice and sounding as much like Gary Cooper as I could manage, "but if you don't strike up a conversation with me immediately, I'm going to have to kill this guy."

She turned slow, smiling golden eyes on me. I felt the impact of her all the way down to my toes. She gave me a huge, wonderful smile, a smile that was pure mean in the nicest possible way. "In that case," she said, in a voice like rum and honey, "I have nothing to say to you."

She turned and looked back out the window.

I was in love.

I mean, I wasn't in love, not really. I couldn't be. I didn't even know her name. She had perfect hands, the most delectable neck I had ever seen, and a great sense of humor. After thirty seconds she seemed so close to my ideal woman that the difference made no difference. But all that was behind me. I couldn't imagine ever dating again. It was foreign country to me, and the only map I had led to those two graves along Sepulveda. The thought of the terri-tory of Love was still tied up with the sound of dirt hitting wooden boxes.

And yet—

"Listen," I said, leaning closer to her and just barely restraining myself from putting my mouth on her neck, "I'll put it another way. If you don't speak to me, I'm going to switch seats with this guy again. Let him sit here in the middle the whole flight. It's five hours to L.A."

She turned back and looked at me. Time slowed. I watched in

helpless fascination as she moved her golden eyes across my face, pausing on the scar, down to my neck and shoulders, back up to my eyes.

"You play dirty," she said finally.

"I play for keeps."

"Well, then," she said, and gave a low, throaty laugh that made the skin walk on the back of my neck. She slid a perfect hand over towards me. My mouth felt dry.

"Nancy Hoffman," she said.

Hoffman, I thought. Hoffman, with that olive tawny skin. I would have thought Mediterranean. Nancy DeLucia. Nancy Sintros. Maybe she was German-Italian. Maybe she was Southern Swiss. Maybe on the day that she was born the angels got together and decided to create a dream come true. It didn't matter. It had never mattered less in my life.

I don't think she noticed me gasping for breath as I took her hand. If she did, maybe she thought it was just the heat. At least my hands weren't clammy. But if this kept up my voice would crack and I'd break out in pimples. "Billy Knight," I said, concentrating on not holding onto her hand for too long. "You're not an actress, are you?"

She laughed again. It sounds stupid to say her laugh was musical, but there it was. Her laugh was as full of wistful harmony as Glenn Miller, as raw as Chuck Berry, soulful as Billie Holiday, pure as Ella Fitzgerald, and clean and light as Mozart.

"An actress? Me? Lord, no. What did I say to offend you? I'm a nurse."

"Fantastic," I said. "I don't think I use that word twice a year, but that's what came out. I could feel this thing slipping away from me fast. "And what does your husband do?"

I think I must have said that to hear her laugh again. It worked. When she was done laughing I felt like applauding. "You cut right to the chase, don't you, Billy?"

While I was trying to think of a clever answer the plane lurched. The air-conditioning came back on, and we were moving out onto the runway again at last.

There was a ragged, sarcastic cheer from some of the passengers and the intercom came on.

"Sorry for the delay, folks," the voice said. "We are now first in line for take-off."

"Hmmph," said Nancy, "Apology goes a lot further with a complimentary drink."

"Flight attendants, prepare for departure," said the intercom, and we were pressed back into our seats as the plane headed down the runway.

We were up in the air very fast. I could just see the clutter of Miami Beach out the window, and then we stood on one wing and turned west: west to the setting sun, west to darkness. I turned and looked at the face between me and the window.

I caught her eye again, that warm golden eye. It held me. "So, uh—you've been on vacation? In Miami?"

"No, in the Virgin Islands. Miami isn't my idea of a vacation."

"Oh, you don't like automatic weapons?"

"I get enough of that at home," she said. "I work at a free clinic and believe me, I get plenty of gunshot work."

I knew the free clinics. They're a leftover from the power-to-the-people stuff that was always a little more potent in L.A. and San Francisco than back east. Some of the clinics are pretty good.

"Which one?" I asked her. "I used to live in L.A."

She made a face. "Crenshaw District."

"Ouch," I said.

"Yeah, I know. I started out there all full of idealism and—I don't know. I've been there for five years and things just get a little worse every year. I think I'm ready for a change. In fact, I've started looking around for something else, maybe in a nicer place. Maybe someplace tropical. I don't know." Her eyes drifted away and she seemed lost for a moment, whether in her past or her future, I couldn't say.

She snapped out of it abruptly, with another of those glorious smiles.

"Anyway. What about you, Billy? Visiting family in L.A.?"

"No. No, I'm, uh—" I had a little flash of thinking I should try to explain it all to her. The feeling went away. "I just, uh, have some stuff to take care of."

It seemed like a bad start. But it got better quickly. Maybe I talked too much to make up for the bad start. Maybe she talked too much to keep me from switching seats with the actor. Whatever it was, we filled up three thousand miles with our life stories. She had a brother who was a reporter, her folks lived out in the Valley.

For my part, I left out a lot; marriage, the Rossmore, that kind of thing. But the rest just poured out. I found it easy to be a human being with her. It was something I hadn't been in a long time.

And far too soon, well before I was ready or thought it was possible, we were sliding down over that red desert, over the last range of mountains, and into LAX.

I leaned over Nancy and looked out the window. The smell of her still made me dizzy—or maybe it was just the plane's loss of altitude.

It was dusk outside. It always seems to be dusk when you land in L.A. They call it the City of Angels, but that's just cheap sarcasm. L.A. is the City of Night.

Something about that last approach to LAX always gets to me. You see the red desert, the soft tan and green and gray of the mountains, and suddenly there it is, the biggest man-made sprawl the world has ever known. From the center of the L.A. basin you can drive for an hour in any direction and nothing changes. There is a bank, a gas station, a convenience mart and a mini-mall at every intersection in all that vast spread.

From the air it is a grid of lights that stretches neat and symmetrical for as far as you can see, from the edge of the mountains down to the ocean. The freeways and larger surface streets are lined by pink lights and marked by the thick ribbons of traffic, yellow dots of headlights running one way and red the other.

Even in a jet it takes a long time to cross that huge and foul basin. It seems even longer when you are trying to think of something to say so the flight doesn't end when the plane lands.

I didn't want to say so long to Nancy and have it end. But the closer I got to L.A. the more that old feeling of dread closed in. As we went into our final approach I couldn't think of anything except that double-casket funeral. Out the window I thought I could see the cemetery along Sepulveda. I knew that was stupid, but I thought it anyway.

So the plane taxied up to the terminal and stopped, and the big guy in the next seat lurched off, sulking. The other passengers jammed into the aisle and started shoving for the exits. I looked for something to say, some way to climb out of the cloud that had settled on me as we landed. I couldn't find it.

Nancy gave it a good long three minutes. She pretended to be watching for an opening in the line of passengers kicking and elbowing past us. She gave me plenty of time to say something to her. I started to say something twice, but I suddenly felt like Jennifer was watching me. The thought paralyzed me. I couldn't even stand up.

Nancy finally gave up. "Well," she said firmly, "thanks for a lovely talk." She stood up. I moved aside to let her out and she grabbed a bag from the bin above our seat. Something witty and endearing was on the tip of my tongue, but it stayed there. She was down the aisle and off the plane and I just sank back into the seat and sat there.

I watched her go. She moved carefully up the aisle, and just before turning left off the plane she looked back at me with a brief, unreadable expression. Then she was gone.

I just sat for three or four minutes. There was no one else left on the plane. I thought I had felt bad when I was trying to talk to her. Suddenly I felt much worse. I grabbed my bag and pushed off the plane, pretty sure I'd just blown some kind of last chance.

The feeling grew on me as I walked into the terminal. LAX is one of the biggest and most modern airports in the world. It always makes me feel fat, cheap, and guilty of something. But this time I didn't pause to watch the anorexic fur-bearing bimbos in their leather jeans. I hurried, just short of running, all the way down the long corridor. I took the escalator two steps at a time.

I found her again outside baggage claim. She had crossed over to the traffic island. One brown canvas bag with leather straps was beside her on the pavement. She was about to climb into a blue van with gold lettering on the side saying SUPER SHUTTLE. The electronic destination sign on the front of the van said WILSHIRE DISTRICT in letters made of yellow dots.

"Hey," I said, sprinting across the road between a stretch limo and a Bentley. "Hang on. Just a second. Wait up." The words tumbled out stupidly as she turned and looked at me, arching one perfect eyebrow. Her right foot was on the step leading up into the van, presenting me with a view of her leg. I took back everything I had ever said about legs just being something you walk around on. Hers were a lot more than that.

"Yes?" she said. There was polite curiosity in her voice, as though the interlude on the airplane was long past and nothing more was supposed to happen.

I came up to her, breathing a little hard. A bus went by. Its exhaust washed over me and I got my first L.A. headache in a year and a half.

"Uh," I said. Not original, not very witty, not a good start. I coughed.

"I think my shuttle is leaving," she said, a light brush of throaty giggle dragging across her words.

"Uh," I said again. "Uhm, I." I stopped. I couldn't say any more to save my life. I looked at her; actually, I goggled at her. My tongue felt like it was twice the size of my mouth and made from some rare heavy metal. She started to smile; that made me blush. I looked away. Another bus went by, followed by a van, a Mercedes, a battered Chevy, a Corniche, and two shuttles.

"You're not very good at this, are you?"

"No. No. I'm not, no."

"Never asked anybody for a phone number before?"

I looked at her, then looked away again. "Not for a long time."

The shuttle driver leaned over, a lean young black man with a goatee. "We leaving now, miss. Got to close the door," he said.

I looked back at Nancy in a panic. I could feel sweat break out over the entire surface of my body. She smiled at me, and for a half-second a different kind of sweat took over.

"Could I, uh—" And I stopped dead, looking into her golden eyes. It had never been this hard the first time around, when I was a teenager.

"Call me sometime? Absolutely. Here." She rummaged in her shoulder bag and tore a deposit slip out of her checkbook. "My number's on here," she said, handing it to me. "Don't wait too long, Billy."

And she was gone into the shuttle. Before I could even take another breath of acid brown bus fumes, the shuttle driver slammed the side door shut, ran around and hopped in the driver's seat, and the shuttle was gone in traffic.

I stood there and watched the spot where it had gone for a good ten minutes before it occurred to me that I didn't know where I was going. I had been so concerned with Nancy that I hadn't thought about what happened next. It hadn't even hit me yet that I was here, back in this place I said I'd never see again.

But here I was. And now I had to figure out what to do with me.

I walked back into the terminal.

CHAPTER
NINE

Somebody once said Los Angeles isn't really a city but a hundred suburbs looking for a city. Every suburb has a different flavor to it, and every Angeleno thinks he knows all about you when he knows which one you live in. But that's mostly important because of the freeways.

Life in L.A. is centered on the freeway system. Which freeway you live nearest is crucial to your whole life. It determines where you can work, eat, shop, what dentist you go to, and who you can be seen with.

I needed a freeway that could take me between the two murder sites, get me downtown fast, or up to the Hollywood substation to see Ed Beasley.

I'd been thinking about the Hollywood Freeway. It went everywhere I needed to go, and it was centrally located, which meant it connected to a lot of other freeways. Besides, I knew a hotel just a block off the freeway that was cheap and within walking distance of the World News, where Roscoe had been cut down. I wanted to look at the spot where it happened. I was pretty sure I wouldn't learn anything, but it was a starting place.

And sometimes just looking at the place where a murder happened can give you ideas about it; cops are probably a little more levelheaded than average, but most of them will agree there's something around a murder scene that, if they weren't cops, they would call vibes.

So Hollywood it was. I flagged down one of the vans that take you to the rental car offices.

By the time I got fitted out with a brand new matchbox—no, thank you, I did not want a special this-week-only deal on a Cadillac convertible; that's right, cash, I didn't like credit cards; no, thank you, I did not want an upgrade of any kind for only a few dollars more; no, thank you, I didn't want the extra insurance—it was dark and I was tired. I drove north on the San Diego Freeway slowly, slowly enough to have at least one maniac per mile yell obscenities at me. Imagine the nerve of me, going only sixty in a fifty-five zone.

The traffic was light. Pretty soon I made my turn east on the Santa Monica. I was getting used to being in L.A. again, getting back into the rhythm of the freeways. I felt a twinge of dread as I passed the exit for Sepulveda Boulevard, but I left it behind with the lights of Westwood.

The city always looks like quiet countryside from the Santa Monica Freeway. Once you are beyond Santa Monica and Westwood, you hit a stretch that is isolated from the areas it passes through. You could be driving through inner-city neighborhoods or country-club suburbs, but you'll never know from the freeway.

That all changes as you approach downtown. Suddenly there is a skyline of tall buildings, and if you time it just right, there are two moons in the sky. The second one is only a round and brightly lit corporate logo on a skyscraper, but if it's your first time through you can pass some anxious moments before you figure that out. After all, if any city in the world had two moons, wouldn't it be L.A.?

And suddenly you are in one of the greatest driving nightmares of all recorded history. As you arc down a slow curve through the buildings and join the Harbor Freeway you are flung into the legendary Four-Level. The name is misleading, a slight understatement. It really seems like a lot more than four levels.

The closest thing to driving the Four-Level is flying a balloon through a vicious dogfight with the Red Baron's Flying Circus. The bad guys—and they are all bad guys in the Four-Level—the bad guys come at you from all possible angles, always at speeds just slightly faster than the traffic is moving, and if you do not have every move planned out hours in advance you'll be stuck in the wrong lane looking for a sign you've already missed and before you know it you will find yourself in Altadena, wondering what happened.

I got over into the right lane in plenty of time and made the swoop under several hundred tons of concrete overpass, and I was on the Hollywood Freeway. Traffic started to pick up after two or three exits, and in ten minutes I was coming off the Gower Street ramp and onto Franklin.

There's a large hotel right there on Franklin at Gower. I've never figured out how they break even. They're always at least two-thirds empty. They don't even ask if you have a reservation. They are so stunned that you've found their hotel they are even polite for the first few days. There's also a really lousy coffee shop right on the premises, which is convenient if you keep a cop's schedule. I guessed I was probably going to do that this trip.

A young Chinese guy named Allan showed me up to my room. It was on the fifth floor and looked down into the city, onto Hollywood Boulevard just two blocks away. I left the curtain open. The room was a little bit bigger than a gas station rest room, but the decor wasn't quite as nice.

It was way past my bedtime back home, but I couldn't sleep. I left my bag untouched on top of the bed and went out.

The neighborhood at Franklin and Gower is schizophrenic. Two blocks up the hill, towards the famous Hollywood sign, the real estate gets pretty close to seven figures. Two blocks down the hill and it's overpriced at three.

I walked straight down Gower, past a big brick church, and turned west. I waved hello to Manny, Moe, and Jack on the corner: it had been a while. There was still a crowd moving along the street. Most of them were dressed like they were auditioning for the role of something your mother warned you against.

Some people have this picture of Hollywood Boulevard. They think it's glamorous. They think if they can just get off the pig farm and leave Iowa for the big city, all they have to do is get to Hollywood Boulevard and magic will happen. They'll be discovered.

The funny thing is, they're right. The guys that do the discovering are almost always waiting in the Greyhound station. If you're young and alone, they'll discover you. The magic they make happen might not be what you had in mind, but you won't care about that for more than a week. After that you'll be so eager to please you'll gladly do things you'd never even had a name for until you got discovered. And a few years later when you die of disease or overdose or failure to please the magic-makers, your own mother won't recognize you. And that's the real magic of Hollywood. They take innocence and turn it into money and broken lives.

I stopped for a hot dog, hoping my sour mood would pass. It didn't. I got mustard on my shirt. I watched a transvestite hooker working on a young Marine. The jarhead was drunk enough not to know better. He couldn't believe his luck. I guess the hooker felt the same way.

The hot dog started to taste like old regrets. I threw the remaining half into the trash and walked the last two blocks to Cahuenga.

The World News is open twenty-four hours a day, and there's always a handful of people browsing. In a town like this there's a lot of people who can't sleep. I don't figure it's their conscience bothering them.

I stood on the sidewalk in front of the place. There were racks of specialty magazines for people interested in unlikely things. There were several rows of out-of-town newspapers. Down at the far end of the newsstand was an alley. Maybe three steps this side of it there was a faint rusty brown stain spread across the sidewalk and over the curb into the gutter. I stepped over it and walked into the alley.

The alley was dark, but that was no surprise. The only surprise was that I started to feel the old cop adrenaline starting up again, just walking down a dark alley late at night. Suddenly I really wanted this guy. I wanted to find whoever had killed Roscoe and put him in a small cell with a couple of very friendly body-builders.

The night air started to feel charged. It felt good to be doing cop work again, and that made me a little mad, but I nosed around for a minute anyway. I wasn't expecting to find anything, and I didn't. By getting down on one knee and squinting I did find the spot where the rusty stains started. There was a large splat, and then a trickle leading back out of the alley to the stain on the sidewalk.

I followed the trickle back to the big stain and stood over it, looking down.

Blood is hard to wash out. But sooner or later the rain, the sun, and the passing feet wear away the stains. This stain was just about all that was left of Roscoe McAuley and when it was gone there would be nothing left of him at all except a piece of rock with his name on it and a couple of loose memories. What he was, what he did, what he thought and cared about—that was already gone. All that was hosed away a lot easier than blood stains—a lot quicker, too.

"I'm sorry, Roscoe," I said to the stain. It didn't answer. I walked back up the hill and climbed into a bed that was too soft and smelled of mothballs and cigarettes.

CHAPTER
TEN

I woke up early the next morning and didn't know where I was. In the pre-dawn darkness I had a moment of terrible panic that took me over, drenched me with sweat, left me gasping, sucking in air that tasted wrong. I was breathing air-conditioned disinfectant instead of the salty-citrus taste of Key West. In a moment of complete disorientation I reached across the bed for Jennifer's hand. There was nobody there.

When I woke up enough to remember where I was and why, it wasn't much better, but at least I could find my feet. I did, and swung them over the side of the bed and onto the floor. I sat on the bed for a minute collecting myself. With my weight on it, the mattress sagged a good three inches in the middle.

All the demons came back at me as I sat there in the dark. It was stupid to come back to L.A. I didn't owe Roscoe a thing. This wasn't my problem at all. But my problem could find me here. It had found me, as I lay there in my rented bed. It had found me and hammered at me and whispered low, horrible things. It was cold in the room but the sheets were soaking wet from the sweat the dreams had squeezed out of me.

I shivered, only partly from the cold of the room. I knew only one way to get rid of night demons. I pulled on a pair of shorts, and a T-shirt that said CONCH REPUBLIC. I got out a pair of Turntec Road

Warriors and tied my room key between my shoelace and the tongue of the shoe, and went out.

I ran up Beechwood Canyon to the small and strange community of Hollywoodland, and then up the hillside to the west. As I pounded back down the hill, with the jam-packed Hollywood Freeway below me on the right, the sun was coming up.

Back in my room I showered, shaved, and dressed, feeling a little bit more like a threat to someone who had killed at least twice. I went down to the coffee shop for breakfast.

The trick to a strange coffee shop is to start simple and work your way up. Charlie Shea, my last partner, once went into a place for the first time and ordered a ham and cheese omelette. That was a big mistake; there are too many chances for something to go wrong.

Charlie hit the jackpot. A new cook, on his first shift, panicked when they ran out of ham and eggs at the same time. So he thickened the remaining eggs with pancake mix, and chopped up some bologna for ham. Charlie took one bite and got the strangest look on his face. All the flavors were familiar, but they were *wrong*. He'd ordered a ham and cheese omelet and ended up with a bologna pancake.

I was feeling fragile enough without any vicious surprises, so I had scrambled eggs, wheat toast, and bacon. I stayed away from the orange juice; it's surprisingly easy to screw up. I stuck with coffee and a glass of water. I've had worse breakfasts.

By the time I was done it was just after seven-thirty. I climbed into my tiny rental car and drove down to the Hollywood substation on Wilcox.

Ed Beasley was already at his desk. Ed was forty-two, black, good-looking in a sinister way, with thick eyebrows and mustache. He had one of those male-pattern baldness hairlines that receded in two fjords on top, leaving a kind of widow's peak running down onto the forehead. It usually made him look rakish.

This morning he didn't look rakish at all. He looked like he'd just pulled a string of all-nighters. He had a Kool smoldering in his ashtray and an enormous Styrofoam cup of coffee in his hand. His eyes were closed and his forehead was wrinkled in deep vees. He was talking on the telephone, the receiver wedged between his shoulder and ear. He looked up at me as I walked over, raising his eyebrows in mild surprise.

"All right," he said into the telephone. "I'll see what I can do. Okay," he said and hung up.

He looked me over. I just stood and let him look. "Well, Billy," he said finally. "Fish not biting?"

There was an edge to his voice that I'd never heard before and I guessed I was right about the all-nighters. I didn't answer, and after a minute Ed just nodded at a chair to the left of his desk. "Took you almost twenty-three hours, Billy. You slowing down."

I sat. Ed slurped his coffee. He half-raised the cup. "Get you some?"

"No thanks. I ate already." He nodded and slurped some more. "Doctor say this shit'll kill me."

"But he won't say when?" I asked him, completing the ancient joke.

"Something like that," Ed said. A young white guy with rolled-up sleeves, a shoulder holster, and suspenders stopped and put a pair of files on Ed's desk. He looked at me, looked at Ed, shrugged, and walked off. Ed watched him go and shook his head. "He wears suspenders," Ed told me, disgusted. "Thinks they make him look like Kevin Costner."

"Why would he want to?"

Ed snorted and slurped coffee. "These new guys, man, I don't know. Half of 'em even think Madonna's sexy."

"That's better than thinking she's talented," I said. "I need to know what you've got on Hector and Roscoe McAuley, Ed."

He gave me the biggest, brightest, toothiest smile he had. It didn't hide the fact that he was mad as hell, and tired almost to the point of no return. "What I got is shit," he said. "And what's more, that's all I'm *gonna* get."

He slurped more coffee. "Word came down from on high. Community relations is *paramount*. So we can't poke at nothing that might disturb the current delicate balance of racial tensions."

He slurped some more and took a long hard pull on his Kool. Through a cloud of smoke, he said, "Which means if a cop dies in the course of investigating a death unofficially, on his own time, and it can be made to look kinda like he was just in the wrong place at the wrong time, we got to leave it alone, 'cause we can't look like we're putting more energy into a cop-killing than into securing a crack dealer's civil rights. And it means that anybody dumb enough to get killed during the riots, meaning Hector, it's like it never happened. 'Cause we don't want nobody having no bad dreams about the riots, I guess."

He rolled his eyes back for a moment and chanted, "Love to see them niggers sing and dance, but they get killed—don't wet your pants. We gave the mother one good chance, he's blown away by circumstance."

I stared at Ed in astonishment. "Sorry," he finally said. He pulled hard on his Kool. It was down to the filter now. "It's a rap number. Kind of an underground hit in the hip-hop clubs since the riots." He swiveled away from the desk and looked off to his left. "It's supposed to be about Hector. And of course it has a lot to say about the current delicate balance of racial tensions. 'Specially on the Force."

There was more of that edge in his voice, a whole lot more. Ed was one of those cops who believe God brought him through hell in his early life so he could be a better L.A. cop. To hear that much bitterness in his voice would have been unthinkable two years ago.

I was sorry for Ed. I knew what it meant to lose your faith in something pure and important. But I hadn't come all this way to pat anybody on the head, not even myself. I pushed on.

"Do you think Hector's murder was racially motivated, Ed?"

He gave me a long hard look. I thought I knew Ed. I'd spent a lot of time with him under tough circumstances. But I'd never seen a look like that.

"*Racially motivated.* That's real pretty. You getting your cop talk back again, Billy?"

"Looks like I need to. How about it? Was it racially motivated?"

He lit another cigarette off the butt of his current smoke. "Roscoe thought so."

"Roscoe wasn't exactly an expert on murder, or on racism," I said. "So why did he think that?"

Ed gave me a slight variation of the look. "Shit," he said. "Every black man in America is an expert on racism." He shrugged. "Why he thought it, I don't know. But it's maybe worth you thinking about."

"Anything in the investigation lead that way?"

"Billy, you just don't get it. Ain't nothin' in either investigation can even confirm somebody's dead."

"So there's nobody investigating either death right now?"

He hissed out smoke through the meanest smile I had ever seen. For a moment he really looked like the devil, the classical one who enjoys your agony only because it hides his own. "Hector was just another black kid who walked into a bullet. We got the paperwork going on Roscoe. There's a team on it, but—" He shrugged and his smile faded into a cold look I'd never seen on him before. "Officially, we are making progress and expect an arrest momentarily."

I nodded. We all know what that means: no progress, no leads, no investigation. "I'd like to see the files, Ed."

Ed knew I'd come here to ask him for the files. Any file on a dead case is public record. Anybody can look at it. But the files of a case that's still open are another thing. They're not supposed to be passed around, even within the department.

These killings were still technically open. If I knew Ed, since I'd walked in he had been balancing the political implications of giving me the files against the possible good that might come of it. He had to decide if he still trusted me, because he could be putting himself in a world of trouble. If he made the wrong choice he'd never be a lieutenant.

He looked at me for a long moment. I looked back. Then he gave a half-shrug and a nod. "Don't see how it can get any worse. I'll see what I can do," he said. "Call you tonight?"

I stood up. "I'm staying at the Franklin," I told him.

"Elegant as shit," he said. His telephone rang and as he turned to stare at it, I left.

It was still just a few minutes after eight in the morning and I wouldn't get to see the files until tonight, if at all. I thought I'd like to see the spot where Hector was killed, on the same goofy theory that looking at the spot where somebody died somehow attunes you to the killing.

I know it's dumb, but cops and fishermen are more superstitious than most. I wasn't sure which I was at the moment—maybe an ex-cop. At this point, maybe an ex-fisherman. Or half-cop, half-fisherman, some strange, mythical hybrid beast that lurches up out of the flats to solve crimes, like Aquaman. Whatever: I figured it couldn't hurt to look at some scenery.

The only problem was, I didn't know where Hector had died. At this hour it was going to be tough to find out.

I left my car at the police station and walked to Ivar Street, where the public library sits next to a strip joint. There were twin ramps crossing in front and leading down from street level to the glass doorway. Taped to the window beside the door was a sign with the library's hours. It opened at ten o'clock today. I glanced at my watch. I had ninety minutes to kill.

I found a newspaper box up on Hollywood Boulevard, and a bus bench with almost six square inches of seat that had somehow been overlooked; there was no gum on it, no vomit, no bird droppings, no spilled chili or melted ice cream. I sat and read the paper.

A battered-looking woman in a greasy green plaid coat was standing at the far end of the bench. As I opened the front page she drifted down to my end and read over my shoulder.

The news wasn't good anywhere. The comics weren't funny, either. The sports reporters hadn't learned to write yet. And the Dodgers were so far in the cellar they had a lock on last place for the next four years. For a saving second I saw my sour mood from outside and found it briefly funny. "Bah, humbug," I muttered at the paper.

"Amen," said the battered-looking woman.

By the time I was done with the paper it was a quarter of ten. I left the paper on the bench for the woman and walked back down to the library.

A fat security guard sat on a stool a few feet inside, chatting to a young woman with a large butt. I stood and waited. At exactly one minute after ten the guard stretched, glanced up at the clock, and sauntered slowly over to the door. It took him a full minute to cross the twelve feet of tiled floor.

He unlocked the door and held it open for me. "Morning," he said. I nodded and headed up the half-circle of stairs to the stacks.

The Los Angeles *Times* for May 2 had what I wanted. On page fourteen of the A section was a small story, three paragraphs long, headed: POLICEMAN'S SON SLAIN. The first paragraph was mostly heavy-handed irony about how even a cop's kid wasn't safe from murder. The final paragraph was a quote from a community leader calling the death tragic and senseless. They made it sound generic.

Sandwiched in between were the two or three facts the reporter had thought might be interesting enough to sneak in. Included was an address near Pearl Street where the killing had happened. I wrote the address on an index card provided by the library for writing down reference numbers.

On an impulse, I pulled out the telephone directory. The free clinic where Nancy worked was only a few blocks away from the spot where Hector was killed. I wrote that address down, too, and stuck it in my breast pocket. Maybe she'd want to have lunch.

Everybody has to have lunch, right?

CHAPTER
ELEVEN

I drove east on Santa Monica Boulevard, then south on Vermont. L.A. was not a melting pot, no matter how many different ethnic groups settled here. The melting-pot idea was dead. It had been swept away as unfair, and as a result L.A. was now a centrifuge. Every new group that arrived was rapidly whirled off to its own area, separated from any cultural contamination like the need to learn English. The new arrivals were all able to preserve the way of life they had fled from when they came to America, and avoid all the dangers and stupidities of this awful place. They could be Americans without ever seeing more of America than the corner store run by someone from their hometown, and whatever they saw on the local TV channel broadcasting in their own language by people from their homeland.

The new immigrants didn't assimilate. They stayed in tight clusters, and there was little interaction. In fifty years America will be made up of a million small neighborhoods that can't even speak to each other.

The area on Vermont I was driving into had become solidly Korean over the last ten years. The Koreans tended to be more insular than most, and they didn't usually care for outsiders, especially anybody that smelled like police. If I needed to talk to someone in this area I would need some leverage, or some luck, or both.

Soon after making my turn on Washington I found the spot I was looking for and pulled off into a small mini-mall parking lot across the street. I stood beside the curb and looked over at it.

Down the block to the left was a row of stores that had been burned. The black smudges of smoke had half-covered most of the graffiti. Fallen beams twisted up at crazy angles.

In the other direction was a large Thrifty drugstore. It was still boarded up. Ads for specials on aspirin, motor oil, and diapers were tacked up on the plywood that covered over whatever might be left of the plate glass.

Directly across from me, in the street, was where Hector McAuley had died. There was a modest four-story building there, with a small grocery store on the ground floor. A sign in the window said PARK HONEST GOOD FOOD GROCERY. Underneath was a neon Schlitz sign.

Next door on the west side was a Pasadena National Bank branch office. It sat in a square six-story building with small windows. The bottom windows closest to the front door were new and still had stickers on them. On the east was a vacant lot with half a car sticking up out of the weeds.

I crossed the street. There were no bloodstains in the road or on the sidewalk in front of Park Honest Good Food Grocery. Either it was already washed away by sun and rain or Hector hadn't bled as much as his father.

There were a couple of young black men lounging outside the store. They looked about seventeen. Both wore clothes that were much too big. One of them wore a porkpie hat and sat on a blue plastic milk crate. The other leaned against the building. He had a Raiders cap on, turned backwards. He said something to the guy sitting as I approached, and they both laughed, looking sideways at me.

I passed them and entered the store. A soft electronic chime sounded in the back of the store as I opened the door and stepped in. It took a moment for my eyes to adjust to the dimness inside. When I could see, I blinked again.

Somebody had crammed an entire full-sized supermarket into a room that wasn't more than thirty-five feet deep and twenty feet wide. Things were hanging off every inch of wall. The shelves went all the way to the ceiling, a good ten feet up, and in the narrow aisles between the shelves more things hung down from hooks screwed into the ceiling.

The cash register was to the left of the door. It was completely enclosed by a heavy metallic mesh. More stuff hung off the mesh: pretzels, potato chips, barbecued bacon rinds, cinnamon toothpicks, and Slim Jims. Farther along there were sunglasses, condoms, and snuff. Almost invisible in all the hanging clutter was the cashier's window.

Through the window, leaning against the wall with his arms crossed, was a Korean man of about forty-five. Koreans have a reputation for being tough and stubborn. It looked like a lot of that reputation was based on this guy. He was simply watching, with eyes that had seen about everything twice. His face seemed frozen in a permanent frown of watchful disapproval. He looked like it would take heavy earth-moving equipment to budge him.

I stepped to the cashier's window. His eyes followed me, unblinking and almost unmoving, like the eyes in a good portrait. I leaned slightly in to let him see me better. "Hi," I said, "Are you Park?"

He just stared. I stared back. "I wonder if you could help me?" I said.

"You no belong here," he told me.

"That's right," I said.

"What you want here?"

"It's about the boy that was shot out front of your store, back in May. I'd like to talk to anybody who might know something about it."

He stared at me some more. Something was going on beyond the dark eyes, but it would take a team of researchers ten years to figure out what. "Why?" he finally demanded.

I had a few choices. I could claim to be a cop, but that would matter less to this guy than a mouse fart on a pig farm. I could give him some shiny lie about insurance, but I had a feeling that would matter even less. Taking a deep breath and holding onto my luck with both hands, I went for the more devious approach. I told the truth.

"His father was a friend of mine," I said. "I promised him I'd find his son's killer."

The man moved. He nodded his head almost a full quarter of an inch up and down. "Father dead too," he said.

"That's right."

He nodded again. He was turning into a real whirlwind. He took a step and leaned his head around the protective mesh. He yelled eight or ten syllables. I didn't understand even one of them. Then he stepped back and leaned in his original position, recrossing his arms. "You wait," he said. His eyes drifted away, back to the front door.

I waited. I had no idea what I was waiting for. It could be a Libyan hit squad for all I knew. But something told me that I had got to Mr. Chatterbox, and whatever I was waiting for would be helpful.

There was a breath of movement, a faint smell of something clean, and a girl was standing beside me. She said something softly to the man in the cage and stood waiting. She was about seventeen and one of the most beautiful girls I had ever seen. She was all the stories about GI's falling for gorgeous Asian girls, all rolled into one.

The man said something harsh to her. She answered, still softly but with a certain amount of firmness.

He interrupted her and spoke a little longer. She hung her head. When he stopped talking she raised her head again, looked at me, and then gave the man six more syllables. He grunted.

She turned to me. "My father says you want to ask about Hector."

There was nothing showing on her face, but there was an awful lot going on behind her eyes, too—too much for somebody that young. Maybe it ran in the family. "That's right," I said. "Did you know him?" Her mask flickered for just a second, and she gave her head a funny half-turn towards her father.

"Oh, yes," she said, a little too loud, "I knew Hector quite well. I used to see him all the time." Her father said nothing, but I could feel the ozone building up. The air between them was as charged as a summer day with a thunderstorm moving in.

I nodded just like everything was normal. "Can you show me where it happened?" I asked, hoping to get her outside before the cage around her father melted.

She turned to me and smiled politely. "Sure," she said, and slid past me and out the door. The chime sounded again. Her father didn't look as I walked past, but I thought I could see a vein throbbing on his forehead.

The two comedians were gone from outside the store when I got out on the sidewalk. The girl was standing on the curb, looking into the street at a point about eight feet out into traffic.

"There," she said, nodding at the spot. "He was standing right there." I looked. It was just another patch of asphalt. The girl was looking at it like she saw something else.

"What's your name?" I asked her. Her head jerked around, the first thing I'd seen her do that was not entirely graceful. She looked at me for a long beat before she answered.

"My name is Lin," she said. "Lin Park."

I held out a hand. "Billy Knight," I said. She looked at my hand carefully, then touched it very softly. Her hand felt amazingly soft, warm and alive. She took her hand away.

"Lin, did you see the shooting?"

She bit her lip fractionally. "Yes," she said.

"What happened, exactly? Do you remember?"

"Oh, yeah," she said, quietly. "I remember."

"Hector was standing there?" She nodded. "What was he doing?"

She laughed a little. It wasn't a very funny laugh. "He heard they were going to torch my father's store and he came to stop them. That's why my father is so mad—because he owes something to a black boy who is dead. And because—" It was all tumbling out, but she caught herself and stopped talking just before the real revelation, which was no revelation at all at this point. Anybody could have figured out by now that there was something between Lin and Hector.

I pretended I didn't know. "Who were they?" She looked at me with eyes that were seeing something else, something that wasn't there anymore. "Who was trying to torch the store?"

She blinked. I had never seen eyelashes like that before, like two great, graceful silk fans waving at me. "Just—you know. A bunch of bangers, I guess."

"Gang members? How do you know they were?"

She shrugged. "I don't know. That's just what everybody was saying."

"Okay. So this bunch of gangbangers comes up to the front of the store?"

She shook back her hair. I held my breath. "No," she said.

"No? Who did show up?"

"Hector. With his posse," she said proudly. "He had this group of kids like him, they were trying to like stop the violence and stuff. And they found out these bangers were going to like torch my father's store. And they showed up to stop them."

Something was slightly off and at first I couldn't figure out what, but it bothered me. I chewed my lip for a minute. Then I got it. "You said he found out the bangers were coming here?"

"Yeah, uh-huh."

"How did he find out?"

She shrugged. She made it look like an elegant gesture. "I don't know. Somebody told him, or one of his posse or something, I guess." She shrugged again.

"Lin, I wasn't here for this thing. But was the looting and burning and all that, was that usually planned ahead of time?"

She frowned, gave her head a half-shake. Her hair rippled. "What do you mean?"

"Didn't people just sort of get mad and then burn and loot whatever was handy?"

She rolled her eyes at me. "Well, sure, I mean they weren't like planning crimes or anything. They just did it, you know."

"But somebody told Hector this was going to happen, and when. And then nobody showed up." She didn't say anything. I let it sink in for a moment. "How did it happen?"

She looked at me again. There was a new look in her eyes now, almost like she was seeing me for the first time, as she chewed on what I'd just helped her figure out. "How did it happen?" I repeated.

She was a little more careful with her answer this time. "Hector was standing there with his posse. He was like, waiting for the bangers. There's one shot, *bam,* and Hector goes down." There was a small catch in her voice as she said it.

"Did you see where the shot came from?"

She shook her head. "I was inside the store with my father. I couldn't even hear what they were saying. But I could hear the shot."

"Okay, you couldn't see the shot. But you saw Hector. How did he fall?"

"What do you mean?"

"I mean, when the shot hit him, how did he fall? Did he go straight back? Did he twist left or fall forward? What? How did he fall?"

She nodded. "I get it. He like twisted down. Sort of—" She showed me there on the sidewalk, in slow motion, a strange watusi of a fall. It was like she was screwing herself into the pavement. I nodded at her.

"Okay. So the shot came from above."

"Hey," she said, and looked very thoughtful. I looked up at the building, and then at the bank next door.

"Can I see the roof?"

She nodded again, suddenly very brisk. "Sure. This way."

Lin led me around to the back of the building, where a fire escape climbed up the side to the roof. She pulled on a rope tied to a length of rusty chain and the lower stair slid down. I held it for her and then followed her up.

Halfway up a woman's voice yelled something and Lin yelled back. She turned and gave me a small grimace of a smile. "My mother," she said apologetically.

She led me up to where the steps turned into one last iron ladder bolted to the wall of the building, and climbed it to the roof. I followed, being very conscious that to look upward at the legs of a seventeen-year-old girl, no matter how gorgeous, was indecent beyond measure. Keeping that thought firmly in mind, I climbed out onto the roof a moment later, and I only looked once.

As I climbed onto the gravel roof I could see Lin ahead, about thirty feet away. There was a desperately ratty lawn chair and a few milk crates sitting in a clump. I came up behind Lin and she spoke without looking at me. "We used to come up here all the time. Just —you know, to talk." She flashed me a furiously embarrassed look. "Not what you think. Just talking. It was like our hangout, the whole posse and everybody."

I nodded and looked at the chair.

"Hector was an amazing guy," she said. "But my father—all he could see was this black boy, and it freaked him out. Told me I couldn't see Hector at all. So I had to like sneak away to talk to him. And Hector wasn't just—he wanted—"

She stopped altogether for a moment. She frowned and stepped to the chair. A worn Dodgers baseball cap was underneath. She picked it up, brushed it off with the back of her hand, and set it on the seat of the chair. "Anyway, I guess he had something he wanted to prove to my father, which is like maybe why he did some of that, you know. Nonviolent confrontation. So my father would see, here's a man. Who was tough and stubborn, just like my father. I don't know," she said, and sat on the milk crate.

So she was feeling guilty about Hector's death, too. It wasn't enough that she had to feel his loss and her father's disapproval. Poor lovely child, carrying a weight so much heavier than herself. Carrying it quite well, too. Tough and stubborn—a chip off the old block. If he could only understand his daughter he would be quite proud of her.

I felt that I should say something, but I couldn't think what. So I watched her for a minute. She just sat, looking down at the roof between her feet.

I turned away to give her some privacy. At the western edge of the building the bank loomed up. It was some twenty feet higher than the roof I stood on, and there was a gap of about twenty-five feet between the two buildings. I walked over to the edge and stood looking at the bank building. There wasn't much to see, but I saw it anyway.

Screwed into the side of the building was a large and healthy-looking stainless steel eyebolt. I pulled at it. It seemed very solid, strong enough to hold my weight and a lot more. I tried to think what might go there that would need a bolt that big. Window-washing equipment? Not on a building like this. Bungee cord?

I gradually became aware of a strong smell of cheap cologne. I stood up and turned back towards Lin.

The two comedians and four of their friends stood facing me in a half-circle, about eight feet away. The friends were stamped from the same mold; young, baggy clothes, Raiders paraphernalia. One of them was Chicano, one of them Korean. The others were black. They didn't look very friendly.

"What's happening, ghost?" said Porkpie Hat.

I nodded. "Something on your mind?"

He took a step forward. "No, man, something on my *roof.*" The others laughed and inched forward. They smelled blood and they liked it. I smelled it, too, mixed with the cheap cologne, but I wasn't happy about it.

"Did you know Hector McAuley?" I asked them.

They got very serious very fast. "What's it to you, ghost?"

"His father was a friend of mine. He asked me to look into Hector's murder."

The kid with the backwards Raiders cap thought this was hilarious. He did a very loose-limbed comedy strut forward to Porkpie Hat. "Yo, check it out, dude thinks he's Magnum P-fucking-I." They cracked up again. And then Porkpie Hat took another step forward. "Look into *this,* motherfucker," he said, and threw a spinning kick at my head.

Off behind my new friends I heard Lin call out, "Spider, *no!*" and then two of them stepped over to hold her arms. She was saying something more, but I didn't listen. I concentrated hard on Porkpie Hat as he spun, stepped, and flung a foot at me.

I let the kick come very close to my head, stepping back a little at the last minute and trying to look clumsy about it. I wanted him to feel confident and try another one. High kicks can be very effective and painful—if the person you're kicking is either intimidated or playing by the rules.

I was neither. And I knew a very good trick for stopping high kicks. You have to be very fast and a little lucky, but I'd done it in the dojo. I hoped it worked in real life, or I was going to have a very lopsided smile.

When the second kick came with all the quick tight moves leading up to it, I was ready. As Porkpie Hat went into his spin, I stepped forward, inside the arc of his kick. As he spun around to kick my face off, I was already too close for his foot to hit me. I let his calf smack into my open hands and then grabbed his ankle with both hands. I pulled hard, letting the force of his kick push him around and off his drag foot. Then I lifted.

Porkpie Hat's hat fell on the roof. Maybe I'd have to call him something else now. He was dangling off the ground upside down, and all of a sudden all the cockiness was gone. "Put me *down,* motherfucker!" He almost squealed it, sounding his age for the first time.

"Why? So you can try to break my face again?"

"Damn right I will! You on my roof! Let the fuck go of me!"

I pulled higher, lifting my arms straight over my head so his face came higher. I wanted him to see my face, but I wanted to impress him with my strength, too. He was still young enough that the adult-child relationship might kick in if I held him up in the air like a bad uncle scaring his nephew.

"Listen, kid," I told him. "Hector McAuley was murdered. I want to find out who did it. If you were his friend, help me. If not—" I paused here for effect. I was going to say something very tough but not too corny—just enough to make him a little wary of trying to kick me again.

It was a good plan. It probably would have worked. Probably—if I hadn't been so busy thinking what to say I forgot about the other kids. I remembered a little too late. I heard a light whirring rattle and half-turned just in time to see the guy with the backwards Raiders hat. He had circled around behind me. He had some nunchuk sticks spinning, and as I registered what they were, he bounced them off my forehead.

From a long way off I heard an epic *boom!* sound, kind of slow and majestic like some great Cambodian temple gong. I thought I heard Porkpie Hat yelling something, too, but it was hard to be sure because the gong rang again.

It got dark very early today, I thought, and then I didn't think anything.

CHAPTER
TWELVE

There were a couple of vague voices coming from far down a dark hall. I couldn't make out what they were saying at first, and I didn't want to. I started to think maybe my head hurt, except it was hard to say if what I was feeling was really pain and anyway I wasn't sure it was in my head.

One of the voices was really getting on my nerves; it kept saying, "Gee, that hurts. Ow. Gee, that hurts. Ow," over and over again in a kind of weak, pathetic moan until I'd finally had enough and said, "Cut it out, you fucking wimp." My voice sounded exactly like the annoying voice.

At that point I started to feel pretty sure it really was my head. And it was definitely hurting.

I tried to open my eyes, but that made the pain come roaring down at me, so I closed them again quickly.

I smelled rubbing alcohol and felt a gentle swab of cool across my forehead, where the thundering pain was blooming out into something sharper. It stung for a moment, and I heard one of the other voices say, very softly, "There." I opened my eyes.

Nancy Hoffman stood over me. She looked so good to me that I forgot to hurt for a second. In her gleaming white nurse's outfit she looked like an angel, except for one small detail: she was smiling at me like she thought it was all pretty funny.

"Hey, there you are," she said as she saw me open my eyes.

"Pretty much," I said. I made the mistake of trying to sit up. It brought the headache into very clear focus, very quickly. I wanted to throw up, except I knew that would hurt too much, too.

So I sat there for a moment with my eyes watering, my stomach clenching rhythmically, and my head hammering. I could feel my skin go cold and green as the thundering agony in my head went on and on until finally, after several weeks of torment, it slowed to a nearly tolerable level.

I opened my eyes again. Nancy was still smiling.

"I don't get it," I said. "Is this funny?"

"Yes," she said. "Very funny."

I didn't feel like arguing. "How did I get here?"

Her smile got bigger. "Some kids brought you in. They looked like gangbangers." She looked at me curiously for a moment; I didn't say anything, so she went on. "Except for the girl, of course. She was amazingly beautiful."

For a moment I tried to feel even worse, but there wasn't room in my head for more than I had going, so I just looked at her.

"Why'd they bring me here?" My voice sounded weak and incredibly irritating to my ears, but I was stuck with it.

"Good question," she said. She held up a crumpled three-by-five-inch card. "My name and the address of the clinic were on this. It was in your pocket." And she put one hand on her hip and raised an eyebrow at me, like a first-grade teacher who caught the class clown with a handful of spitwads.

I tried to organize my answer. I was making some progress with my head, but it still took me a moment to put together a thought with as many parts to it as this one had. There were several different things to say, and I knew they had to go in the right order. So I let my head roll forward and I just breathed for a moment before I answered.

"Oh. It—I wrote it down. The—address. I was going to be down here . . . on business . . . I wanted to stop by. Maybe— have lunch." It was tough, but so am I; I made it through the whole sentence without fainting.

I looked up at Nancy. She looked very serious.

"You could have just called," she said. "You didn't have to go to all this trouble." She watched my face as I figured out she was kidding. Then she gave me a little of her warm, low chuckle and I closed my eyes. I opened them up again after a moment and she was still looking at me.

"Would you like to have lunch now?" she asked.

I gulped some air and closed my eyes. "Not if it involves eating," I said. "Or even looking at food."

"Hm," she said. "Well, that's the way I usually do it, so I guess lunch is out."

Nancy leaned forward and put a thumb on my eyelid. She peeled it back and looked inside, then whipped a small penlight up and into my face. She looked a moment longer, switched eyes, then nodded, putting the light into a pocket of her uniform.

"I think you'll live," she said. I closed my eyes again, remembering the last time I'd heard that. "Do you remember what happened?"

I shook my head. It was a bad idea.

"Well, somebody apparently gave you a pretty good knock on the skull."

"Yeah. That seems about right." I started to remember the outline of what happened. The details were still too much work.

I raised a hand to feel my forehead. The hand was trembling. The forehead was throbbing. There was a brand-new place on my head that stuck out about four feet further than it ever had before. I felt like a very sick unicorn.

What they never tell you in the movies is that getting whacked on the head can ruin your whole day. It's like the cinematic tough guys who say, "It's just a flesh wound," and yank a hanky on tight with their teeth and then jump on their horses, draw their sabres, and fire two shotguns with their lips.

Sorry: I've had flesh wounds. They hurt. They make you want to gnash your teeth and howl, and when the pain settles in to a constant throbbing you just want to sit quietly by yourself and whimper.

A good head-whacking is about the same. When you come to, you're not sure where you are, or even *who* you are sometimes. You want to crawl into a dark, well-ventilated corner, preferably with some kind of drain in it, and stay there until you can stand to take aspirin without gagging. It can take a day or two for things to settle down and lose their bright yellow edge.

Nancy put a cool, dry hand on my forehead. It felt very good. "You had me worried," she said.

That was the best news I'd had for a while. "Really?" I asked her, managing to get one eye opened and pointed pretty much in her direction. I thought maybe opening one eye would only hurt half as much, but it didn't work out that way.

She smiled. She didn't take her hand away. It felt good. "You did not look good when those kids brought you in. You still don't."

"Thank you," I said, leaning my head gratefully onto her hand.

"But the doctor had a look at you. He said whoever hit you got you in a good place, hit mostly bone." She chuckled again but had the good taste not to make any of the obvious jokes about bone and my head. "Anyway, he doesn't think you'll have a concussion or any other serious problems. Just a headache."

"It's a serious headache," I told her weakly.

"Maybe. But it could have been a lot worse. Two inches lower and it would have been the bridge of your nose. Off to either side and it could have been your temple." She touched each place as she named it. "They're not as hard as your forehead."

I was starting to feel a little better. And as her hand moved over my head, I was starting to feel other things, too. Her hand had an almost electric feeling to it as it passed across my face. It made my skin feel like a Santa Ana wind was blowing over me and charging all my pores with static electricity.

I stood up. For a minute I forgot all about Nancy. Then light and sound came back and I was still standing.

"Thanks," I said. I managed to make the room hold still long enough to look her in the eye. "I appreciate the TLC. Sorry about lunch."

"That's okay." She smiled a little. "You can spend a little extra on dinner."

I had actually turned away before I registered what she said and it took me a couple of seconds to turn back and wait for the sloshing in my head to slow down.

"Di-dinner?"

She raised a perfect eyebrow at me and waggled it once. "You don't want to take me to dinner? I'll take my Band-aid back—"

I managed to stammer out that I'd love to take her to dinner. We settled on Friday night and a few moments later I was out on the sidewalk with my head spinning in two directions at once. I must have looked kind of scary with the big knot pounding on my forehead and the big grin on my face, because two young black women made a wide arc around me as they passed me and went into the clinic.

It was just five blocks to the mini-mall where I had left my car, so I managed it in only about an hour. I had to stop a lot and wait for my head to catch up with me, but by the time I got there I was feeling better—better enough to drive, anyway.

As I pulled out into traffic I thought I saw something move in the window of Park Honest Good Food Grocery, but with all the junk hanging and the glare off the glass, I couldn't be sure.

By the time I got back to the hotel the throbbing had faded to the background. As long as I didn't make any sudden movement or try to sing "You Light Up My Life" it wasn't bad. Anyway, it was no worse than brain surgery without anesthetic.

In my room I pulled off my shoes and stretched out on the sagging bed, just breathing deeply for a while. I remembered hearing that it's bad to fall asleep if you might have a concussion because you can slip into a coma and not wake up, so I fought against sleep, just lying with my eyes closed, just breathing. I would just relax for fifteen minutes, soothe myself a little, try to get the pain to ease off, not fall asleep, definitely not . . .

CHAPTER
THIRTEEN

The sun was down when I woke up. I guess I don't have a concussion, I thought. Either that or I'm dead and this is heaven. I sat up carefully and glanced out the window. It was dark. A row of lights gleamed dully through a thick blanket of smog.

Not heaven—not even close: Los Angeles.

I put a finger on my forehead. The swelling was down a little but it still felt like I was wearing a rhinoceros costume. The pain was a lot less, and I was hungry as hell.

As I swung my feet onto the floor, the telephone rang.

"Well, Billy," Ed Beasley's voice purred at me, "I'm surprised you're not out sampling our night life. Too much excitement for you after sleepy Key West?"

"What time is it?" I asked him. He chuckled.

"Still right on top of things, huh? Well, truth is, it's dinnertime. And I got something for you."

It took me a few seconds to figure out what he meant—the case files. Like I said, a whack on the head slows you down for a few days.

"Oh. Well, how about Mama Siam?" It was a Thai place near the Greyhound station, and Ed loved Thai food—the hotter the better. I'd seen him eat things a circus fire-eater wouldn't touch and grin while the sweat rolled off him in buckets.

But he hesitated just a moment, so I prodded him a little. "Hey.

I know you're saving up for those lieutenant's uniforms, Ed, but it's on me."

He chuckled again, a little strained this time, and said, "Okay, Billy. Mama Siam's, twenty minutes." He hung up.

It took me a while to get myself together, but I was surprised at how much better I felt. Now the problem was not so much the pain as it was that the circuits weren't quite connecting properly. I would look for my shoe, see it, and have to hesitate just a moment and think, yes, *shoe,* before I could reach for it.

This had happened to me once before, back when I was in the Rangers. I had mouthed off to a drill instructor before breakfast and woke up after lunch. For the next day or so reality had been a slightly grainy movie running on a projector with bad sprockets. But at least I had learned how much punishment my head could take. I had also learned not to talk back to people with black belts in more than one discipline.

I figured out my shoes. It wasn't so hard if I just took my time.

Exactly twenty-six minutes later I walked in the door of Mama Siam's. Ed Beasley was in a booth, already working on a pair of egg rolls accompanied by a few dozen slices of Thai pepper.

Most Thai places have small pots of them on the table, thin slices of green pepper about as big around as a pencil. Each piece is about the size of a thumbtack's head and if you eat a whole slice you will pass out from the pain.

Ed was shoveling in five or six slices with each bite of eggroll. Sweat was pouring off him, and he was smiling like a kid with an all-day sucker.

"Billy," he said as I slid into the booth across from him. His grin was so big I could almost count his teeth. But I'd have needed a team of MIT researchers and a Cray computer to count the drops of sweat. "You walk into a door?"

"Some kids beat me up," I told him. He nodded like he was expecting something like that.

"Right," he said. "They do that here." I guess he thought I was being funny, so he didn't smile.

"Well," he said, after looking at me for a minute. "You really been working on that tan, huh?" He took a big bite with a half-dozen of those terrifying peppers clinging to it, and shook his head slightly as he swallowed. "Damn, that's good."

Ed took a big swig of water and then smiled, just a little. It made me think of how he had always been known for that big Cheshire cat smile and how I hadn't seen much of it this trip.

"You don't look so hot, Ed," I said. "How's business?

He just looked at me. There might have been some good humor left in him somewhere, but I couldn't see it. "This keep up, I be on the boat next to yours, Billy. They got Thai food in Key West?"

"I thought you were almost a lieutenant. What's the problem?"

"Shit floats, man. The closer I get to the top, the more of it sticks to me." He pointed a large finger at me, thumb cocked. "You got out just in time, boy. Things going straight to hell since the riots. Awful lot of guys thinking about early retirement all of a sudden." Ed pushed another hunk of eggroll into his mouth, followed by a forkful of peppers. "*Oo-ee*," he said softly, happily, as he chomped down on the peppers.

"Come on, Ed. It couldn't be that bad."

He gave his head a half-shake. "The fuck it can't. We still not back on our feet from the riots. Not just what happened, but *how* it happened. Like somebody tried to fuck us up on purpose."

He ate a couple of peppers all by themselves. "Fact is, Billy, morale is so bad, I'm just not having any fun lately. Everybody running around trying to catch everybody else doing something or other, and staying out of it their ownselves at the same time. My ass is out the window if they find out I'm letting you see the files."

"Is that them?" I asked him, nodding at the seat beside him. There was a brown paper grocery bag, wrinkled and folded over, sitting beside him. It said RALPH'S on the side. It was nearly full.

"That's it." He popped in the last bite of eggroll, finishing the pot of peppers with it.

I stood again and leaned across the booth, snagging the brown bag and sitting down with it on my lap. I wanted to tear it open and start reading; that surprised me. I had not expected to be so eager.

I put a hand on the top of the bag, then rolled the paper over tighter and placed it beside me. "What can you tell me about Hector?"

Ed swallowed, took a sip of water, and leaned back from his empty plate. "Roscoe was very damn proud of that boy." He wiped his forehead with a napkin. The napkin came away soaked.

"Hector didn't have to hang out in that kind of 'hood, you understand. He made that choice for himself."

"Why?"

Ed saw the waitress across the room and raised a finger to her. "He was his daddy's boy, Billy."

The waitress arrived. I thought about what Ed had said while he ordered dinner. Then I ordered, too—a Thai beer and a special hot-and-sour soup Mama Siam makes that is the best I've ever had. When you're sick, whatever you've got, it cures you. The waitress, a middle-aged Thai woman, looked at the lump on my head and nodded approval. She made a few of the mysterious, elegant marks that are Thai writing and vanished into the kitchen.

Maybe my head was still working at half-speed, but I couldn't quite figure out what Ed was hinting at. Roscoe had been making decent enough money—and his wife was an attorney. They could live where they wanted, and Hector could have gone to private schools, or Beverly Hills High, or whatever he felt like. So why would he choose the inner city?

"His daddy's boy—" Did Ed mean that Hector was a political animal? Then why—

"Are you saying Hector hung out in the inner city just to get a political background? So someday he'd be, what, authentic?"

Ed looked very serious. "Yes, Billy. That is what I am saying." He said it in a kind of low, Presbyterian voice with no accent and no inflection. Then he laughed, the first real laugh I'd heard from him since I'd been back. It was a deep, raucous yell of joy. A few of the other customers looked up at us, then looked away. "Shee-it, Billy. You been away too long." Still laughing, he shook his head some more. "I thought eating a lot of fish supposed to make you smart—man, that bump on the head must of got you all stupid."

"I guess so. What about Hector?"

He pointed a long finger at me. I could see where the nail was chewed all the way down to the quick. "You know what Roscoe was like—coldest black man I ever met. Never did a thing unless it was for a reason he'd thought out years ago. Boy started out the same way."

"But he changed?"

He gave me all those teeth again. "Good for you, Billy boy. Good for you."

"What changed him?"

The waitress set two beers on the table and poured half of each one into the two glasses, pushing one to me and one to Ed.

Ed took a big sip, then poured the rest of the beer into the glass. "The ghet-to changed Hector, Billy. It marked him like it marks everybody. It made him care." He took a big swallow of beer. "Worst mistake he could've made."

I didn't say anything. If Ed wanted to be cynical and mysterious, I'd let him. If he wanted to dance naked with a rose in his teeth I guess I'd let him, too. He had been my partner for two and a half years and in some ways he still was.

He finished his beer and waved for another one.

"Then there was this girl, too."

"You mean Lin Park."

He raised one boomerang-shaped eyebrow at me. "Yeah-huh. That's right." Then his gaze moved up to the knot on my forehead and he nodded again. "Well, well . . . ."

"Yeah," I told him, seeing he had put it together. "Maybe you should eat more fish, Ed."

He showed me the teeth. "Don't need to be smart, man, I'm almost a lieutenant. I just need to cover my ass." He pointed his head at the Ralph's bag. "Don't you leave my ass hanging out, honky."

"Sure. So Lin changed Hector?"

"Not the way she changed you, Billy." He snorted. "The way she changed him hurt a lot more. Lasted longer. Made him start thinking about being black, and that's no way to get a career to happen."

"What career?"

He gave me his devilish smile and leaned back. "You got to understand how important it is for a black politician to be able to say he's from the 'hood, he grew up in the ghet-to so he understands what it's like to be *really* black.

"Roscoe knew that, and he got Hector to understand it. They were all set for that boy to be the first black president, Billy, and they were serious about it. You want to be major league, you got to start young these days. Ain't nobody walks in off the street and throws a perfect knuckleball.

"Then he meets this Korean girl and the whole beautiful plan is in the shithouse. 'Cause her daddy'd rather see his girl dead than doing the horizontal boogie with a black boy. So now Hector's gotta think about Black Identity, Black Pride and Black Culture, Racial Context, the Politics of Assimilation, and the Meaning of Color." He rattled it off like it was a list of classes he had taken at L.A. City College, and maybe it was. But he meant it, too.

I shook my head. "Kid's what—sixteen? And he's thinking like that?"

Ed started to look serious. "He'd already been thinking that way, Billy, that's the point. But now he wasn't thinking about it tactically—he was thinking what it *meant*. Why it meant that, what he could do about changing it."

He looked down at the table, almost like he was embarrassed. "Boy started out Jesse Jackson. All of a sudden he's turning into Martin Luther King." He shrugged. "And all he ever wanted was a background."

"Which he thought he would get by hanging with the homeys."

Ed nodded. "Until he met Lin." The waitress set another beer in front of Ed and he poured it into his glass. He slurped the beer. "Now this is a girl who is not in any way a black person."

"Yeah, I noticed that."

"I bet you did. That would explain the lump on your head." He poured the rest of the beer into his glass. It fit now. "On the other hand, it occurs to some folks that Hector is in no way a Korean person. And so now we got a situation."

"Romeo and Juliet."

"More like Young John Kennedy and Juliet. 'Cause he can't even get in the door with the Koreans, and since an Asian girl does not fit the presidential agenda he's getting no support about it from home."

"So he's between a rock and a hard place."

Ed snorted. "Yeah, Billy. Either that or the devil and the deep blue sea. Whichever's worse."

"I never could tell the difference. And then the riots happen."

"Right on cue. Right when Hector is standing at the bottom of his soul, looking for a way up. And hey-bop-a-ree-bop"—he snapped his fingers—"there's his ladder . . ." He took a long pull on his beer. When he set the glass down again and wiped his lips with the back of his hand his face was serious. "A lot of guys could get cynical here and say Hector just went crazy for some pussy."

"You don't think so."

"No, Billy, I don't. I like to think there was more to it than that. A man can be changed by love, but—"

He saw my look and shrugged. "You call me a romantic if you like, but I still think there's a difference between love and pussy-crazy."

"Sure," I said, seeing that Ed was a little embarrassed. "Probably a matter of degree."

He waved it off. "Point is, the boy was for real. You don't face down a mob if you bluffing. 'Cause they'll roll right over you and grab onto that new Sony Watchman you standing in front of. And that's what Hector was doing. He was facing 'em down, making 'em think what they were doing and what that meant, how the rest of the world would see them for it. He was taking a mob and turning it into a group of *people* again, just talking to 'em. Word was all over the city, everybody knew about Hector. New Times was working on a cover story on him. What he was doing—it was like magic, man, and it got to you like nothing I ever saw, like maybe only that I-been-to-the-mountain speech—"

There was a catch in his voice and Ed stopped talking, either because he was aware that he was being sincere, emotionally involved in his memory of Hector, and he didn't sound like himself —or maybe because the food arrived and he was looking forward to another beer and a second pot of peppers.

I knew Ed Beasley about as well as one cop can know another, and I had never seen him like this before. Something about Hector had gotten to him. Ed had grown up in the worst of South Central L.A. and spent his whole life since in the LAPD. If something could get to Ed and move him like that, it was for real. It could get to anybody.

For a few minutes we ate and didn't talk. The food was good and it felt good going down. But I was not sure either of us could fill the uncomfortable hole Ed had made in the evening.

And so for the rest of dinner we slipped into old-shoe talk about the people we knew and had worked with and who was doing what.

And until we stood up and walked out to our parked cars he did not say another word that was not ordinary. Then, as I was sitting in my tiny rental car with a hand on the key in the ignition, he leaned into my window for just a moment and said to me in a soft, hurt voice, "Find this guy, Billy. It's important."

And then he was gone.

I went back to my hotel room with a sinking feeling I couldn't fight and I couldn't pin down.

I still didn't know who killed Hector. But for the first time I felt his loss.

CHAPTER
FOURTEEN

Back in my hotel room I ripped open the Ralph's bag and waded into the two case files Ed had given me. I wanted to start with Hector's—and not just because of what Ed had said. I was pretty sure Roscoe was murdered because he had been looking into Hector's death. And anyway, Roscoe's case file was just a day old. There wouldn't be much in it.

Hector's file was another matter. It was a good-sized stack of folders and manila envelopes. I opened it up.

If you grew up reading murder mysteries, you probably wouldn't recognize modern homicide files. They're not done in pencil by a half-smart bulldog. They're not typed out sloppily on a thirty-year-old Underwood by a fat guy in a stained shirt. There are no eraser marks and no splotches of chili on the margin.

What you see is a series of computerized forms that looks more like an inventory control report from an office-supply warehouse than a document examining the violent death of a human being.

The first several pages are almost identical with one of those computer dating-service questionnaires. The pages are filled with neat rows of numbered boxes. The detective in charge of the investigation puts a check or an X in each appropriate box to fill in all the details about victim, location, and procedure.

I looked at a top sheet marked (017) Black (023) Male (41) Gunshot.

That's what Hector came down to. All summed up in a neat row of Xs.

The next form was the lead sheet. It carefully spelled out who would check into each predetermined compartment of the case:

WITNESSES—Mallory
BACKGROUND CHECK—Rodriguez
AREA—Spitz

There's a lab report, of course. It's usually spit out by the lab's computer. The lab techs and coroners generally have blood, brains, bone splinters, and feces up to the elbow. They don't mind, but the guys with nice offices who have to read the reports do. To keep things neat, which is important nowadays, the lab guys generally have the computer fill in the boxes for them.

It went on—page after page of neat, computerized forms. I didn't much like it, but that never seemed to be as important to the department as it was to me.

Ed was the guy who had tried to explain it to me, back when he was first bucking for detective and we were sitting in a patrol car together for long hours.

"When you got ten murders a year, Billy," he had told me, "then you can be creative and go by instinct, get the feel of each murder, each one different. When you got ten murders a week you got to be organized. So you set up grids, make a pattern based on all the other kills. You fill out forms. Play percentages. Everybody do it the same each time so you know where you are."

"Uh-huh," I had said. "And that way, when you fuck it up at least you got your name spelled right on a nice-looking piece of paper."

He had given me the kind of look a sheepdog gives a lamb that keeps getting tangled in the fence.

It still seemed to me that somewhere along the way detective work, like everything else, got to be a bureaucratic procedure. When it did, it started to be about covering your ass.

Because of politics—in the department and in the community—a detective needs to prove he has all the reasonable angles covered. That's okay as far as it goes. But murder was not reasonable. A lot of times it didn't fit in the little boxes and you could not track it with a grid. But nobody ever argues with computer-generated forms. Nobody would dare.

So all homicide investigations are handled pretty much the same way. Columbo, Kojak, and Dirty Harry just fill out the forms; no more raincoat, lollipop, and make my day.

But there are still a couple of places in a homicide file where you can find some hint of individuality, and that's what I was looking for. First I looked to see if the detective filled in the boxes with an X or a check mark.

It was a personal quirk of mine. I had a theory that if you use a quick check mark you're trying to finish the bullshit and get on to the real work. An X means you take this stuff seriously.

Detective R. Cole had used an X: a careful guy. The arms of the X went up exactly into the corners and did not spill out of the box.

I flipped through the report, scanning for anything interesting; statements, lab reports, background, memos, and so on, all in neat manila folders.

The coroner said it was a gunshot. The entry wound was relatively small, consistent with the type produced by a military or hunting weapon of a caliber in the range of a .257.

It was pretty large for modern military, but R. Cole had jumped on it, commenting that it tended to indicate the shot was fired by an overzealous shopkeeper trying to protect his store.

The problem with that was the exit wound. It looked like it had been made by a high-velocity bowling ball.

I flipped through to the scene report. No slug had been found.

So whatever the weapon, the bullet used was a hunting round. Military rounds are jacketed. They leave neat exit wounds. Hunters use unjacketed lead for maximum expansion. Hunting rounds with a powerful load disintegrate when they hit something solid, like pavement. So there would be a big exit and no slug—exactly what we had here.

And Park didn't strike me as a hunter somehow.

I filed it away and moved on.

Next came the pictures.

You might expect the pictures from each crime scene to be unique. They're not. After a while death begins to look the same, whether it's a grandmother skewered with a bread knife or a roadkill armadillo.

It's just part of the spiritual downside of being a cop. Sooner or later that piece of you that is revolted and offended by the indignity of death gets turned off and it's all just scenery, whether it's an armed robber scragged by a security guard or a Sunday school teacher pulled in seven sections from a blown-up car. It stops bothering you because you could not do your job if every death bothered you the same way.

So you learn to look at death. You learn to look at pictures of death, too. The bodies in these photos never look quite human. The victim is just a lump of cold meat in its own gravy.

I turned to the sheaf of glossies in Hector's file, not expecting much.

The first shot took my breath away.

Hector was lying on the pavement. He looked incredibly graceful. He lay in an artful heap, almost as though some great painter had posed him there after weeks of sketching and study. His right leg was bent back at an angle too severe for comfort. His left arm was spread wide, beckoning. His right arm lay across his chest.

It was the face that really bothered me. I had never seen anything like it. Hector's face was peaceful, noble, *important* somehow. It looked like a romantic death mask from some great leader who had said beautiful things and then been shot down.

I knew this was a shot Ed had spent hours looking at, knew it without even seeing the smudges on the margins. All he had tried to say and been too embarrassed to finish—this picture said it all.

And I thought of what Ed had said about Hector. Cops don't spend much time with what might have been. They know too much about what is. But looking at the picture of this dead teenager, I could see why Ed was thinking that way. It made me think what if, too—what if Hector really had been able to become all Ed thought he might be?

Homicide pictures hadn't bothered me since I saw my first set. These were making my head spin.

What got to me was the same thing eating away at Ed Beasley— the thought that this kid might very well have been more important than the rest of us, and that by letting him die quietly like this we were blowing it big-time.

I didn't have the stomach for computerized forms anymore. But I thumbed through all the stuff anyway. By the end of my rookie year, two of my classmates had been shot by not being thorough. Dull routine is part of the turf.

There were a couple of items that were interesting. But the one that caught my eye was in the crime scene report. It listed a piece of HARDWARE, STEEL, UNIDENTIFIED found on the west edge of the roof.

It was typical of this investigation: UNIDENTIFIED. They had weighed it, measured it, analyzed the composition of the steel—stainless—and they hadn't figured out what the hell it was. But there was a full page of reports on the thing to prove that the investigation was thorough. Their ass was covered.

I had been looking at an eyebolt in the west edge of the roof when Lin Park's friends had done the drum solo on my skull. I couldn't tell from the picture what this thing was, but I wondered at the connection. I made a mental note to check it out and moved on.

What I really wanted to see was the summary. It took me forty minutes but I finally got there.

If you know what to look for and can decipher the convoluted high-tech cop-ese, the summary tells you all you need to know. Not because it gives the whole story from start to finish in too much detail, but because it tells you how the detective in charge was thinking.

Reading between the lines, you can see how much the detectives were allowed to do in a case—how far they could take it, how creative they could be, how much pressure they were under to nail the killer.

And in the summary of Hector's file the answer was crystal clear: not much.

Nothing written in the file spelled that out. That would be too obvious, and this summary was not obvious, not at all. In its own way it was a masterpiece of political ice-skating.

I had never seen anything so carefully arranged to give the impression of tremendous work under impossible conditions resulting in a regrettable but inevitable lack of results in a matter that was possibly better left alone for other reasons, which were in any case more in line with departmental policy on the allocation of man-hours with specific reference to overtime on homicide cases.

It all added up to a long-winded and meaningless but important-sounding conclusion that said, We didn't really do a whole lot here except make all the right gestures and generate the politically correct amount of paper.

But the subtext could not have been plainer. Somebody had put pressure on the investigating team so they went through all the motions, checked in all the boxes, and covered their asses without actually doing anything.

It didn't have to be malicious. Any time an investigation approached a sensitive area, a competent cop might back away, unwilling to do what is known as stirring up shit. That just means, stay away from trouble. There's enough of it looking for you already.

It looked like that's what had happened here. To anybody but an insider it would seem like an exhaustive investigation. It wouldn't have fooled Roscoe. It didn't fool me.

I turned to Roscoe's file. Since this one was still technically a fresh case, Ed had given me a photocopy of the initial paperwork. Detective W. Mancks was leading his team through the same kind of exhaustive orgy of box-checking. He had filled in the boxes with an X, too. Aha, I thought. A pattern was beginning to develop.

The cover sheet said Ed had been assigned to do a background check. It made a lot of political sense. The paperwork would show that a dedicated black cop, above reproach, had been in on the investigation, but background would keep Ed out of the way of all the important non-work. I didn't know any of the others on the team. I assumed they were all a little more pliable than Ed.

I thumbed through the file and then pulled out the envelope with the pictures. I knew the way Roscoe had died, so I knew the pictures would be bad. I didn't expect them to bother me too much.

But the pictures were worse than I thought. Roscoe looked like a tired puppet. Some kid had thrown a snit and pulled the head off, then thrown the puppet into the gutter.

I flipped through the report. All the boxes were filled in. There was no summary yet, but I could see it was already adding up to the same thing: somebody with a very heavy hand wanted this investigation to go through the motions without rocking the boat.

The results were identical, but each team was different, headed by a different cop. That didn't necessarily add up to conspiracy. It wasn't hard to find a cop who would walk softly on just one case—

especially if you threatened his career, his pension, his place in the fraternity. Besides, he would have all the forms filled out right, proving he had done his job.

There were a lot of people with enough clout to twist an arm that hard, from the commissioner on down to the rep from the union. Even a few local politicos, one or two businessmen, and at least one movie star I could think of would be able to swing it.

The only question was, who would do it? Who would deliberately sabotage an investigation into the murder of a brother officer? And why?

I sat with the pictures on my lap and just thought about it for maybe two hours. I started to get a nightmare feeling of wading through something that didn't make sense and couldn't be stopped. I finally put the pictures down and turned out the light.

Just before I fell asleep I realized my head didn't hurt anymore. I was finally getting somewhere.

CHAPTER
FIFTEEN

The morning came a couple of hours before I was ready for it. It might have been jet lag, or a last reminder of my bang on the head. Or it could have been just some leftover uneasiness about being in L.A.

Whatever it was, I woke up feeling like there was something terribly important I had to do and I couldn't figure out what, just that it was vital. I lay in the sagging bed with my heart pounding for a good five minutes trying to figure out what it was I was failing to do before I decided it was just a dream.

It was after seven by the time I got to the coffee shop downstairs in the hotel. I ordered coffee, eggs, and toast. In a spurt of real bravery I got a small glass of orange juice. It had a weird aftertaste that made me think I had a mouthful of rotting copper. Somehow that made the bad-dream feeling linger as I went to look for a telephone.

I didn't want to use the one in my room. Hotels tend to charge exorbitant rates for telephone calls, and anyway my room was all the way upstairs, and I was feeling penned in. I just wanted to get outside. I went out and looked for a booth.

That was a mistake. The air was a thick brown sap that could bring on a headache in a statue. I couldn't find a phone that wasn't broken or covered with stuff that smelled like the rest room at Venice Beach. After a few minutes of frustration, my eyes tearing from the smog, I decided I didn't need a phone anyway. I packed myself into my tiny rental and drove the few blocks over to Hollywood bureau.

Ed was already at his desk when I got there. He looked even more tired and sour. He was wading through a stack of papers and he glanced up as I sat in the chair by his desk.

I put the case file on his desk, rewrapped in the Ralph's bag. The weight of the papers caused smoke to swirl away from the smoldering Kool in the ashtray and into Ed's eyes. He blinked. He looked at the bag and then at me. "Good morning, Ed," I said after he had stared at me for a few moments.

"If you get cheerful at me, I'm gonna have to shoot you," he said.

"Farthest thing from my mind," I told him. "What do you know about this?"

I flipped a page from the file at him, marked with a paper clip. He glanced at it.

"Uh-huh," he said, sounding like he looked, tired and sour. "What about it? You want to file a complaint about police incompetence?" He dropped the sheet on the desk with a weary shrug.

"I'd rather take a look at that unidentified hardware," I said.

He didn't say anything for a minute. Then he gave me one short nod. "Yeah. Maybe somebody ought to." He swiveled away and picked up the telephone on his desk. I couldn't hear what he said, but in a minute he turned back to me.

"It's down at Crenshaw," he said. "I told them it might be connected to Roscoe, which is on my turf. So I'm sending an expert to take a look. That's you, you understand." He gave me his new smile, the mean one.

"I got that."

He scribbled on a pad and tore off the top sheet. "Get on down there. Sergeant Whitt waiting for you." He handed me the slip of paper. It said SGT. WHITT in Ed's small, precise handwriting. "Let me know about it, huh, Billy?"

I said I would. I tried hard not to notice how important it was to him.

Crenshaw bureau is not the worst in the city. But that might just be because of the competition. The station is not as pretty as the one in Hollywood. It has the look of something blunt and functional, like a hammer. In a way, it is.

Sergeant Whitt was waiting for me in a room in the basement. There was a cage around the room, and a small window was the only access.

Whitt was almost a cartoon cop. He must have been close to retirement; his belly looked like it had taken at least twenty-five years of hard work, punishing doughnuts, arresting chili dogs, and sending whole pizzas away for the big fall. If potatoes were bright red, somebody would have baked his nose by mistake a long time ago.

He sat at a desk about fifteen feet inside the shelf-lined room and glanced up at me when I appeared at the window and leaned on the sill. "What do you want?" he grunted.

"Detective Beasley sent me," I said. I managed not to add, "Ho, ho, ho." After all, the guy didn't even have a beard.

He grunted again. "McCauley case," he said. "Don't know if I can find it." He still hadn't moved. He looked away again, down at his desk, where a hoagie, fries, a Coke, and two jelly doughnuts were sitting in a small cardboard box.

I straightened up. "Okay," I said, with a cheerful smile. "Where's the captain's office? He'll want to know you've lost some evidence from an open case file." I very helpfully showed him all my teeth.

Sergeant Whitt grunted and stared hard at me for a good thirty seconds. He took a huge bite of the hoagie. A normal human being could not fit half of a sandwich that size into his mouth, but Sergeant Whitt did. He chewed twice and swallowed. Then he shoved his chair back explosively from the desk and barreled across the room on his wheeled chair. He must have hit forty-five or fifty miles an hour before sticking out a foot and stopping at a shelf. It was startling to see an old fat curmudgeon move that fast. But at least he didn't grunt again.

He grabbed at something and rolled over to the window. He plopped a sealed bag onto the counter, staring at me with mean, hard little eyes. "You're not a cop, are you?" he said.

"I'm an expert," I told him. "Just ask anybody."

He nodded without taking his eyes off me. "I didn't think you

were a cop," he said, and he sat there and watched me as I took the
hardware out of its bag.

It was a flat chunk of stainless steel about the size of a pocket
knife. The tag was hanging from a hole in one end of it. The other
end had a similar hole, except that there was a small grooved slot in
the side of the second hole. I turned it over in my hand a couple of
times, but I didn't really need much of a look. I knew what it was.

I had seen one only a few weeks ago, back home in Key West.
My charter had been for only a half-day, and while I was cleaning
up my boat I had heard an impressive amount of swearing coming
from a sailboat moored at a dock across the channel from my slip.

I had walked around and over to the slip where I found Betty
Fleming, a leathery forty-five-year-old sailing woman, trying to re-
rig the spreaders on the mast of her forty-two-foot sloop. She re-
sented needing help, never needed help from *anybody,* but eventually she let me haul on a rope and send her up the mast on her
bosun's chair. She'd even given me a beer afterwards.

The piece of metal Sergeant Whitt was guarding so carefully was
identical to part of the rig of Betty's bosun's chair. Betty, with
much amused swearing, had said it was called a brummel hook.
"Nobody much uses 'em nowadays," she had said. "Just old-fashioned assholes like me."

So the lump of stainless steel in my hand now was familiar—but
it just added to the dream feeling with which I'd started the day.
This was a pretty uncommon piece of hardware. Why would somebody have anything nautical on a rooftop in an inner-city neighborhood in L.A.? It was one hell of a place to sail off into the sunset.

Anyway, it was easier to understand why none of the detectives
knew what it was. Of course, that didn't make it easier to understand why they hadn't tried to find out.

I snapped out of thinking about it to see that Sergeant Whitt was
still staring at me.

I stared back. "Do you ever blink? Or do you have one of those
inner eyelids like a frog?"

I don't believe he thought it was very funny. In fact, I couldn't
tell if he thought anything. He just stared. Finally he grunted. "You
all done?"

I gave up. The man could outstare a rock. Even if the rock was smarter, and better looking. I dropped the brummel hook on the counter. "Yeah, I'm all done. Thanks for your time, Sergeant."

He grunted.

I climbed up the stairs and out of Sergeant Whitt's dungeon, and as I turned for the door a hand came down on my shoulder from behind. "Billy," a soft voice said. "Hey, well—Billy Knight."

I turned into the big grin of Charlie Shea, the friend who had talked me down that bad morning so many months ago.

I shook his hand, happy to see him. He looked me over with the interest of a guy who has saved your life and now feels responsible for you.

"Geez, Billy Knight. Man, you look great. Look at that tan. You look great. You really look great." He sounded like that made him happy and he held onto my hand a moment too long, peering into my face. "How you doing, Billy?"

I pulled my hand away. "I'm doing fine, Charlie. Just fine."

He didn't look completely convinced. "Uh-huh. What, you're doing the, uh, the fishing boat?"

"That's right, I'm a fishing guide. You come on down, I'll give you a discount."

He blinked for the half-second it took him to realize it was a joke. "Right, a discount, okay." He paused for his gentle and vague smile. "Hey, you look great. I mean—really. Geez, lookit you."

I was starting to get the idea that I looked great. Before Charlie could enter me in a beauty contest I figured I should say something. "You have time for a cup of coffee, Charlie?"

He hesitated. Charlie was not the brightest guy alive, and it took him a minute to decide things. But his heart was good. He took some ribbing about his low IQ—cop humor tends to be basic—but he was well-liked. "Coffee, huh? Well—sure. Sure. Sure, I got a few minutes here. Come on."

He led me out the front door to a place about a half-block away. A pencil-thin black man with a tiny mustache and a crisp white hat stood behind the counter in the cleanest apron I had ever seen. He nodded to Charlie. "Officer," he said, very distinctly.

"Hey, Philbert, how are you today?"

They chattered for a few moments and I stood waiting. I was used to it. One of the disadvantages of being partnered with a guy like Charlie is that everything takes twice as long. He can't go anywhere without seeing somebody he knows, and if he knows them he has to talk to them.

Eventually he got two cups of coffee out of Philbert. Charlie remembered how I liked my coffee, and we sat and sipped at a small round table in the front window.

There was really not a lot to say, but that was never a problem with Charlie. We spent close to half an hour just gossiping. Charlie told me Putz Pelham never did come down with AIDS, but the thought that he might had scared him badly and he was now Born again in the most self-righteous way possible.

There was other stuff, little things, mostly about buddies we shared, new things we wanted to mention. It was more like college roommates meeting by chance than two guys who had been cops together in one of the worst urban jungles in the country.

As I said goodbye and walked back to my car there was really only one thing that stuck in my mind from the whole talk, and I couldn't even figure out why it was sticking until I was pulling out of the parking lot.

At one point Charlie had given his head a sad little shake and said something about maybe quitting, maybe going into business with his brother who was a plumbing contractor.

"You don't mean that," I told him. "Not really."

He looked away, out the cluttered window. A bus went by. "Ahh. I don't know," he finally said. "Hasn't been much fun lately. Maybe I really shouldn't be a cop."

"It's not that bad, is it, Charlie? Come on."

"Yeah, well. Since the riots. The riots were—you know, it was like nobody knew what to do and we were waiting for orders that just never came." He crumpled his empty Styrofoam cup. "I really don't like that feeling. Like the brass either doesn't know or doesn't care. I don't like that."

And as I pulled out of the lot into traffic I realized why I was replaying that small chunk of talk.

This was the third time I'd heard the same message: cops felt like the command structure had let them down during the riots. Roscoe had said it was "almost like deliberate sabotage." And he had wanted an outsider, somebody he could trust—because he had a suspicion that somebody on the inside was guilty?

Ed had mentioned having the same feeling of mistrust, like the high command wasn't quite right. "Like somebody tried to fuck us up on purpose," he had said. And now Charlie—for Charlie to mention it at all it had to be something everybody was thinking about, even talking about.

And when I added all that to my notion that somebody with major clout had been leaning on the investigations into Hector's and Roscoe's murders, it started to add up to—

To what? Was the bump on my head making me stupid? Did I really think somebody in the command structure was behind Hector's murder? And Roscoe's? If it was bribery or nepotism, sure. No problem. Easy. That happened every day.

But murder? Cops killing cops? A cop on the roof with a sailboat? That wasn't even farfetched. It was stupid.

It was just too whacko. I'd just been away too long. I wasn't thinking like a cop anymore—I was thinking like Nicky, like one of his New Age conspiracy theories.

No, cops were still cops, even if they wore suits instead of blues. The idea was totally nuts. I let go of it and headed for the freeway.

CHAPTER
SIXTEEN

Before I could buy into a whacked-out idea like cops killing cops, I had to chase down a few more obvious leads. The first one was the paper trail.

Roscoe was an administrator. His earliest training and his personal instincts for political survival would guarantee that he had left some kind of hint on paper somewhere. I was as sure of that as I could be. His first commandment was Thou Shalt Cover Thine Ass, and a political cop's favorite ass-cover would be paper: memos, reports, briefings, summations, anything he could think of.

There had to be something. Knowing that, *what* and *where* were just a matter of poking.

I went to a sushi place not far away and called Ed. The telephone smelled like Windex, but at least it worked.

"It's me," I said when he answered. "You said you had Roscoe's datebook. You have any other personal papers?"

He blew out smoke. "I got the datebook cause I'm checking background. The other stuff, it's all in a box somewhere, but I can't get at it without some kind of official reason."

"For an official reason, would an anonymous tip do the trick?"

"Works for me. If it's from a usually reliable source."

"Uh-huh. Well, here's an anonymous tip for you, from a usually reliable source. Roscoe's personal papers will reveal something about his background that has a lot to do with his murder."

"You sweet–talking devil. Call me later, I'll see what I can do."
He hung up.

It wasn't even a hunch. It was just a routine piece of investigative
footslogging. Sometimes that stuff pays off—that's why it's routine.
Maybe we'd get lucky and the papers would turn up something.

I sat at the bar and thought about what to do next. The bar
surface was clean, highly polished dark wood. I ordered a beer and
a couple of California rolls, just to have something to do. It was
good. When it was gone I had decided.

I was close to Park's Honest Good Food Grocery, and I still had
some questions. I got in my car and pointed it that way.

The neighborhood hadn't changed since my last visit a couple of
days ago. The Thrifty had the same specials going. The burned-out
car hadn't moved. I guess once you find a good parking place, you
hang onto it.

I parked across the street again. I looked up at Park's roof and my
head throbbed. I crossed the street.

An electronic chime sounded as I pushed open the door. It took
me a second to get my bearings in that frantic clutter.

Park didn't help. He stood in his cage, completely motionless. I
stepped over in front of him. "I need to talk to your daughter
again," I said.

His eyes moved fractionally, up to the knot on my forehead, then
down to my eyes. "Black boy do that?" he asked.

"That's right."

He looked at me for a long moment. I couldn't tell what he was
thinking. Maybe that's just as well. Then his eyes moved away. "Lin
not home."

"When will she be home?"

The slight lift of his right shoulder was almost a shrug. "After
school," he said.

I looked at my watch. It was close to three. "I'll wait."

Park didn't even shrug. He just went back to motionlessness. He
reminded me of an alligator waiting for something to walk into
range.

I stepped back into the street in front of the store. The blue
plastic milk crate was still there to one side of the door. I sat on it.

A few cars went by. Some buses passed, too. A thin black kid,
about eight, ran past like a werewolf was after him. A few minutes

later a group of kids about the same age came by in more casual style. They laughed and hit each other until they came even with me. Then they got very quiet and filed by, looking at me with gigantic eyes. As soon as they were past they laughed again. Life goes on.

I watched them until they were almost out of sight. Then I heard a soft swish. I turned into a faint clean smell.

"Oh," Lin Park said. "Mr.—ah, it's you." Her eyes flicked to the knot on my forehead and she colored faintly under her flawless skin.

I stood up. "That's right. It's me."

"Oh. Well—" She could obviously think of a few people she'd rather talk to.

"I need to ask you a couple more questions," I said.

She bit her lip. "I—don't know. I just—like—what kind of questions?"

"I just need to know a few things about Hector's posse."

Lin shook her head hard. "I don't—that's not like a very good idea."

"Why not?"

She hesitated and looked around out of the corner of her eyes.

"Lin, I'd like to try to find out who killed Hector. I can't do that until I know a couple of things."

"Like what?"

"Like were any of the posse not there when Hector was shot?"

She frowned, an incredibly elegant expression on her. "Why would you want to know that?"

"Because Hector was set up. So somebody had to set him up. So whoever set him up might not be there because they knew it was a setup." If she looked like Roseanne Arnold I probably wouldn't have been so patient. But she didn't look like Roseanne, not by two hundred pounds and a few yards of creamy skin. "So was anybody missing?"

She shook her head. "Just Spider. The guy that, you know." She nodded slightly at my forehead. "But that wasn't—he had to, like, go to the hospital."

"Why?"

"He like fell off the roof? And was busted up for a couple of weeks. So it couldn't have been Spider."

"When did he fall from the roof?"

Lin raised one shoulder in a graceful shrug. The collar of her blouse opened slightly and I fought not to look. "It was like almost the same time. He rode the ambulance they brought for Hector."

I nodded. "I need to talk to him."

Lin hissed. "That's not a good idea."

"Why not?"

She raised a hand. I watched it flutter for a moment like a small lost bird, then it dropped. "He hasn't been—you know. Since Hector got shot, Spider has been kind of wild? Like, not a real good person to bother? I mean—" And she nodded at my forehead again.

"I'd still like to talk to him, Lin. It might be important."

She shook her head again, but it didn't mean no this time. It was just something to do while she was thinking about it. So I pushed. "Can you get him here?"

She smiled, a very old and very feminine smile. "Oh, I can get him to come here. If I ask him, Spider will come. That's not the problem."

"What is the problem?"

She bit her lip and looked away.

"What do you think Hector would want you to do?" It was shameless and probably wouldn't have worked on anybody but a sixteen-year-old. But it worked on her, or something did.

She looked carefully up and down the street. "I'll call him," she said. "But be real careful, okay? Meet me on the roof in like ten minutes?" And she was gone into the store.

I looked up and down the street and didn't see anything. Of course, I didn't really know what I was looking for. But at least I didn't see it.

Lin was acting more like somebody stuck in a moral dilemma than somebody afraid. I thought she might be tough to scare. So I guessed she wanted to make sure nobody saw her talking with the enemy.

I walked down the alley between the bank and the grocery store. Park's dumpster was there. It stank, but it was neat. Enigmatic, too.

Around back I pulled on the tattered rope and climbed the stairs to the roof. I walked across the gravel and tar and stood looking down into the street.

What had Spider seen? If he had been on the roof at the same time Hector was shot, I was willing to bet my boat he had seen something. There was even a chance he could identify the killer.

But he hadn't come forward and said anything at the time—why? It smelled like guilt to me. Guilt about what, I couldn't say.

But the more I thought about it, the more sure I was that I was right. Spider had been one of the good kids, helping to cool down violence with Hector's posse. Now he had gone bad. It could be simple bitterness, but he was young for that. Guilt would be a lot stronger as a motivation.

There was a clatter and Lin came up the ladder, followed moments later by Spider, the kid with the porkpie hat.

He stopped dead when he saw me and then turned with a sour look and said something to Lin. She shook her head. Her hair whirled around her face like shredded silk. She spoke passionately for a moment, her face serious, animated, heartbreakingly lovely.

That was not lost on Spider. He watched her, licked his lips, and shrugged. When she placed a hand on his shoulder he stiffened, then slowly nodded.

He turned to face me, then strutted across the roof to where I stood.

"Hey, ghost, sorry about your face, man."

"Shit happens," I said.

"Yeah, but whoa. Look like shit happen to your face a lot, man." He shook his head, reached a finger toward the knot on my face. "You get beat up a lot, ghost?"

I snatched at his hand. He tried to yank it back, but I caught his wrist. I didn't pull or squeeze or anything dramatic. I was trying to get him off balance mentally, not physically. I just held his arm motionless while he struggled to retrieve it, giving him a friendly smile the whole time.

After a few moments he gave it up. "Damn, man, okay, you can hold my hand, that what you want?"

"No. That's not what I want."

"Then what *is* what you want, motherfucker?"

"I want to know something only you can tell me, Spider."

"Goddamn, you let go my arm I'll tell you anything."

"Okay. How does it feel to kill your best friend?"

For a long moment he didn't breathe. All the blood left him. He sagged and if I had let go of his arm he would have fallen to the tarpaper.

When he finally gathered enough air to speak, it sounded like a small boy talking from the bottom of a well.

"Didn't kill nobody," he whined.

I kept smiling. "Sure you did, Spider. Have you forgotten him already? His name was Hector McAuley. He thought you were his friend. I guess he was wrong about that, huh? Because you set him up."

"I—I didn't think—don't know what you're talking about, man."

"Of course not. You just keep thinking that," I said. "Because if Lin finds out—"

He twisted so violently to look at her that he almost managed to pull away from my grip. She still stood near the ladder. She smiled encouragement at Spider.

He turned back to me. If possible, he looked even more scared, but not quite so young now. "What you want from me?" he husked.

I let go of his wrist. "The truth, Spider."

He licked his lips, rubbed his wrist. "I didn't kill him."

"I know that. But you know who did."

Nothing. He looked at the roof, moved a pebble around with his toe.

"He was your friend, Spider. That ought to mean something."

He switched feet. The pebble rolled out of reach. "What's gonna happen to me?"

I was pretty sure I knew what that meant. "She doesn't have to know. That's up to you. But I have to know. And you might have to tell the cops. Maybe identify a picture."

He shook his head and looked for another pebble.

"He's dead, Spider. You can't bring him back. But you can help get the guy that killed him."

A tear rolled off his face and slapped the roof. "I didn't mean for it to happen." Another tear landed by the first one. "I didn't mean for him to die like that."

"What happened?"

He shook his head. "White guy," he said, still looking down.

"A white guy killed Hector?"

"Yeah."

"Who was he?"

"Dunno." The new pebble rolled over beside the old one.

It took some work and a lot of patience, but I finally got the whole thing from him.

A white guy had approached him the morning of the shooting. He said he was a reporter and had seen Spider with Hector when the posse was facing down a mob. Spider remembered seeing a car, heavily tinted windows, white face inside. It was the reporter.

Did Spider want to be on TV? Spider did. Spider was in love with Lin Park, but she couldn't see anyone but Hector. Spider was just one of the posse. But if this reporter put him on TV, explaining what was going on, making it sound like Spider was maybe a little more important . . .

Anyway, Spider had agreed to get Hector to show up. He had even suggested Park's store as the place. The plan was for Spider to stay on the roof with the cameraman and talk about what was happening. He'd be the star.

The reporter was already there when Spider climbed up onto the roof. But that was not a camera he was holding.

It was a gun.

Spider ran to stop him. The white guy just smiled and picked him up like a rag doll and threw him off the roof. Just threw him like he didn't weigh anything at all, with one hand.

The guy hadn't even looked. Spider landed in Park's dumpster on top of some spoiled produce. He'd broken a leg and an arm, two ribs, like that, instead of getting killed. Been in the hospital for a week.

But the last thing he saw before he crawled away down the alley was that white guy. He was going hand-over-hand up a rope to the roof of the bank next door. Hand-over-hand, like on a jungle gym. Fast, smooth, making it look as easy as walking.

Spider sniffled like a scared kid, and maybe that's all he was. "I close my eyes I still see that," he said. "That great big white motherfucker zooming across that rope like Spiderman. And I'm just lying in the goddamn garbage."

At least that explained the brummel hook. The killer had retreated across the rooftops and got away.

I looked at Spider. He had collapsed into himself. All the swagger and toughness were gone. He looked like a small, lost kid.

"Why didn't you tell anybody?"

The look he gave me was haunted, pure misery. "What's that make me look like? I'm either a punk or a chump. Ain't no choice."

His face was old, ravaged, but the kid he was showed in the eyes. Just a scared, miserable, guilty kid with no idea how to do what was right, and it was eating him up.

He looked down again, not even bothering to kick at pebbles.

"You didn't kill him, Spider. This other guy killed him. And you're going to help me catch him."

He said nothing. He was crying again.

"You're doing the right thing," I said.

"Fuck you, ghost."

He was still standing there like that when I walked back to the ladder and followed Lin off the roof.

CHAPTER
SEVENTEEN

Parker Center is a big modern building with plenty of parking. It sits on the corner of First and Los Angeles streets, in an area they keep trying to clean up—I think *revitalize* is the word the mayor's office is using.

It's only a few short blocks from the Nickel, but worlds apart. It's close to a few major corporate offices and banks, and close to the Japanese area, too, so you're more likely to see a dark blue business suit than a bottle of Mad Dog.

When you walk in the front door, you almost always walk in with a crowd. I was surrounded by two three-piece suits, both navy blue, a woman in a dark green power suit, and two uniforms. We all moved in together. The others showed some ID and moved on past the reception area.

They stopped me at the reception desk. There were a couple of uniforms sitting behind a raised desk. With a cold politeness that only a cop can really master, they gave me a can-I-help-you-sir that really means who the hell are you.

I told them they could help me. That didn't make them burst into song, but they did say I could see the information officer. I had to turn over my driver's license before they would let me past the desk.

Then I had to fill out a couple of forms describing the documents I wanted to see. I sat in a small room on a hard chair and filled out the forms with a pen on the end of a chain.

I still wasn't quite sure how I'd ended up here. Somehow the whole idea of somebody in the command structure killing the McAuleys was still too dumb to take seriously.

And somehow that made me take it seriously. At least my subconscious did. I really had thought I was driving back to the hotel; instead I found myself standing in the street in front of this building.

The talk with Spider had left a bad taste in my mouth. At first I thought it came from pushing the kid the way I had, breaking him down to get what I wanted.

But then I realized I hadn't had to push that hard. Like Nicky's front door, he was ready to collapse under the lightest touch.

No, the bad taste was coming from the killer. He had used the kid up and tossed him in the garbage—literally into the dumpster, from the roof. It hadn't mattered to him whether Spider lived or died.

What kind of person was I looking for? A white guy. A white guy who had been cruising the worst area of the city during a riot, apparently unafraid. That could easily be a cop.

But then he had picked up about one hundred sixty pounds of kid with one hand and flung him through the air. Then he had shot Hector perfectly, casually, gone hand-over-hand up a rope and disappeared—

What the hell kind of person was this?

My thoughts had started steering the car. While I wondered who could do all that and still put pressure on an investigation, my thoughts continued to drive without me. I was lost inside them, and all the time moving down the freeway and out into Spring Street.

And I came to standing in the street in front of Parker Center.

I had just stood there for a while, looking up at the building and feeling stupid. This didn't make any sense. I didn't want to be here. I wanted to be home, on my boat, poling across the flats towards a tailing permit. I didn't want to be in Los Angeles, trying to find out if a killer kept office hours in Parker Center.

But it had started to make sense. All the complaints I'd heard about the high command during the riots—there could only be a few people in a position to do any real damage. What if one of them had?

Astronomers have a theory. If planets don't act the way they're supposed to, then maybe there's a dark planet, an unknown source of gravity.

If the high command didn't act the way it should have in the riots, and if there was somebody in high command leaning on the investigations—two very unlikely events—then it could have been the same somebody.

So suppose for a minute that there was a racist in the high command. Not just somebody with an attitude problem about black people, but somebody with an active, secret agenda.

A big if, but let that go. What would somebody like that do? Stir the pot a little to keep the riots going, make them a little worse. Intercept orders, delay them or fail to send them. Issue contradictory instructions and sit back and watch things get worse.

And then, when rumors about Hector and what he was doing had come out, this hypothetical ranking cop had gone in, tracked down the posse, and eliminated the threat to all that disorder. Then he'd come back and leaned on the investigation, and that was that.

Did that make sense?

No, it didn't. It was stupid. The LAPD was not perfect, but it didn't promote people who did those things.

Still, what did make sense?

I finally decided that no matter how stupid the idea made me feel, I'd feel a lot more stupid if I was right and never checked it out. I went in.

The quickest way I could think of to check on the idea of a guilty insider was to look at the duty roster for the day the riot broke out. If somebody in the command structure on that day was even remotely suspicious or out of the ordinary, I had a starting place.

The documents were supposed to be a matter of public record. I just had to ask. So here I was filling out the forms.

When I was done I handed them to a young man in a small cubicle. He looked me over suspiciously, glanced at the forms, and disappeared.

I waited. There were no magazines to look at—not even a copy of True Crime.

After about ten minutes the suspicious young man came back and pointed back the way he came. "Sergeant Brandon will see you," he said. I started down the hall. I looked back once, halfway. The young man was still watching me. Probably afraid I was going to steal a slab of linoleum from the floor.

The law says the department has to let the public see any documents they ask for, within reason. There's no law that says it has to make it easy. That was lucky for Sergeant Brandon. If it was illegal to be a pain in the ass, Sergeant Brandon would be doing hard time at San Quentin.

Apparently the suspicious young man and Brandon had figured out I was an ex-cop. Easy enough: a quick glance at my driver's license, then a check with computerized records. Out pops the file of Billy Knight, formerly of the LAPD.

And unless there was always spittle foaming on his lips and his face was always bright red, I'd have to say that something about ex-cops requesting documents made Sergeant Brandon especially mad.

He started right off with a snarl. "Didn't they teach you at the Academy it's illegal to investigate without proper credentials?"

"You should cut down on salt," I told him. "Maybe lose a few pounds. Otherwise you're looking at a stroke."

I think the color he turned is called vermillion. Until now I had only seen it in crayon boxes.

I thought he was going to pop or at least stand on his chair and call my mother names. But he surprised me.

Sergeant Brandon got up and left.

I waited half an hour before I decided he wasn't coming back. I was really making a lot of new friends on my trip.

I stood up and looked around the cubicle. There was a file cabinet. It was locked. There was a desk with three drawers. They were locked, too. There was no lock on the telephone, but I couldn't think of anybody I wanted to call.

He'd have to come back someday, unless I had driven him into early retirement. I couldn't wait too long—I was already getting hungry.

I had just decided to come back tomorrow—and tomorrow and tomorrow—when there was a slight, delicate throat-clearing sound behind me. I turned.

A very proper-looking young woman in uniform stood in the

doorway. Her light-brown hair was in a bun and she held a manila envelope in her hand. "Mr. Knight?"

I don't know where these impulses come from, but I very badly wanted to say, "That's my name, don't wear it out." I fought the urge down and settled for, "That's me."

She gave me a very proper one-eighth inch of smile and slapped the envelope into my hand.

"Sergeant Brandon said to give this to you." She turned and tick-tacked off down the hall in her regulation shoes.

For a moment I worried that it might have been too easy, but when I gave myself credit for waiting patiently for half an hour I felt better. I got my driver's license from the receptionist and headed out.

CHAPTER
EIGHTEEN

I really was hungry, and in a way that only seems to happen in L.A., I was hungry for something very specific. Nothing else would do, no matter how delicious. If somebody had waved filet mignon and lobster under my nose I would have pushed past on the run. It wasn't a great treat, but I couldn't get it out of my mind.

I'm not proud of it, but all I could think of was a chili-cheese dog from Pink's. Maybe it was the force of Sergeant Whitt's personality.

As I drove I thought about what I might have in the envelope, and what I might do with it. Every time I got hold of a really good thought, my stomach growled.

But it came down to this: the duty roster would tell me who in the high command had been in a position to act—or refrain from acting—when the riot broke out. After that, I could check on who actually had, or hadn't.

Of course, I would have to eat first. A chili-cheese dog. Maybe two. Two sounded about right—man-sized, but not greedy.

I drove west on Olympic to La Brea and turned north. Pink's was on the left-hand side, and crowded. It was always crowded.

I ordered two chili-cheese dogs and a cream soda and, when they came, I squeezed into a seat at the back of the room, under a row of eight-by-ten pictures of famous people I'd never heard of.

I inhaled the first dog, and as I stopped to breathe I opened the manila envelope.

The first reports of rioting had come in about four o'clock. The log showed that the chief of police was on his way to give a speech at a spot about an hour away. He heard about the trouble en route but continued on his way and gave his speech anyway.

I thought about that one for a few minutes. Was it suspicious for the chief to keep going, an hour out of town, when a riot was breaking out? Wouldn't it be normal for a police chief to head back, cancel his speech, be on the scene? Did it mean something when he went ahead with a speech and left his men on their own?

It could—but chances were it was simpler than that. The chief had no way of knowing how bad it would get. There were plans in place, capable people to get things moving. In an image-conscious town like L.A. he might have felt that he had to show a calm, unruffled front. Business as usual would calm people down, let them think things were under control.

Anyway, whatever else you said about Chief Gates, he was all cop. I couldn't even fantasize about his being guilty of anything more serious than an overdue library book.

I glanced down the sheet. Three other top administrators were on duty: Doyle, Tanner, and Chismond.

Douglas J. Tanner was new to the LAPD. He'd come from Miami, where he had made a name for himself at Metro Dade Homicide with a new system of computer-generated personnel record-keeping. I remembered the jokes when he arrived, only about six months before I left. They were calling him Software Tanner— only partly because of his interest in computerizing everything.

Albert Chismond had been a fiery black radical in his younger days. Somewhere along the way he'd become so outraged by the police that he'd decided to become one. He was smart, streetwise, and ambitious. He'd come up fast. I knew him slightly; he had been behind Ed Beasley's decision to buck for Detective.

Warren Francis Doyle was the third man. He was from one of the old L.A. families, had lots of money, was in the department for idealistic reasons. His brother had been on the city council for a while. A family tradition of service, like the Kennedys.

All three had been on duty when the trouble started. All three had, at least in theory, access to the civil disturbance planning and the power and duty to act.

I had a starting point: three names that might or might not have done something, or not done something they should have done. But where did I go with them?

Two young men sat down at the table with me. They were so pale they were almost green, and their long scraggly hair clacked when they moved. They were dressed in slashed black leather vests, with lots of things hanging off their necks, arms, and heads. Things like twisted chunks of metal, skulls with green eyes and devils. One of them wore a bright red penis dangling from his neck.

"Fuck, *no!*" one of them screamed as they sat down. "That shit *sucks*. Michaels is a *cunt!*" Neither of them even looked at me. They just launched into their lighthearted witty talk.

"He can suck my dick," the other one agreed.

"What the fuck *IS* this shit, huh? Can somebody tell me what this shit *is?*"

"He's a fucking douche bag," said the other one.

"It's *my* fucking *band!*"

L.A. is the cultural capital of the western world, I thought.

"Fuck that shit!"

"Fucking right."

I got up and walked back to my car.

Ed was still at his desk. That was no surprise, and neither was the sour expression on his face. He looked like his ass had sent out roots into his desk chair and it hurt like hell.

His face didn't improve as I told him what Spider had said, and what I had figured. He lit a series of Kools, slurped his coffee, and made mean faces. Then I showed him the documents from Parker Center. He bit the filter off his Kool.

"Figures," he said when I was done.

"I don't like the idea. But it would explain an awful lot."

"Explaining is one thing. Proving something like this, man, that's gonna be a little more complicated."

"Roscoe would have left some kind of paper trail. If it doesn't prove anything, it might at least point towards something that does. So now I'd really like to see Roscoe's papers," I said.

"You ain't the only one." I raised an eyebrow, and he nodded. "Talked to Roscoe's widow. Didn't know nothing. I don't think she has a lot of joy in her heart about the LAPD being on the job. She put her maid on the phone."

"Maid?"

"Uh-huh. A maid of Central American origin. *Poco Ingles. Tiene miedo de los policias.*" He threw out the Spanish casually, with a pure South Central accent.

I whistled. "When did this happen?"

He shrugged. "Gotta talk the talk if you gonna walk the walk."

"You mean the walk up the ladder?"

"You know it. So anyhow, the maid say a man showed up and took away all the papers. I asked her what man? Very nice man, very good. Polite. He showed a badge. Oh, so the Señora let him in? Oh, no, she says, the Señora was at the funeral. *Que lástima.* What kind of badge, I say? She say a badge. Like the poor señor's, but different maybe."

"The papers are gone?"

"That's the bad news."

I let out a long breath, some of it wrapped around a bad word. "What's the good news?"

He hoisted both eyebrows all the way up to his hairline and looked at me with mock surprise. "Why, Billy," he said, "good news is we know there really is something in those papers. 'Cause I checked all over the damn department, and nobody the LAPD knows about was anywhere near those papers."

"Which means the killer grabbed 'em."

"Yeah-huh."

"That isn't very good news."

He smiled. "Sure seem like it, way things been going."

CHAPTER
NINETEEN

I was up early the next day and into my new routine: run up the hill, run back down the hill. Shower and shave, and then go downstairs to experiment with the menu in the coffee shop. I tried waffles, Canadian bacon, and a fruit cup.

The waffles were frozen; one was still cold in the middle. The fruit cup was from a can, except for one slice of really sour grapefruit. On the plus side, none of it actually killed me.

As I finished a second cup of the pale, soapy coffee I realized that without thinking about it I had decided to concentrate on Hector's murder. It made sense to me that Roscoe was killed to cover up Hector's death. It was theoretically possible that the two deaths were unrelated, but it seemed a lot more likely that I would become the next king of Norway.

With Roscoe's papers missing I had a couple of choices, and none of them were very good. But since I was not tied down by police investigative procedure, the best idea seemed to be to skip trying to prove anything and just assume I was right.

I thought about my three suspects: Chismond, Tanner, Doyle. I knew almost nothing about them. I needed a starting point. All I really knew was that the killer was pretty good with a rifle. But with three cops for suspects, that wasn't going to help much.

Of the three, which one had anything to gain from Hector's death? Come to think of it, what had anybody gained from his death? The black community had lost a promising young leader—who could possibly profit from that?

Chismond seemed unlikely. He was black, too, and this was looking like a racially motivated crime. But if he was guilty, he'd had help; Spider had seen a white man.

Still, Chismond had been a radical in his youth and might still be. On the old theory of the worse things are the better, he could have arranged for someone to shoot Hector. Or he could have thought the kid was taking the movement in the wrong direction. It was possible; it seemed pretty unlikely.

Doyle was almost as unlikely. There wasn't a more squeaky-clean officer in the history of the department. With his rank, his wealth, and his standing in the community, I couldn't see what he might possibly have to gain from a couple of murders. Besides, his whole life had been dedicated to improving the city, and a strong black leader in the figure of Hector would have helped.

That left Tanner. He was relatively new to the department, and I knew less about him than the other two. He was an appealing suspect in a couple of ways. First, he was primarily a bookkeeper, and I have a lifelong prejudice against bookkeepers. Second, by reputation he was so dull and ordinary and gray I couldn't help thinking of the old saw about how ordinary evil has become in the twentieth century. And I knew Miami was a place where racism flourished.

I could picture it perfectly: the quiet, boring man, sitting at his desk with a blotter and a neat In basket, carefully plotting out the survival of the white race in a double-entry ledger.

Even if the picture was a cartoon, I had to start somewhere. I would start with Tanner.

Now the question was, *how* would I start?

One way would be to go through my contacts on the LAPD and get a look at Tanner's personnel file, try to get any kind of handle there might be to get. But I didn't want to strain my favor account too early. I might need it later.

Another way would be to go through the L.A. *Times* for the last year and find anything with his name on it that popped up. Or maybe I could call Miami—I had one friend there in the Florida Department of Law Enforcement.

But probably the best way to start was with routine surveillance.

That way I could get a feel for Tanner right off. And I'm good at surveillance; I was pretty sure he wouldn't know I was on his tail. He might go somewhere, do something, meet somebody he shouldn't. I might catch him picking up his Klan robes from the dry cleaners.

I got out the phone book. There were a column and a half of Tanners listed. D. J. Tanner had an address in Eagle Rock. I figured he was my man.

I drove over on the freeway. Most of the traffic was going in the other direction, so it took only about thirty minutes to drive the seven miles to Eagle Rock.

Eagle Rock is a kind of bastard child of Glendale and Pasadena. There are some very nice areas, and there are some pretty tough neighborhoods, too. Sometimes they're right next door to each other.

I couldn't tell from Tanner's address which kind of area he lived in. When I got there, I was mildly surprised to see it was one of the border areas: nice houses, racially mixed neighborhood.

In fact, as I drove slowly past Tanner's house, a woman yelled something out of what looked like Tanner's kitchen window at the house next door. I heard a loud caw of laughter and a black woman leaned out the side door of the house next to Tanner's and yelled something back with a big smile.

Three kids raced past her as she stood there, two black and one white. The kids ran into Tanner's house and disappeared. There was more yelling, most of it good-humored.

Okay. It didn't mean anything. It might be a clever cover. Probably lots of racists lived next door to black people. Probably once you lived next to them, you had to let their kids run in and out of your house, just to avoid confrontation. And hey, maybe the murders had nothing to do with race. Maybe Tanner was in love with Lin Park.

I drove once around the block and didn't really convince myself. But I still pulled in about a half a block down and waited, watching the house.

In about five minutes Tanner came out with a big smile. He was pulling at his jacket. The three kids were pulling on the other side of it. They were shouting and laughing and wouldn't let him go.

After twenty or thirty seconds of this, Tanner did a pretty good

King Kong imitation and the kids let go, squealing and running for cover.

Still smiling, Tanner walked to the curb, smoothing his jacket down over the soft roll of fat at his waist. He didn't look like the kind of super-strong guy Spider had described. He didn't even look like a cop. Tanner got into a year-old Lexus and headed for work. I followed.

The traffic was a lot worse in that direction. It took forty-five minutes to get to Parker Center. I watched Tanner pull into the parking garage, and then I kept driving around the block.

I stopped and bought a newspaper, a bag of doughnuts, and a cup of coffee. I expected to get something to eat later, when Tanner went out for lunch, but I wanted to have something in the car in case I was sitting there for a while.

I drove back and parked down the block from Parker Center, where I could watch the parking garage. I had decided that Tanner would not do anything incriminating at his desk in police head-quarters. I just had to follow him if he left the building.

So I read the paper, glancing up from time to time to make sure Tanner didn't sneak out to a Nazi rally while I was reading about Darryl Strawberry's back problems.

I finished the paper. I ate one of the doughnuts. It tasted like somebody had deep-fried a wad of old newspaper and dipped it in a solution of lightly sweetened paraffin. There was some red goo in the middle that might have been jelly. It might have been melted crayon, too.

I fiddled with the radio for a while. You can find almost anything on the radio in Los Angeles. I listened to some Haitian rock and roll, some Japanese ceremonial drumming, a Bach guitar piece and "Spoonful" by Cream. Lunchtime came.

Lunchtime passed. Maybe Tanner was eating at his desk. If he was as hungry as I was getting, maybe he just ate the desk. I had a couple more doughnuts. They didn't taste any better than the desk might have.

By three o'clock I was hungry enough to eat the rest of the doughnuts. But as I took one out of the white paper bag and stared at it, I decided I was already above and beyond the call of duty. I threw the doughnut into the gutter and drove the three blocks to the nearest convenience mart. I got a couple of sandwiches, a bottle of apple juice, and used the rest room.

Fifteen minutes later I was watching the garage again, from a slightly different spot. A tour bus had pulled into the parking place I'd been in before, but I got one almost as good.

I ate one of the sandwiches. I decided it had been made by the same person who made the doughnuts, except with yellow crayons instead of red.

Tanner didn't come out until after six. The guy was starting to annoy me: he worked straight through lunch and then stayed late, too. There was such a thing as too much devotion to duty.

I followed him home through the miserable, honking, crawling, tire-biting traffic and watched from a half-block away as he went in the front door. I thought I could hear somebody shouting, "Daddy!" but maybe I imagined it.

And that was it. I sat there until almost midnight and there were no muffled gunshots, no burning crosses, no unusual hole-digging —nothing. Tanner went in. It got dark and the lights came on. The purple glow of television filled the front window. The purple glow went out. The lights went out.

I had plenty of time to think about all kinds of things. I thought about Darryl Strawberry's back problems. I thought about the Burrito King down on Eagle Rock Boulevard. I thought about that voice yelling "Daddy" when Tanner went in the house. That took me in directions I didn't want to go. But I thought about it for a while anyway.

At 11:47 the last light went out. I waited a few more minutes to be sure Tanner didn't sneak out wrapped in a Nazi flag. Then I started the car and left.

I drove slowly down to Eagle Rock Boulevard and found the Burrito King. I had two beef burritos and a bottle of Corona from the liquor store next door. I barely made it back to the hotel, where I fell onto the bed and slept the night through.

CHAPTER
TWENTY

I overslept the next morning. I hadn't left a wake-up call but I still felt guilty and stupid about sleeping so late. I dragged myself out of bed and into the shower without running. I felt like a weight was hanging from the back of my head and a family of mice was camping out in my mouth.

It was nearly nine o'clock when I got downstairs to the coffee shop. I don't know what I was thinking, but I ordered French toast. I took the first bite, and all I could think was that if I walked back into the kitchen I could finally discover how yesterday's doughnuts had been made.

I decided I wasn't hungry anyway. I drank my water and left the sugar-heaped, fat-fried cardboard on my plate. I went back up to my room.

I was already having the kind of morning where you can't figure out why you bother. It must be blood sugar. Or maybe it was geographical. Whatever it was, I sat on my bed for a half hour or so and tried to figure out what I should do and why.

The whole shape of the day was just adding to the feeling of stupid futility I had about tailing Tanner yesterday. One day of surveillance doesn't generally tell you anything, but my gut was insisting that Tanner was exactly what he seemed: a hardworking, ordinary family man. Clean, decent, God-fearing—he probably had season tickets for a local church.

He was a typical police administrator, no more. He had the swivel-chair spread to prove it. I had watched him all day, and the idea of this agreeable family man flinging Spider off the roof with one hand was laughable.

That's what my gut said. But Tanner could have had help. He might be the point man for a racist conspiracy. And listening to my gut made me think I was wimping out, whining about futility when I should just stick with it, no matter how long it took.

Should I stick with Tanner? Tail one of the others? Or do something else—like get on a plane and go home?

I turned it over in my head a few times, but I couldn't decide. I could feel myself slipping backwards again, back into the dim, clenched-stomach place where nothing mattered and everything was gray. I missed my boat. I missed Nicky and Captain Art and the smell of the cat under my house. I wanted to feel the water moving me again, the fresh salty tang of it on my face. I didn't want to be here.

But I *was* here. And if I let myself start thinking about that, it was going to lead me down again.

For my own sake, and for the sake of solving a couple of murders that seemed to matter more than a lot of others, I had to keep moving. What I did wasn't important; I just had to do *something*. Anything.

That took some of the pressure off. Surprisingly, I felt a little better. I felt so much better I was hungry again. I went downstairs, got in my car and drove to Norm's down on Sunset. I had a ham and cheese omelette, whole-wheat toast, and orange juice. It tasted pretty much like it was supposed to taste. I decided that was a good omen.

I used the phone book outside the restaurant to look up Doyle and Chismond. Most of the book was missing, ripped out by people with no pencils and short memories. The page that would have listed Chismond was gone, but I found Doyle's address.

Okay, I thought. Another sign. This was my day.

I drove over to Hancock Park, where Doyle had one of the beautiful Tudor homes they grow there. It sat behind a high hedge, with a couple of big trees in the yard. I could just see the top of a tree house sticking up. Doyle wasn't married; maybe it was from a previous owner.

I pulled in under a tree across the street and looked at the house for a minute.

It was a very quiet neighborhood. All the lawns were neatly mown. There was no litter in the gutters. No traffic passed through on the way to somewhere else. In fact, about all I could see or hear was one mockingbird, sitting on a wire a half-block away and warbling with measured dignity.

Doyle was almost certainly at work. I wasn't sure what I could expect to get from looking at his house, but in a way it was out of my hands. I had been led here by a good breakfast and a savaged telephone book.

So I looked at the house. I had been looking at it for about five minutes when my car door was snatched open and something cold pushed into my ear.

"Neighborhood Watch," a soft voice said. "Can I help you with something?"

Out of the corner of my eyes I could see the gunman. He was in his thirties, big, with short dirty-blond hair and a Hawaiian shirt. He looked very fit. He'd moved up on me quietly and smoothly and I was caught.

I was more pissed-off than scared. I hadn't heard a thing. I was supposed to be street-smart and I had let this goon into my lap without noticing anything.

And now he was leaning his weight on the top of the car door and moving the tip of his gun against my ear with a nasty grin.

So I did something stupid. I jerked my hands up in front of my face, as if I was scared. I mumbled, "Oh, please—" while I half-turned and got my foot on the door. Then I kicked at the door as hard as I could.

It was a bad idea. If somebody has a gun in your ear it's generally good form to ask politely what they'd like you to do, and then do it.

But I was mad. This was supposed to be my lucky day. Things were supposed to go my way this morning. If you can get a decent breakfast in L.A., anything can happen. So I moved without really thinking.

What happened was that when I kicked the car door it caught him squarely on the chin and the Neighborhood Watch clown went sprawling on his butt. I was out of the car as he fell back and clunked his head on the pavement.

He lay there for a moment, dazed. I moved to him quickly, plucking the gun from his fingers. I shook my head in surprise when I saw the weapon. It was a Glock 9mm with a fifteen-shot magazine and something that looked an awful lot like an illegal silencer on the end.

If this guy was Neighborhood Watch, what was in this neighborhood? The Corleone family's summerhouse?

I checked the chamber on the gun. Sure enough, he had a round in it. The maniac could have blown my head off. I pumped the round out and into the gutter.

I leaned over and grabbed a handful of Hawaiian shirt. I pulled him to his feet and shoved him up against my car. As I did, I felt something under his shirt, so I gave him a quick frisking.

I came up with a large bronze medallion on a chain around his neck.

His pockets were empty, except for a wallet and a set of keys on a large ring. There was a small silver sword hanging from the keychain. On the blade were some tiny characters. As near as I could make out they said, *Is Thusa Mo Thua Chatha.*

I opened the wallet. He had a driver's license in the name of Phillip Moss, and an Orange County address. "I think you're in the wrong neighborhood," I told him as he grunted and shook his head to clear it.

He glared at me. "Who are you?" he demanded, with a very tight-lipped snarl.

I shook my head. "I'm sorry. You had your chance. Now it's my turn." I held up the gun in front of him. "It's not polite to stick your gun in a stranger's ear. But I've got your Q-tip now. So why don't you tell me what you're doing wandering around with a cannon?"

"It's my weapon," he said.

"I'm sure it is. So what was it doing in my ear?"

"You have no right to take that weapon."

I sighed. "You don't get it, do you? It's not about the weapon anymore. It's about you, Phil. Who are you and what are you doing here?"

His eyes narrowed, and he nodded slightly as if something finally made sense. "Zog," he said, in a tone of voice like he was saying *Eureka*.

"Well, you've got me there, pal," I told him.

"Z-O-G," he said. Maybe he figured that anybody who moved fast enough to get the drop on him couldn't spell.

"I'll need a receipt for the pistol," he said.

I gave up. L.A. was the kind of town where any damned fool could show up and put a gun in your ear, and this was getting me nowhere.

"Here," I said, sliding the clip out of the handle. "Take the damn thing," I told him, and put the pistol in his hands. "Go play with your acorns."

He just looked at the gun in his hands, then looked up at me again. His eyes narrowed. "What the hell is this?" he asked.

"It's a Glock nine-millimeter," I told him. "I'm keeping the clip."

"Just like that, huh?" he said. I could see now that he had the gun back he thought he was going to get tough again. "I don't think so—" And he raised the gun up, pointed it at my nose, and pulled the trigger.

He had obviously not seen me jack the round out of the chamber, but I was still shocked. Neighborhood Watch was getting damned unfriendly.

"I don't think so, either," I told him. I slapped him hard and fast on the face. His head rocked to the side and met my left hand coming across for another slap on the other side of the face. His head swung the other way and I gave him one more.

"I don't like guns in my nose, or my ear, or any other body cavity. If I ever see you again I'm going to pull your head off and shove it so far up your ass you'll be looking out your own neck. Now get moving."

He put a hand up to his face. It was the hand with the gun. It looked like it hurt. "Your day is coming, you filthy—"

I held up my hand again like I was going to hit him. He tried to step back and ran into the car. So he slid along the car and scrambled onto the sidewalk, grabbing for his dignity.

"You haven't heard the last of this, mud-boy," he said. And then he turned and marched off, disappearing around the corner without looking back.

I climbed back into my car. I suddenly had a lot to think about.

CHAPTER
TWENTY-ONE

"He called you *mud-boy?*" Ed asked me, his inverted *V* eyebrows climbing up until they were almost lost on top of his head.

"And Zog," I said. "He called me Zog twice. He even spelled it for me."

"Damn," said Ed. He let his eyebrows slide back down into position and fired up a Kool. "What you make of that shit?"

I shook my head at him. "I don't know what to make of it. I never heard any of it before. But the more I thought about it, the more I thought it might mean something. You can take coincidence only so far."

"And you already there, Billy."

"Yeah. Past there."

Ed leaned back. He reached his hand all the way around the back of his head and scratched the other side, puffing on the Kool that dangled from his fingers of his other hand. "So you think maybe he wasn't really Neighborhood Watch, huh?"

I shrugged. "Hell, I don't know. Maybe he's with Pinkerton's and he thought I was Jesse James. But there was something about this guy."

He gave me a lazy smile. "Uh-huh. Must be something, he get his gun in your ear like that."

"That's part of it," I admitted. "The guy moved pretty good. He looked like he was in very good shape, knew how to use the gun, all that. But—" I stopped talking, because I couldn't figure out how to say it.

I didn't have to figure it out. The Kevin Costner lookalike sauntered over and dropped a folder on Ed's desk. He looked at me, then looked at Ed.

Ed stared back without touching the folder. After a few seconds Kevin shrugged and walked away.

Ed sighed and opened the folder. After a moment he gave his head a slight nod. "Well, well."

"Isn't there supposed to be a third *well?* So it goes, 'Well, well, *well'?*"

"Billy, you can have all the *wells* you want. You just hit a gusher."

He flipped the folder over to me. It was a rap sheet for Phillip L. Moss. I scanned it.

Phil was a very busy guy. When he wasn't helping out with Neighborhood Watch he was spending a lot of time eating public food. He'd been inside for assault, aggravated assault, disorderly conduct, attempted murder, and public nuisance more times than the whole local chapter of Hell's Angels. He was also a known former member of CSA.

I looked up at Ed. "CSA? Like Confederate States of America?"

The famous Cheshire grin appeared. This was making Ed happy. "The Covenant, the Sword, and the Arm of the Lord." He said it like it was the tag line for a sermon. "I'm not sure if they still in business, but we can find out."

"I'm sure we could," I said, "but why would we want to?"

Ed looked at me and shook his head sadly. "What we gonna do with you, son? You gettin' all pathetic on me. CSA was one of the original white racist gun clubs, Billy. You know, crawling 'round in the mud with an AR–15 pretending you shooting at evil niggers trying to integrate your wife. Survivalism mixed with racism. You never hear about that shit?"

"Oh," I said. I had a vague memory of something like that. "They had a commune in, uh, Mississippi or something."

Ed pointed a finger at me and dropped his thumb: *Pow.* "Arkansas. Had a big spread up there to train for the survival of the pure white race."

He turned and punched four digits into the telephone. I couldn't hear what he said and he didn't tell me. But a minute later a guy strolled over.

He was a very impressive-looking guy; about six-three, with the kind of silhouette you get only from a lifetime in the gym. He had a shaved head, an eyepatch, and a diamond in his left ear.

"Billy," Ed said, "this is Detective Braun."

I gave him my hand. He didn't rip it off and eat it. But it throbbed for a while.

"Detective Braun here is our expert on the survival of the pure white race." He showed Braun some teeth. "He don't look Jewish, does he?"

"I was undercover last year," Braun told me. He had a very soft, high voice. "You know the Stompers?"

I said I did. They were a bunch of smelly, overweight yahoos on Harleys. Even the other bikers avoided them.

"We got word they were in on a bank job. I hung out with them."

I was impressed. I looked at him a little harder.

Braun smiled. "I washed since then."

"Point is," Ed cut in, "Stompers got down with Aryan Nations. Must of caught it in jail. So Detective Braun got to go to the convention."

"The what?"

Braun nodded. "All the right-wing God-and-gun nuts get together every year. They swap guns and knives and books and pictures of Hitler. You get to see who's coming up and what ideas are going around."

"This guy called me Zog. Then he said I was a mud-boy."

Braun nodded. "Aren't we all. Zog is Z-O-G. Stands for Zionist Occupation Government. Means a fed, or a cop. They believe America—and the world—has been stolen away by the Jews and their puppets."

Ed couldn't let that go. " 'Scuse me, boss, but could I borrow Montana?"

Braun ignored the interruption. So did I. "And mud-boy?"

He smiled. "That's a little nastier. Anybody who isn't one hundred percent pure Aryan has tainted blood. They're mud-people, not really humans."

"What about that keychain, Billy?" Ed asked me.

I nodded. "He had a sword on his keychain. It had an inscription." I closed my eyes and pictured the sword. I've always had a good visual memory, and in a moment I could see it. *"Is thusa mo thua chatha,"* I said.

Braun whistled. Now he looked impressed. "This guy keeps fast company," he said to Ed.

He turned back to me. " 'You will be my battle ax,' " he said. "It's Gaelic, it's the motto of the Brothers of the Righteous Sword."

"Oh, my," said Ed.

"Can I take it that the Brothers are not a fencing club?"

"And they ain't *brothers,* neither," Ed tossed in with a cackle.

Braun turned his one good eye on me. I could see why the Stompers let him hang around. It was like looking into a cold dark well.

"Die Bruders are an elite group of shock troopers. They call themselves Aryan Warriors. They've taken all these oaths to God about death before dishonor, defending the white race to the last drop of their pure white blood, and so on."

"The usual shit," I said.

"Nope," Braun told me. "So far, these guys mean it. We never took one alive. And they always take down a couple of ZOGs when they go."

"So how does Moss go from CSA to the Bruders?"

Braun smiled. He had a gold tooth in the front with a small diamond set into it. "There's only so many of these guys to go around. The feds bust one bunch, the leaders go to jail, and the troopers need to find a new outfit." He shrugged. "I'd bet most of the soldiers in Die Bruders were in two or three other groups before this one. It's what they do. They're professional racists."

"My, my," said Ed. "What you into now, Billy boy?"

"I don't know. I'm just a mud-boy. What would this guy be doing hanging around that neighborhood?"

"These are not the kind of guys that go for a walk in the park," said Braun. "If he was there, it was for a reason."

"Bingo," said Ed.

I shook my head. "We still don't know what that reason is. Okay, he's a member of a racist group—"

"A racist *paramilitary* group," Ed butted in. "Which ought to make you feel better 'bout him cleaning out your ear. Man's had some *training.''*

Braun stood up. "One last tip on these guys," he said.

"What's that?" I asked him.

He winked that single cold eye. "Don't fuck with 'em." He nodded to Ed and strolled away, back to his desk.

"All right," I said. "So either this guy was following me—which is possible, considering how rusty I am. Meaning he picked me up when I was tailing Tanner. Or else—"

"Or else he was already there when you got there. Which means somebody in the neighborhood got a very unusual security system."

"Or it's a complete coincidence. The guy is a nut case, and he just happened to go off while I was around."

Ed looked at me sadly. "Yeah, Billy. I think I could buy complete coincidence. You probably right, let's go for a few beers. How 'bout those Dodgers, huh?"

I watched him look at me. Neither of us had anything much to say for a few moments, so we just stared.

Ed didn't believe it was a coincidence. Neither did I, but I hadn't believed it was going to be this easy, either. I realized I had been looking for a difficult task—no, a quest.

I needed a quest to redeem me—something tough and pure and close to impossible. If I could work through a long fight against overwhelming odds, it would help make all the heartache and night sweats mean something. It wouldn't bring my family back—nothing would. But it might give some focus to a reason for going on, something beyond fishing.

And I realized, too, that fishing wasn't enough anymore. After just a few days and one medium jolt of adrenaline, I realized I needed to do this. I needed the feelings that only this kind of work gave me.

But it had to mean something. And it had to be tough. I needed penance. I needed to work for it, work hard, not have some geek in a flowered shirt fall into my lap waving a pistol.

If it was too easy, it wouldn't count.

I smiled at myself, at the games Billy played with Billy. Silly, yes, but true anyway. I had to do this, and—

And what? Hope it got harder?

Ed cleared his throat. He was just waiting for me. I wondered how much of this he had figured out.

I let out a long breath. I knew I wasn't giving up. "Let's take a look at who else lives in that neighborhood."

Ed nodded, like that was all he was waiting for. He made a small note on a pad. "I can get that easy enough."

I reached over and took the pad and pencil that had rolled up against his Out basket. "Here." I sketched out the street as I remembered it. "I was parked here—Doyle's house was here. So these five houses ought to do it."

I pushed the paper across the desk at Ed. He glanced at it and nodded. "Okay, Billy. Meantime I'll put out a BOLO for Moss." He waved the paper at me. "This take me a couple of hours. Say this evening?"

"Sure, uh—" It suddenly dawned on me that today was Friday. And Friday night was my date with Nancy Hoffman. I tried to sound casual, knowing how good Ed's radar was. "Make it easy on yourself. Let's say tomorrow morning."

It didn't work. His eyes fastened onto me immediately, and the old Cheshire cat grin spread across his face. "How about I call you this evening?" he said, pretending innocence.

"I'll call you in the morning, Ed," I told him. I could feel a blush spreading across my face, like a teenager caught holding hands.

"Well, ain't you something. In town three days and already dated up."

I stood up. "I'll call you," I said, and turned to go.

"Don't forget to use a condom, Billy," he called after me.

I could hear him hooting with laughter almost all the way down to my car.

CHAPTER
TWENTY-TWO

There's an old L.A. joke that goes: What do Porsches and hemor-rhoids have in common? Answer: Sooner or later every asshole in Marina del Rey has one.

There's some truth to the joke. Marina del Rey is a ridiculously upscale area, loaded with single millionaire dentists and plastic sur-geons, Saudi princes, retired drug dealers, and other playboys. A high percentage of them seem to enjoy roaring around in Porsches, gold chains flapping in the breeze.

No one knows why they decided to infest this particular area. It's not centrally located, it's not close to Beverly Hills or Melrose Ave-nue. Of course, it's on the water, and that counts for something.

And there's the marina itself. I grew up around boats, and a marina is a marina to me, no matter where it is, but Marina del Rey is not really a marina.

You might say there are boats, lots of them. Boats that would make anybody drool. But in the setting of Marina del Rey, they're not boats so much as marks on a tally sheet for the big cribbage game of L.A.

Make no mistake. These are not really boats. In fact, there are no boats at all in Marina del Rey. They're yachts, and that makes all the difference. A yacht is a boat with an attitude.

I didn't care much for the attitude, but it was good to look at the yachts, and I could half-close my eyes and pretend they were only boats. Besides, when the smog has gone inland for the night, the area is pretty.

It's also got some pretty good restaurants, and at eight o'clock that evening I found myself sitting in the bar of one of them, staring into Nancy Hoffman's eyes over the rim of a margarita.

I have never read a whole lot of poetry, but the good stuff sticks with me, and I was trying to remember something about eyes being bottomless pools of light. I wasn't having any luck remembering. Maybe it wasn't really poetry. Maybe it was a cheap novel.

It didn't seem to matter much since I was looking into the real thing. Nancy's eyes were golden, unlike anything I had ever seen before, although the longer I looked the more sure I became that I had dreamed something similar many times.

We had been sitting for about twenty minutes and were on our second drinks. Through some horrible computer error, the management of the restaurant had somehow overlooked firing the bartender, who was over thirty, not particularly attractive, and knew how to make real margaritas instead of the canned kind you pour out of a blender.

The drinks tasted very good. They had a flavor of new love, old promise, and cool, elegant jazz. They were starting to remind me of all the things I had liked about Los Angeles before things got bad for me.

And it might have been the drinks, but Nancy Hoffman looked as good to me as anyone had ever looked. And she was making me remember what life had been like once upon a time.

I wasn't sure I was comfortable with these feelings. But they felt so good, I didn't care.

So I stared into Nancy's bottomless pools of light—until she reminded me that just sitting and staring made me look like an idiot.

"Hello?" she said, and a moment later she repeated herself, "Hello?"

I shook my head and looked at her instead of through her. "What was that?"

"Echo," she said. "I suddenly felt all alone."

"Sorry," I said.

"You looked like you were pretty far away."

"Um, actually, I was maybe a little too much right here."

She raised a perfect eyebrow. "Then where was I?"

"I couldn't see you at all," I said. "There was this goddess in the way."

She nodded. "You're going to hurt your neck, looking up at pedestals like that." And then she smiled. It was a very good smile.

"I was just thinking how good you look," I said.

She fanned herself with a hand, all mock southern belle. "Oh, la," she said. "All this before dinner. You'll turn a girl's head."

"I mean it."

She reached a cool hand over and put it on top of mine. "I know you mean it, Billy. But I think you've been out of L.A. too long. People here don't say what they mean. It's embarrassing." She gave my hand a light squeeze. I turned my hand over and held onto hers. My whole body tingled.

"Besides," she said, "you're not so bad yourself."

The headwaiter called my name right then to tell me my table was ready. I guess it was just as well. The bartender probably didn't perform weddings anyway.

It was a popular restaurant, and I wasn't a millionaire dentist, so our table wasn't right at the window. But we were only a tier away, on a raised level, so we had a pretty good view of a row of people with great teeth. Beyond them, out the window, were the water and the moonlight.

I really didn't spend much time looking at the view anyway. Nancy even had to remind me to look at the menu.

Looking at the menu was a waste of time. I don't remember what we ate. What I remember is the way Nancy looked when she turned her head to the left and the soft light played over the hollows in her shoulders and neck.

But I guess the food was pretty good, too. We ate all of it, and I didn't try to sneak out without paying.

After I paid we walked out along the docks. They are very solid docks and go out a good long way. We went all the way.

We admired a number of the yachts in their slips. We stopped to look at one that impressed me. It was a fifty-foot sailboat, the *Warrior*. Hanging off its spars I could see every electronic device in the catalog, and some I could only guess at.

Nancy asked about them, and I explained the difference between GPS and Loran and what a waypoint was, and VHF and sideband, and what digital mapping and plotting were, and how radar was used on small boats, and how an autohelm worked. And I guess I was talking a lot more than I had been, and Nancy started to find it funny and then so did I, and the two of us stood on the dock by the *Warrior,* hooting like loons.

Two men came out from below and stood on the deck, looking at us. They were tan and very fit-looking.

As we stopped laughing for a moment, one of the men leaned forward and took a photograph of us. The flash nearly blinded me. Nancy thought it was pretty funny. I don't think the two guys did. Anyhow, they didn't laugh.

We did. But we moved on, stifling our laughter as we strolled to the end of the dock.

At the end of the dock we stood and stared at the water for a while. The laughter died down and we talked about a lot of things, picking up where the talk on the airplane had ended.

There's something about a night by the water in Southern California. Somehow it gives amazing potential and promise to whatever it is you're doing or thinking about. Maybe that explains a lot about the area. Maybe it's not cocaine and ego at all, but a drug made of pure moonlight and water and a breeze so dry and soft you feel it as an emotion instead of a sensation.

And maybe that explains how I was able to come so far back from the grave, back from the bad memories and nightmares and from all I had done to run and hide, and in just a few hours of Southern California moonlight come all the way back to life, to kissing Nancy Hoffman, in the moonlight, on the dock, by the water.

Nancy Hoffman kissed me back, too. A lot of people who have tried to describe a kiss usually sound like elfin dorks. So I won't try, beyond saying it did everything a kiss is supposed to do and then some.

Nancy came up for air first. I could have stayed under, lips to lips, all night.

"Whew," she said. "Slow down, Billy."

"It's too late to slow down," I said. My lips felt tight and heavy. My whole body did, like my blood supply had just doubled.

"Yeah, well, you better try. While I can still stand up." She ran her fingertips across her lips, then across mine. I almost bit them off. Nancy chuckled. "Billy," she said. "Oh, Billy, Billy, Billy-boy. What am I going to do with you?"

"You're doing it," I told her, and dove back into another kiss. It started a little slower this time. I chewed softly on her lower lip. It tasted like fresh lemons, tart and coppery at the same time.

Sometimes you kiss someone and you're thinking about what comes next. You use the kiss to lever open the door to other kinds of pawing and snorting.

But kissing Nancy Hoffman, all I was thinking about was the kiss. It was the most complete kiss I've ever been a part of. Time stopped, and nothing else mattered.

The next time we came up for air, we paused a little longer. It was pretty clear where we were headed, and I guess both of us needed to think about whether we really wanted to go there.

So we sat on a dock box, snuggled together close, and watched the ripples in the water break up the reflection of the moon. We talked some more.

"Where does all this passion come from?" she wanted to know.

"I'm not sure," I said. "I guess I've been alone awhile."

"Uh-huh."

"I guess I've needed to be."

She looked out over the water and squeezed my hand. "I just don't know if I'm ready for this."

I squeezed back. "Me either. But here it is."

"I'm not quite sure what I want."

I reached a hand over and gently turned her chin. Just seeing those golden eyes again stopped my breath for a moment. "I know what I want," I said.

She gave her low, honey-throated chuckle. "I'll bet," she said. "Let me guess."

She leaned in and rubbed her cheek against mine. "Mm-hmm," she said. It was part sigh and part laugh. I felt the warm wind of it ricochet into my ear. All the hairs on the back of my neck stood up.

Right then, I wanted her more than anything else in the world. And not just blind passion, not just wham-bam and to hell with the consequences. I wanted all of her, for all time. I wanted to drag her away to my cave forever and hide from the dragon together until we got too old and slow and it finally got us.

I settled for another kiss.

This one was every bit as good as the first two. I could feel myself sliding farther and farther away from where I thought I was, where I was supposed to be. For a few minutes I didn't feel bad or guilty. I didn't think about Hector McAuley and his sad, slick father.

And for a few minutes there, that was almost as good as the kiss. Almost.

CHAPTER
TWENTY-THREE

The inside of Nancy Hoffman's apartment was spare and restrained. It had a kind of old-fashioned feeling to it, even though the furniture was modern. Everything was clean and the surfaces gleamed.

In the living room there was a small and stiff couch, an easy chair, a coffee table, a floor lamp, and an end table. A small hooked throw rug was on the floor by the couch. Off in the corner stood a large stereo cabinet with a glass door. A stack of about thirty records leaned against it, and a larger box of cassettes and CDs sat on top.

There was a doorway at the far end of the room where Nancy had disappeared a few minutes earlier. I guessed it led to the bedroom and bathroom. Either that or she slept on the small couch. A neat row of windows took up about half of one wall. I stepped over and looked out.

The apartment was on the fourth floor of one of those old stone buildings they threw up in the thirties for people who thought they were stars. Out the row of windows I had a grand view of an oak tree that couldn't quite hide a liquor store. Beyond that was a tremendous glare of bright colored lights.

Nancy had the great good taste to keep heavy curtains across the windows, and I let them drop back in place and turned to look at the room.

I'm a toucher. I admit it. I try not to be a pain in the ass about it,

168

but if I'm left alone in a room, I'll touch things. I knelt by the stereo and touched the records. She had some good old Motown albums, three by Funkadelic, some Miles Davis, Herbie Hancock, Josef Zawinul, and a recording of Tchaikovsky's Violin Concerto featuring David Oistrakh.

Above and behind was a small alcove with a standing bookshelf. There were a couple of standard-issue best-sellers, three travel books on the Caribbean, and a stack of coffee-table books on ballet, tropical sunsets, and so on.

On the top shelf stood a row of photographs in silver frames. There was one of Nancy in a cap and gown. A large, bearded man was handing her a diploma. There was another of Nancy wearing a white nurse's uniform, smiling against a studio background.

In the center was a picture of a group of people clearly celebrating something or other. At the center of the group were a thin, balding man and a very nice-looking black woman, both middle-aged.

I picked the picture up for some clue. Off on the left edge of the shot I could see a beaming Nancy, her hands held together in mid-clap. A very handsome black man stood next to her. There was a table on the other side of the picture. I could see a cake, a punch bowl, and some plates on the table. But no clue about the purpose of the celebration, or who the people were—

"My parents," Nancy said. She had snuck up behind me. I almost dropped the picture.

Nancy took it from me as I turned, smiling fondly down at it. "Their thirty-fifth wedding anniversary."

I didn't get it. "Your parents?" I said stupidly.

Nancy was still smiling, but it might have been a little forced at this point. "That's right," she said.

I leaned over and looked at the picture again. I still didn't get it. "Which ones?"

Her finger moved right to the center of the picture, to the thin man and the black woman. "Right here," she said. "Mom and Dad." And then she gained a little steam, pointing to the handsome black man. "And that is my brother, the reporter."

"Oh," I said. Her tawny olive skin, the rich, tight curls of her coppery hair, the luscious lips: oh. "They seem very nice."

She slammed the picture down, back on the shelf. "You mean, she seems very dark?"

"Nancy—"

"You mean, nice for a white man who married a black woman?"

"Come on, I was surprised, that's all."

"Because I don't *act* black? You jes ain't seen me dance is all."

She had turned nasty so fast I wasn't ready for that, either. It did not matter to me whether Nancy was half-black. It really didn't.

She glared at me, waiting for some feeble defense. I opened my mouth to make it, but nothing came out. It was just—

Just what? Was she right? I was surprised because she didn't "act black"? What did that mean? How *did* you act black? Pretend your skin is dark? Why did we think of it as acting?

And here I was, caught in the classical liberal dilemma. Damn it, some of my best friends really *were* black. But maybe friendship was a different level of intimacy—I sure didn't think of Nancy the same way I thought about Ed Beasley.

So *was* I disturbed? Put off by the revelation of her blackness? I didn't like to think so. It didn't fit with my self-image at all. But I *had* been shocked. I had acted differently than the way I would have if she had revealed she was half-Polish.

Self-image—did it come down to that? Was I more worried about how I looked than what I was doing?

There's a real jerk inside all of us. Like most jerks, he has a simple job on this earth. Whenever you least expect it, whenever it's most inconvenient, he steps out from behind the couch and puts an arm around your shoulder, so everybody knows he's with you.

And the thing is, he *is* with you. He's with all of us. He won't go away and we are permanently stuck with him. And if we can't make him funny, it becomes very sad indeed.

So I did the only thing I could. I laughed.

I laughed at pure, unprejudiced Billy Knight, caught in a blind-side trap he had made for himself. I laughed at me, up to my neck in the outhouse and worried about how I was going to get my socks clean. I laughed at my good friend, the jerk inside, who had surprised me into seeing something about myself I didn't know and wouldn't have guessed.

And mostly I laughed because, now that I had seen the truth about myself, it really *didn't* matter. If Nancy had been completely black, or Irish, or anything in between, it wouldn't matter—now. Because she was the nicest and most interesting person I had met in six or seven years, and that was all that mattered.

Nancy watched me laugh with a polite coldness for about thirty seconds. Finally one corner of her mouth started to twitch, then the other. Then she opened her lovely mouth and let out such a hoot of laughter that it almost scared me.

And in just a minute we were both rolling on the tiny couch, laughing, arms around each other, gasping with laughter.

And after just a few moments of that, my hands suddenly became aware of where they were and what they were doing, and started doing other things.

And after several minutes of that, we quickly became aware of one more thing.

"The couch is too small," Nancy whispered to me.

"No problem," I told her. I picked her up in my arms, dizzy with the solid warmth of her weight.

"Down the hall, on the left," she said, chewing on my ear. She put her tongue inside the ear and hummed softly.

I made it all the way down the hall and into the bedroom, but it was a close call.

By the time I got through the door Nancy was working on my neck, and standing up suddenly took a lot of thought. I stopped thinking about it and tumbled us both onto the bed.

Her skin felt silky and responsive to the touch and alive. The surface of her skin all over felt like it was humming gently. I could almost feel the pores purring.

In spite of my urgency I spent long minutes exploring her, marveling at the feel of that skin, at the rounds and hollows of her, and feeling her hands moving over me, too.

And at some point her breathing broke rhythm for just a moment and I heard her gasp.

Soon after that I stopped hearing and thinking.

In pitch darkness I woke up. My heart was hammering and my mouth was filled with a dry, bitter taste. A line of tears was still wet on the side of my face.

I had been walking with ghosts, listening as they explained their

terrible disappointment in me. I knew I had done something un-
forgivably stupid. The ghosts explained it to me, told me all about
it. But when I woke up I couldn't remember what it was.

Nancy was lying with her back to me. It was a wonderful back,
smooth, satiny, lean, and sleek. I couldn't understand why looking
at that back, remembering love with Nancy, could make me feel so
bad.

Beyond Nancy was a small bedside table with a digital clock
radio. The time flashed as I watched: 3:47.

What the hell was I doing here?

I've never been awake at 3:47 A.M. without asking that question.
But now there seemed to be a really good reason for asking it.

What *was* I doing here? I was thinking with my gonads, pursuing
pleasure when I should have been at work on a couple of nasty
murders. Christ Almighty, my wife and child were buried just a few
miles from here. What was I thinking about?

Clearly I wasn't thinking about anything. I wasn't thinking at all.
I had become a cartoon, a caricature of myself, a Billy Knight with
a perpetual erection, little horns sprouting from my head and steam
coming from my nose.

I swung my legs over the side of the bed and sat with my head in
my hands. As the bed shifted under me Nancy made a slow snug-
gling motion with her shoulders and asked me, "Hmmmdrble?"

Now I had something else to feel bad about. Nancy was a sweet
person. She didn't deserve a monster like me, somebody so far
gone he couldn't even manage anything more complicated than
fishing.

And now I couldn't even manage that. Here I was, three thousand miles away from my ocean, and I was drowning. I was losing
time on a cold trail, hurting Nancy, being unfaithful to the memory of family—oh, God, this was so wrong . . .

What the hell *was* I doing here?

I didn't know. But I knew I had to get out before I did any more
harm.

I slipped quietly into my clothes. Nancy didn't stir again. I was
out the door and down the four flights of stairs in just a few minutes.

When I started my rental car to head back to the hotel, the clock
said 4:02.

CHAPTER
TWENTY-FOUR

I got back to the hotel room at 4:42. It was still small and smelled bad. But it was home. My back hurt just looking at the tiny warped bed. The room seemed so oppressive that I started to feel noble and justified. I must be doing something right—I was suffering again.

I knew even Ed wouldn't be at his desk at this hour, but I called anyway and left a message for him to call me. Then I fell out of my clothes and onto the bed, face down. I was asleep instantly, having just enough time to realize that my feet and my head were six inches higher than my navel.

I was having one of those vivid, backlit dreams that make you yell, but there was no one to wake me up and tell me. The ghosts had come back. This time I stood in the center of a ring of their cloaked and hooded faces. They were all dead and they hated me. They were moving in on me so slowly I couldn't see them move, but every time I turned, they were closer.

I turned one last time just as one of them was reaching to touch my face. Its claw came out of the robe, part machine and part skeleton. One terrifying digit stretched out for my eye.

The sound of the phone ringing jerked me up out of sleep just before the thing touched me.

I sat up. I was sweating heavily. My back felt like someone had been pounding on it with brickbats. I rubbed my eyes, trying to get enough blood flowing into my head to figure out what to do. The dream was so disorienting that I wasn't sure how to answer the telephone. Suddenly all the normal, everyday things we take for granted were no longer clear and certain but instead had turned into slippery, sinewy, evil possibilities. The world was a snake basket, and I had pried the lid off and seen its writhing contents.

But the phone was still ringing. I was sure it had to be Ed. I was sure that if I just picked it up and said something, reality would click back into place and I would be me again, sitting in a cheesy hotel room in solid reality.

I reached for the telephone. Just in time I remembered what to say. "Hello?"

"Well," said the honey-and-rum voice on the other end. Then she paused.

It wasn't Ed. It was one of the shapes from my dream. The snakes wriggled as solid reality tilted sideways.

I guess I didn't say anything for a little bit too long, because when the voice spoke again it sounded a little irritated.

"Well, don't knock me over with sweet nothings, Billy," she said, and I recognized the voice. It belonged to somebody alive.

"Uh, Nancy?"

"Very good. May I ask how many women you might expect to call you this early?"

"I don't—I was having a bad dream."

"Good," she said, and I could hear the satisfaction in her voice. "That's what you get for running out on me. You might have been enjoying an eye-opener right now instead of a nightmare."

"What time is it?" The disorientation was fading, but it was being replaced by a sense of impossibility. The idea that I had been making love with her just a few hours ago was absurd.

"It's just about seven A.M. and I have to be at the clinic in half an hour. I just wanted to talk to you first."

I couldn't think of anything to say about that, so I didn't. I heard her sigh heavily on the other end. "Oh, shit, what have I gotten into now? You sure had plenty to say last night."

I felt a panicked sense of my own worthlessness rising up in my throat. I was still stupid from sleep, but I didn't want to hurt Nancy —it wasn't her fault.

"Look, uh, I'm sorry. I'm not real sharp yet. I was asleep."

"Sounds like you still are, Billy. I have to get going. Why don't you call me at work later?"

"Yes. Okay, if I can."

"I think you *better* can, baby. 'Bye."

And she hung up. I was left with a clear sense that she was peeved with me. Maybe that was for the best. Maybe she should realize right away that it wasn't going to work, could never work. And that she deserved better.

I fell asleep again almost instantly. I woke up an hour later thinking about Nancy. What a jerk I was. This was an incredible person, and she liked me. I had a real chance at something here, and I was about to blow it for—for what? A sense of duty or honor? Low self-esteem?

I thought about the last look I'd had of her as I snuck out, that taut, sleek back. I thought about the other side, too. I wanted her again, right now.

How could that be wrong? What did it have to do with what I was doing? Didn't Lancelot go home at the end of the day, home to a hot bath, Guinevere, and a few hours of sleep?

I sat on the side of the bed and looked at my feet. I wiggled my toes at myself: *Hello, head.* I nodded my head at my toes: *Hey, how's it going? Things are getting a little rocky on this end, toes. Would you guys like to do some of the thinking for a while? We're not doing so great up here.*

Sure: dialogue between self and toes. Why not?

I stumbled into the shower and started to feel a little more like part of the world again. As I climbed out, the telephone was ringing again. I leaned out the bathroom door and looked at it for a few seconds before deciding it couldn't possibly be Nancy. I took the three steps over and picked it up.

"Hello?" I said.

There was a long breath blown out on the other end, the sound of amused exasperation expressed as cigarette smoke. "It's my day off, you know," Ed said.

"You won't make Lieutenant sitting around on your ass, Ed," I told him.

"I won't make it at all, they find out I'm talking to you."

That didn't sound good. "What does that mean?"

Another long exhale. It was so loud and clear I could almost see the smoke trickle out of the receiver. "Means you not doing so good making friends, Billy. Means from now on you best leave any messages you got on my answering machine at home. And try to disguise your voice, all right? You Typhoid Billy now, and I sure don't want to catch nothing from you."

"When did this happen?"

"Happened yesterday. Suddenly they don't want nobody having nothing to do with you. I'm in deep shit and officially told to mind my own fuckin' business and stay 'way from you. Came down last night, while you out muff-diving."

I let that go. "Who is *they*, Ed?"

I heard him fire up another Kool, blow out the smoke. "Hard to say for sure. Situation like this, pressure works kind of sideways. You know, somebody suggest something at the water cooler, then they walk it down the hall to somebody who mention it to their buddy while they trading memos. Hard to say where it started."

"Uh-huh. Would it be too corny to ask if the pressure's coming from upstairs?"

"Oh, my, no," said Ed. "That ain't corny at all, son. Upstairs is just exactly where the pressure is coming from, Billy." He had never sounded more sardonic.

"What did you find out about Doyle's neighborhood?"

"Funny you should ask. I checked those five houses. One of 'em been empty for six months. Probate thing. Another one got the dean of arts at USC."

"It could happen."

"I don't think so, Billy. Not really."

"No," I said, "I don't really think so either. What else?"

"One of 'em belong to Eddie Jackson."

"I think we can rule that one out," I said. Eddie Jackson had a record in the Billboard Top Forty at least two times a year. He was black. "What else?"

Another hiss of smoke. "Real estate man. Wife's a teacher. Three kids."

"Possible?"

"Anything's possible, Billy. But this the guy that sold Eddie Jackson the house, so it don't seem too likely."

"Which leaves Doyle."

"Which leaves Doyle," he agreed.

I heard another hiss of breath. But this one was mine.

"Something else kind of interesting," Ed said. "I took a couple of pictures over and showed 'em to McAuley's maid. Asked her if the nice man with the badge that picked up Roscoe's papers was one of them. Guess who she picked out?"

My stomach flip-flopped. "Doyle," I said, sure that it was.

Ed laughed. "Nope. Phillip Moss."

I didn't say anything for a long moment. My head was spinning. "You think Moss is the killer? Maybe protecting Doyle from something, even without Doyle's knowledge?"

He laughed again. "I don't think so, Billy. Remember that BOLO I put out on Moss? Well, we got him."

"Where is he?"

The laughter gurgled out of control into a cough. I waited, not very patiently. When Ed had calmed down again I asked him again. "Where's Moss, Ed?"

"He's in the morgue, Billy. Broken neck."

"Doyle is covering his tracks," I said. "Making sure nobody can connect him."

"Uh-huh. Guy that shot Hector could have been Moss."

"It wasn't Moss."

"No, but all you got is one gangbanger witness, and his description could be Moss easy as Doyle."

"What do we do now?"

Ed laughed one last time. "What you mean *we*, white man?" he said, and hung up.

I listened to the dial tone for a good twenty seconds before I could convince myself that he meant it. Then I put the receiver back in the cradle and stood up.

Okay. Maybe he was kidding, but if Ed had to choose between his career and saving my ass, I wasn't sure what he'd do. I'd just have to try not to push him into a corner where he had to decide. I was on my own. No big deal—I had expected to be.

Now I had one good question Ed couldn't answer: what had I done in the last twenty-four hours that had pushed somebody one step further than they could go without pushing back?

I thought about it for a half-hour. I kept thinking of Nancy, too, but I tried to be tough and spend at least half my thinking on the real problem.

After half an hour I realized two things. The first was that I was still naked. The second, as I pulled on my shorts, was that whatever this hypothetical last straw was, it had to be accidental, if it had happened while I was with Nancy.

I had gone to see Sergeant Whitt, and nobody had cared—not even Sergeant Whitt. I had taken some documents from Parker Center, and nobody had even written me a parking ticket.

So what had I done since then that was more threatening? Talked to Detective Braun. Requested a rap sheet for Phillip Moss. Gone to Marina del Rey with Nancy for dinner. Looked at some boats. Admired one of them until we got chased off. Kissed some. Gone to her place, made love all night . . . nothing threatening there, not one single thing that might—

Whoa, son, as my Uncle Mack used to say. Slow down here. Back up half a step. What if it wasn't *one* thing? What if it was a combination, something somebody perceived as a pattern?

Except there still had to be something final, some last piece that had fallen into place while I was with Nancy, and I had no idea what it could possibly be.

I thought about what I knew. It didn't seem like much: the hunting rifle, the brummel hook. A white supremacist staking out Doyle's house.

Maybe the visits to Sergeant Whitt and Sergeant Brandon or the little chat with Moss had triggered small alarms. Had Doyle started to feel the hounds sniffing at the edge of his grove? Would something else make him feel like they were at the foot of his tree? He would feel the noose getting tighter around his neck. So the one thing that would tip him over would be—

What? Something that happened while I was with Nancy, which didn't make any sense. Not at all.

Unless—

I called Ed at home.

"You just can't take a hint, can you, boy?"

"One quick question, Ed."

"It have to be quick, I'm in the middle of cooking my famous Arkansas flannel cakes."

"Does Doyle keep a boat at Marina del Rey?"

He chuckled around a mouthful of smoke. "Oh, yass. He got a boat all right. Big sleek motherfucker. He's one of them old-timey ocean racers, they all go out every year and try to kill themselves going to Hawaii or some damn thing. That's a big thing with him, have to *prove* himself with all kinds of wild shit. He keep another boat in Texas just so he can get a shot at dying in either ocean."

"You know the name of the boat he keeps here, Ed? Is it the *Warrior*?"

"That's two questions, Billy. But I think that's the name. The *Warrior*." He chuckled, a throaty, smoke-filled sound. "Only a honky would name a boat something like that."

"You're probably right," I told him. "Thanks."

CHAPTER
TWENTY-FIVE

It was one more small, circumstantial link to Doyle. I had stood on the dock by his boat. The two goons had taken my picture. And sometime that night Doyle had seen the picture, figured out who I was, and put out the word. It all added up; there was not the slightest doubt in the world, and there was even less proof that a prosecutor would buy.

It's a classic cop dilemma. I thought I had left it behind when I turned in my badge, but here it was again. I knew exactly who was guilty and where they were; and I couldn't prove anything. All I had was circumstantial soup.

I could show a really flimsy connection from Doyle to one deranged neo-Nazi. I could extend that connection to ownership of a sailboat. They might provide motive and means, and they might be nothing. *Might* didn't seem like enough.

I needed more, and that's part of the cop dilemma, too. But Doyle was a very public figure, and I couldn't dig around him without tripping on roots.

My choices were limited. Anything I did was going to alert Doyle, one way or another. And then he would take action of another sort. If he wasn't afraid to kill a well-connected, serving police officer like Roscoe, he wouldn't hesitate to kill me either.

And that thought brought me up short, too. Roscoe had been an administrator. He had no street-smarts at all, and even less idea of

180

how to investigate something as tricky as this. Yet Roscoe had found something, and it must have been something solid, because Roscoe had died.

What could Roscoe have found that I couldn't?

The idea chewed at me. I was a competent investigator; Roscoe was a chair-warmer. I was at a dead end, and Roscoe had found something important enough to get him killed.

What had he found?

The answer didn't come in one big, bright lump. In fact, I pushed away pieces of it a couple of times, irritated at the shape it took. Finally, when I had been grinding my teeth for a half-hour and had nothing else to think about, I sat down with it, looked it over.

Roscoe was good at only one thing. So whatever he had found to implicate Hector's killer had to be political or administrative. Somewhere there were faint vapor-trail markings in the upper echelon of command that only an expert like Roscoe could read. I would never have been able to find it. But he had followed the trail, found the trail-maker, and wound up headless in the gutter.

And that led back to the same place. Only a high-ranking cop could leave the kind of trail that Roscoe could find. The only high-ranking cop who had left any kind of footprint at all here was Doyle. That left me at the same dead end.

I got dressed slowly and went down to the coffee shop. I tried to find a safe choice on the menu while I turned the Doyle problem over in my mind.

Because my mind was churning furiously, I ordered blueberry pancakes. They were terrible, with a strong taste of lard and pesticide.

I ate them anyway, and maybe they were to blame for what I decided to do. After watching so many killers laugh their way out of hard time with defenses like eating junk food and watching TV, maybe it's only fair to say it was the pancakes, Your Honor. They clouded my judgment.

More than that, though, it was probably a combination of frustrations. The son of a bitch was a cop, and he was getting away with something he shouldn't, and that made me mad.

When I had been a cop I hadn't felt this kind of anger at anybody I busted. They were playing their parts, I was playing mine.

There's a funny kind of understanding between cops and crooks. They both stick to an odd set of rules.

But Doyle wasn't playing by those rules. He was trying to play both sides. I wanted him to pay for that. So I decided to do something against all the rules, too.

After breakfast I drove over to Hancock Park and pulled up in front of Doyle's gigantic Tudor-style house.

If there were no loose ends sticking out for me to pull on, maybe I could snag some of my own. I wanted to hammer at Doyle's smug sense of safety, push him off balance, make him do something he shouldn't. And then, of course, hope I survived to nail him on it.

I looked at the house. I didn't know if he was at his office or at home. But I could find out.

I parked the car well down the block, under a large oak tree that shielded my spot from Doyle's house. I got out, crossed the street, and approached his house.

There was no sign that anyone was there. The garage, attached to the house and off to one side, was closed. I moved into the neighboring yard and approached Doyle's house from the side.

It was a nice house, nicer than anything I'd ever seen this close. Nobody I knew had ever lived in a house that nice. I pushed through a hedge and got closer. I tried to move quietly, carefully, the way Uncle Sugar had taught me to move through jungles. This wasn't much of a jungle. Aside from the hedge there was almost no cover, except for the big oak tree with the tree house in it.

I slipped over to the tree and stood with my cheek against it, watching the house. There was still no sign of life in the house.

I thought about what to do next. While I thought there was a rustle and a soft thud behind me.

I turned fast, but the guy behind me was faster. He had his gun in my face before I was more than halfway around. It was a Glock 9mm with a silencer, the twin of Phillip Moss's piece.

And this guy was almost Phillip Moss's twin. He was large and looked fit. He had thinning light brown hair and wore a camouflage suit instead of a Hawaiian shirt.

I put my hands up. "Neighborhood Watch?" I asked him.

He gave me a nasty smirk. "Tree patrol." He jerked his head up at the treehouse above us. "We thought you might be coming. Thanks for making it easy."

"Don't mention it."

He took a half-step back, very careful, and waved the gun toward the front door of the house. "Move along."

I moved. He marched me across a manicured front lawn and right up the four steps to the door.

"Knock," he said.

There was a massive door knocker shaped like an eagle's head. I could lift it without a winch, but just barely. I let it crash down, listening for distant thunder or the scream of terrified horses. All I heard was a huge echo ringing through the house.

After a few moments the door swung open.

I was ready for a lot of things. Sudden violence, certainly. Surprise, fear, hate, no question. I was ready for a picture I had of who Doyle was and what he had done and might do.

I was not ready for Doyle.

Warren Francis Doyle filled the doorway. He didn't do it with his size, although he was a big man, maybe six-two, and broad across the back and shoulders, with short reddish hair. He was wearing a tank top and a pair of sweat pants. A light sheen of sweat covered his skin. He looked very fit, very strong, and completely in charge of everything in sight. If he told the trees to bow I would expect them to obey.

There was something in the way he stood, something in his eyes, some special quality that just seemed to come out of his pores. It made you want to drop to one knee and put a knuckle to your forehead. Doyle filled the doorway with his presence.

Presence: It's a word for romance novels. It's a quality so rare and undefinable, most people have never really seen it. If you haven't, all anyone can tell you about it is, you had to be there.

I was there. I'd had a lot of things I was going to say. Doyle's presence took them all away from me. So did his action.

If he'd pulled a gun I would have been ready. Instead, with a pause so slight I couldn't be sure it was there at all, he looked at me, nodded twice and said, "Good. You're here. Come on in." And he held the door wide, nodding to the guy with the gun, who turned and headed back for the treehouse.

I stepped into Doyle's house. I was thinking about the old rhyme, the spider and the fly, trying to remember how it ended for the fly. I didn't think it was a happy ending.

The door opened into a wide marble hall, white and cool, accented with soft grays and a few pieces of oak furniture. Doyle closed the door and led me toward the back of the house. He didn't say anything more, and didn't seem to mind turning his back on me. His confidence was so overwhelming I started to take it for granted, too. Of course I couldn't hurt him; why shouldn't he turn his back on me?

I followed Doyle to a large room at the back of the house. It had a highly polished wooden floor and a high ceiling with a row of skylights. A mirror stretched along one wall.

The room was filled with the most complete home gym I have ever seen. I once paid seven hundred bucks a year to belong to a gym that had a lot less.

There was a complete set of Nautilus machines along one end of the room. Something about them looked wrong. It took me a minute to figure it out: they were all specially modified so that the maximum weight on each machine was more than double what you might see in a health club.

I stared at the machines, the racks of free weights, the heavy punching bag and speed bag, the narrow wooden door that must lead into a sauna.

"I was working out," Doyle said behind me, and I jerked around to face him again. I didn't have the confidence in his good intentions that he seemed to have in mine. The fact that I'd turned my back on him was just one more instance of his presence; I'd forgotten he was dangerous. I wouldn't forget again—I hoped.

He seemed to know what I was thinking. He smiled, tilting his head just a little. "You don't mind if I continue, do you?"

The truth was, his personality was so powerful I would have had a hard time objecting if he had wanted to eat babies. "I don't mind," I said.

"Good," he said, and stepped over to a large free weight bar on the floor by the mirror. I tried to add up the plates on the bar and guessed it weighed around two hundred fifty pounds.

Doyle squatted beside the bar, placing his hands on the grips. He grunted slightly and stood, raising the bar to a position just under his chin. "I think you'll find this game has been rigged against you," he said. There was a merry twinkle in his eye. I caught myself smiling and nodding without knowing it.

I was about to say something back when he lifted the weights straight over his head and began to do military presses. A very strong man could do ten at that weight with a lot of effort. Doyle, with no effort at all, began to move the weight up and down in a smooth and quick motion. He was at fourteen reps before I recovered enough to stop gaping.

"What do you mean?" I asked him. The smooth up-and-down of that impossibly heavy bar did not even slow. I couldn't have taken my eyes away if my life depended on it.

"I mean," he said with no strain in his voice, "that you're swimming with sharks, and you're going to be eaten." He flashed his teeth at me over the bar, and then smoothly raised it again. "There's no way you're ever going to get anything out of this. You should go home."

"*Can* I go home?" I asked him.

The teeth again. "Of course you can. What's stopping you?"

"I don't know," I said. "If we leave out honor and duty and all the other funny words, how about you?"

He gave a small chuckle. The weight went up and down. "Why would I stop you? More important, *how* would I stop you?"

"I bet you'd think of something," I said. Up, down—he had to be near fifty reps.

"I'm a sworn officer of the law," he said. "I can't imagine what you think I might do."

"Only what you've already done," I said.

He paused, holding the weight halfway up, his arms bent. It was hurting my arms just to see him do it, but there was not the slightest trace of a quiver or tremor. If he was trying to impress me, it was working. "What have I already done?" he asked me with amusement in his voice.

"I think you killed Hector McAuley. Then when his father started sniffing too close to your trail, I think you killed him, too."

He nodded. "What've you got?" he said, and it startled me to hear him say it like that, the way one cop would say it to another.

"The brummel hook on the rooftop," I said. "It's something you would know about, you might have one. It's pretty unusual."

"But not unique."

"No."

His eyes were twinkling merrily again. It's a terrible, strange word, *merry,* but it's the only one that fit. This was a happy person, doing what he loved, bringing good cheer. "And what did I do with the brummel hook? Use it to rig a line? Run over from the roof of the bank, shoot Hector McAuley, and then run back up the line again?"

"Yeah," I said, fighting the stupid feeling he was trying to create. "That's about right."

Doyle gave a happy little chuckle. "Okay. What else? What about the weapon?"

I hesitated, and he laughed aloud. "You don't have the weapon? You don't even know what it was yet?"

"A two-fifty-seven," I said. "Hunting rifle."

He nodded. "Probably a Webley, because that's what I own, isn't it? A two-fifty-seven Webley hunting rifle. A brummel hook. That's it? That's all you have?"

It suddenly didn't sound like much. Maybe it wasn't, but what I couldn't tell him, couldn't call evidence at all, was a lot simpler.

I *knew.* I had known since I came into this house that Doyle had killed the McAuleys, knew it without the smallest doubt. And he knew I knew it, and that suited him just fine.

"That's about it," I said.

Doyle laughed. "What do they call you—Bill? William? Surely not Willy?" He laughed again. He looked like somebody's portrait of a Greek god at the peak of his power.

"Billy," I said.

"Well, Billy. I know from your record you're smart, too smart to risk a libel suit and a possible jail sentence by saying things like that in public. That's why you came here to see me, right?"

"Right," I said. I was still fighting down the good warm feeling I got when he called me smart.

"And you're thinking to yourself that if you confront me with it, just blurt it out like that, maybe I'll get flustered enough to do something foolish, right?"

I didn't answer. He made it sound like a stupid idea. Maybe I should have taken the warning from the blueberry pancakes.

Doyle dropped the weights. They made a tremendous crashing sound. I sucked in my breath and took an involuntary step backwards. He took a step closer. If lightning had started to come out of his eyes it would not have surprised me.

"Well, what would you like me to do? Confess? Go with you to Parker Center and turn myself in? Did you think the power of your moral righteousness would knock me off my feet and sweep me into a jail cell?"

He took a step closer. I realized I was holding my breath.

"Or did you think I might lose it altogether and attack you? And then you could subdue me and take me in?"

Another step. I couldn't even move my eyes away from his.

His voice dropped. There was something very intimate in his voice as he said, "Would you like to try to subdue me, Billy?" His hand lashed out, faster than anything I had ever seen before, and slapped my face. My head rocked around to the right and I felt a quick spurt of blood along my back teeth. "You're welcome to try."

The hand came again. I was ready and ducked. It still caught me —just the tips of his fingers, but it felt like it took off a yard of skin.

"Good," he said. "You're very fast." And he swung again. There was a merry little smile on his face and his eyes were sparkling. He looked like he was telling a favorite niece about the Easter Bunny. His hand smacked my face, just the tips of the fingers, and I was already getting punchy.

Smack. "Wonderful," he said. *Smack.* "You have superb reflexes." *Smack.*

I was anticipating, and moving as fast as I had ever moved, and he was tagging me. It was like playing one of those hand-slapping games with a kid; the adult is simply moving on a different and much faster plane. So you make encouraging noises so the kid will keep trying, not grow discouraged about life in general. But no matter what you may be saying, the kid doesn't have a chance.

Neither did I. But Doyle was making the same encouraging noises, smiling his bright, cheerful, encouraging smile, and continuing to rip off the sides of my face.

Smack. "It's not really fair, is it?" *Smack.* "I don't know what it is." *Smack.* "I was just born this way." *Smack-smack smack,* a double with a backhand. "Stronger, faster, better than everyone else." *Smack smack.* A trickle of blood started above my eye.

"Better?" I said, and dodged hard. For the first time he missed completely. It seemed to make him very happy; he laughed aloud.

"Ha!" he said. "Good! Yes, of course better. Some kind of genetic accident. I take no credit for it, but it's true." *Smack smack smack.* One miss. "If I am better at everything I do than those around me, why shouldn't I say it? They all say it, they know it, I know it. It's *true.* Yes, better." *Smack smack smack,* like he was proving it.

I couldn't take a whole lot more of this pounding. I had never seen anybody so fast hit so hard. There was already a ringing in my ears and the coppery taste of blood filling my mouth.

Doyle still looked like he was playing kid's games, a jolly smiling uncle. He was just warming up. I had to do something fast or I was not going to get a chance to do anything.

Anybody, no matter how good he is, settles into a rhythm with any physical effort. A very regular internal meter develops and consciously or not you start thinking one-two-three, one-two-three. Muhammad Ali figured that out, and with his Ali Shuffle, settling a rhythm and then deliberately breaking it, he brought a lot of guys to a taste of canvas.

I thought I had caught Doyle's rhythm. By anticipating it, I thought I could make him miss. I tried it once, and it worked. I had a chance, but it was a slim one. If I could catch his hand and step inside I might be able to land a couple of my own. And no matter how strong he was, if I could hit him, he'd go down.

I ate two more slaps while I waited for the right opening. I wanted him slightly off-balance, weight forward, leaning into the punch I was planning to throw. I would catch his arm, step inside, and uncork a haymaker.

The moment came. I made him miss a left and as he followed with his right I grabbed his forearm. It was like holding onto steel cable.

Before I could move, Doyle pulled his forearm up and lifted me straight into the air. With a very warm smile, like he was very pleased with me, he said, "You really are very good, Billy."

Then he brought his other hand within six inches of my face. *"Very* good," he said. He moved the fist. That's all I remember.

CHAPTER
TWENTY-SIX

The drunk tank has a sound all its own. It's a combination of low moaning, like you might find in the waiting room in hell, and the raspy gargle of a TB ward that's part choking and part snore. There's the occasional scream or bellow and, just to make things perfect, the odd snatch of song here and there.

The drunk tank has a smell, too. Oh, boy, does it have a smell. If you take fifty or sixty incontinent, unwashed alcoholics who have been living in sewers and dumpsters and cram them into a space the size of an average living room, you get a smell that's hard to mistake. It's hard to take, too.

It was the smell that clued me in. The noise might just have been the sound track from some of the dreams I'd been having lately. But my dreams hadn't been coming with a scratch-and-sniff card.

I opened my eyes—or one eye, anyway. The left one seemed stuck. I wet a finger and worked around the lashes. I held the finger up to my eye; dried blood.

I looked around the room with my one eye. I felt like Popeye after a bender. The cell was packed with bodies. Most of them looked like they'd been found in the dumpsters behind really cheap cafeterias.

Over in one corner was a small sink and a toilet with no seat. I managed to stand up and work my way across the floor to the sink. I felt a little dizzy. My face was throbbing, and something was wrong with one of my back teeth. The right sleeve had been torn off my shirt. My watch was gone, and my wallet and shoes.

I bent over the sink and turned on the tap. A rusty trickle came out into my hands and I used it to scrub at my eye. After a couple of minutes I got the eye open.

It wasn't an improvement. None of the drunks got any prettier. The smell didn't go away, either.

Over in the corner by the door I noticed a very large, very hairy white man. He was sitting with his back propped against the wall and glaring at me. I glared back.

"What the fuck are you looking at, fuckface?" he asked me politely. I couldn't think of a clever answer so I turned away, back to the spot where I woke up.

I sat down again and put my head in my hands. I hadn't expected to wake up in the drunk tank—I hadn't expected to wake up at all. Why hadn't Doyle killed me? What the hell was I doing here?

I remembered the last time I had thought that question—was it really just a day ago? With Nancy. I hadn't called her. She would be mad. Maybe she wouldn't want to see me anymore. Serve me right.

My head was hurting. I guess I should have been used to it, but I wasn't. I felt as bad as if I really belonged here, sitting in the tank on a Saturday night.

Feet scuffed. I opened my eyes.

My new friend with the attitude was towering over me, glaring down at me with comic-opera fierceness. "I asked you a question, fuckface," he said. He kicked at me, popping my knee with his foot.

It made me mad. My knee was one of the few places that didn't hurt. Had I really sunk this low, that I was getting kicked around by a bully in the drunk tank?

I hit him in the balls and stood up as he doubled over in pain. I was ready to peg him again, but he was already falling gently to his knees, so I just stood there. "It's *Mister* Fuckface to you," I told him. I felt a little better. Maybe a superhuman racist could beat me up without working up a sweat, but I was still a terror with drunks —even big drunks.

I sat back down again. The bully didn't move for quite a while. Then he sat up suddenly, looked at me, and scuttled away, back to his place, without taking his eyes off me. I didn't feel so great about hitting him anymore.

I sat there feeling sorry for myself for one of the longest nights I can remember. Five or six times a couple of cops showed up and pushed somebody new through the door.

Sunday was even worse. If there is a place deader than the drunk tank on a Sunday I don't want to know about it. The whole day plodded by at slow speed, every minute dragging out to a full half-hour.

I guess the smell stayed the same, but after the first night my senses went numb. The moans continued; the singing tapered off. Small blessings.

There was a battered clock behind a wire mesh over the main door. Every time the door opened, every eye capable of movement would swing to the door, glance up at the clock, and swing back again to whatever patch of wall they were staring at.

It was just after ten-thirty on Monday morning when Ed finally came for me.

He stood at the bars for a little too long, just looking at me. Then the famous Cheshire cat grin spread over his face. "Billy!" he said with real delight. "You lookin' good!"

"I feel great, Ed. Come on in, have a seat."

He didn't lose the grin, but he shook his head. "I'd love to, Billy, but I can't afford to burn my suit. How 'bout you come on out instead?"

"If you're sure—"

"Oh, I'm sure, Billy. I'm very damn sure."

I stood up. It was a lot harder than it should have been. My knees creaked, and my back didn't want to straighten out. But after a few moments I got them to do what they were supposed to do, and we all went over to the door.

"Can I assume you had the weekend off, Ed?"

He nodded. "Otherwise I never would have missed this," he said.

"Are you going to get me out?"

He smiled a little broader, nodded. "In a minute. Let me look a little longer. This the most fun I had in a long time."

There was a certain amount of paperwork before I got my belt and wallet back. They didn't have my sleeve. Or my watch, or my shoes. I asked for a copy of the arrest report and they gave it to me.

I looked it over as we walked to Ed's car. Ed shook his head. "It'll be clean, Billy. I already checked."

"You know these guys?" I asked. The two arresting officers were M. Stokes and G. Pietsch.

Ed nodded. "Stokes a brother. I know him, he's all right. Little too serious, but—" He turned a hand over and raised an eyebrow. "Pietsch wouldn't hurt nobody. All he cares about, the triathalon twice a year and his wife."

"So they're clean?"

"I don't know they *clean*, Billy. But they ain't got nothin' to do with a asshole like Doyle, I know that." He pointed his finger at me. "You got set up, man."

"What else did you find out?"

He smiled and shook his head. "They got you off Boyd Street. Alarm went off in one of those toy warehouses. Pietsch and Stokes get there, you lying in front, covered with broken glass and stinking like old, cheap muscatel." He looked at me with mock disappointment. "Thought you a chardonnay man, Billy."

It was a pretty good set-up. It even looked like they were showing leniency, reducing the charges from breaking and entering to drunk and disorderly. Two honest cops, and it was their word against mine.

And my defense? Well, Your Honor, a high-ranking police official beat me unconscious and I guess he must have brought me down here and broken the window himself so it looked like I did it.

Why? Well—you got a minute, Your Honor?

We were at the car. Ed walked around to the driver's side and I climbed in the passenger seat. I had to move a huge pile of papers into the back. It didn't quite fit.

Ed's car was a 1967 Mustang. The engine and body were in perfect condition. The inside looked like somebody had dumped a filing cabinet onto the couch and then emptied ashtrays on it for a week.

Ed slid in, pushed the keys into the slot, and then just sat back. "So how come you ain't dead, Billy?"

I looked at him. He wasn't smiling now. He looked more like

the Ed I'd seen briefly at the Thai restaurant, the one you could still hurt.

"I thought about that a lot," I said slowly. "I think it works out like this. If somebody sort of credible is walking around saying Doyle is a killer and a racist, things could get tough for him. Even if there's no real proof, it could be enough to get somebody good to start digging into his background. And sooner or later, somebody would find something. Nobody is so good they can hide everything forever—he's got to know that."

"But if the somebody saying all that bad shit have a record of Drunk and Disorderly, and shows up barefoot, smelling like his ten best friends been peeing on him for two weeks, that's a little different, huh?" said Ed, nodding. "Yeah-huh, I can believe that."

"And in a way, it's better to have somebody saying this stuff if that somebody is hard to believe. Because that way if it comes up again, it's old news from a crank. So he makes sure I'm not credible anymore, and then the charges of murder and racism aren't plausible ever again. In a way, I'm a lucky break for him," I said. "As long as he can make me look bad enough."

Ed looked at me from the driver's seat. "Don't have too far to go with that."

"He's taking away my options, Ed. And I would guess that he'd have something cooking for you, too."

Ed started the car. "Shit," he said. "My ass already cooked."

"Maybe," I said, "but you better just drop me at the hotel and forget about me."

"Too late for that," he said. "What you gonna do? Go home?"

"I don't know yet. But not that."

"But you want me to?"

I looked him over. He was smiling, but his eyes showed the hurt again. It might be true what he said, that he was already marked by this thing. If that was true, then the only thing he could do to salvage his career would be to make sure I took Doyle down.

Besides that, the killings had hurt him, hurt the things he believed in, from the hope Hector had made him feel all the way down to his bedrock, the LAPD. He wanted in on the end of this, one way or the other.

The only problem with that was that I still didn't have a clue what I was going to do.

"All right, Ed," I said. "But drop me at the hotel anyhow. I need to think."

"Sounds dangerous," said Ed. "Considering how you done so far."

CHAPTER
TWENTY-SEVEN

I put my clothes in a plastic bag I found in the closet and threw them into the trash. Then I took the longest shower I can ever remember taking. After the first ten minutes I no longer felt like things were growing on me. The next ten minutes took most of the knots, bumps, and dead spots out of my muscles. The final ten minutes were just because it felt good.

Then I sat on the bed and picked up the telephone. I'd done an awful lot of thinking over the weekend, especially considering that I'd been surrounded by a group that was louder than the average college fraternity party and smelled even worse than the next morning at the same frat.

I'd thought mostly about two things: first, Doyle, and how to bring him down. I hadn't come up with a whole lot. He seemed to have all the chips and all the cards. On the other hand, I had moral superiority. I would have traded it for one thumbprint.

The other thing I had thought about might be a little easier if I could do it right. So I called.

"Hello?" Nancy said when the receptionist at the clinic put her on. Hearing her voice sent a wave of goose bumps over my skin.

"Hi," I said.

There was a pause. "I'm not sure I want to talk to you," she said finally.

"I know," I said, "and this sounds really stupid, but I can explain."

"Boy, I'll just bet you can."

"Nancy, listen, I'm sorry. I got caught up in something, and I couldn't call."

"Couldn't call? Really? And there were no telephones anywhere around?"

"That's right."

"Well, I'm sure the telephone company would *love* to know where you were so they can rush over and put in a pay phone," she said, and I could hear in her voice that she thought that was a pretty good line to hang up on.

"I was in jail," I said, as fast and clear as I could.

Another pause, a long one. Then that wonderful throaty laugh started and rose to a middle A before it stopped again. I realized I was holding the phone in a death grip, shoving the receiver hard against my head, so I wouldn't miss a note of it.

"It figures," she said at last. "All right, Billy. You got one explain coming to you. What were you in for?"

"Drunk and disorderly," I said. "But I was innocent."

"This just gets better," she said.

"I know how that sounds."

"Uh-huh."

I could feel it going against me. It was the same feeling I used to get in court, trying to explain how the good-looking, clean-cut guy in the well-tailored suit did all those awful things I had arrested him for, and seeing the jury eat up his innocent expression and admire his tailored elegance. No sale.

"Nancy, just give me a chance to lay this all out for you. None of this is what it seems."

"It never is," she said.

"Please," I said.

She gave it one more long pause, for effect or for real, I couldn't tell. I felt my greasy jail breakfast knot in my gut while I waited. "All right," she said at last. "Meet me after work. Six o'clock at my place."

"I'll be there," I said.

"You better be," she said, and hung up.

I lay back on the bed and thought about what to do with Doyle.

My first thought was to take the whole thing to Captain Spaulding. He would figure he owed me, and he was the ultimate stand-up guy.

The problem was, there was really nothing he could do. He would have to turn it over to Internal Affairs, and then it was back in Doyle's court and Doyle had enough muscle to squash it. If Spaulding investigated it himself, he would hit the same blind alleys Roscoe had hit.

I needed somebody with even more clout than Doyle. I could think of only one person. I didn't exactly have a warm relationship with him, but I was pretty sure he'd let me in the door.

I put on clean clothes, the best I'd brought with me, and headed out.

A police cruiser blocked the entrance to the small parking lot outside the hotel. The lights were flashing, and two officers stood beside my car, looking into it.

They looked up as I approached. "This your car?" asked the first one. He was maybe twenty-eight, white and baby-faced with a small, fuzzy mustache.

"It's mine," I told him. "Is there a problem?"

"Could I see some identification, please?" He asked it politely, but his partner had moved into the Academy-approved position to cover his partner in case I had a bazooka in my wallet.

I took my driver's license from my wallet and handed it to Babyface. He glanced at it. "It's him," he told his partner, and they drew their guns.

"Against the car. Move!" Babyface said. I leaned against the car.

"Am I allowed to ask what this is about?"

He kicked my feet apart, frisked me, and put his cuffs on my wrists without answering. "In the car," he said, and he walked me to the cruiser.

Three and a half hours later I was still wearing the handcuffs. I was sitting in an interrogation room at the Hollywood bureau where Babyface had dumped me while he filled out paperwork.

I had one anxious eye on the clock. I wasn't worried about spending another night in jail, but I didn't want to miss my appointment with Nancy.

The door swung open and a potbellied guy about forty came in.

He wore a cheap suit, a vague expression, and several gallons of cologne that smelled like he'd found it in the rest room of a disco.

"You Knight?" he asked, turning a chair around and leaning thick forearms on its back.

"That's right."

He put a grimy toothpick in the corner of his mouth and started chewing. "Detective Mancks. I'd like to ask you a couple of questions."

"Too bad," I said. "Because I don't have any answers at all."

He cocked his head to the side. "That so?"

"Yup. I'm afraid my lawyer has all my answers. He'll be happy to talk to you."

"I'm investigating a capital crime, Knight."

"And I bet you're doing a bang-up job, too." I held up my wrists with the cuffs on them. "This one of your investigative techniques?"

He licked his lips and shifted his eyes to the wall behind me. "I told them I had some questions for you. I guess they went overboard. I can get the key."

"Good to know. But I have some questions for you, too."

He looked cautious. "Like what?"

"Are you the Detective Mancks who's investigating Roscoe McAuley's murder?"

"Yeah. So?"

"So who's leaning on you not to find anything?"

He looked at me for a full two minutes. I looked back. It wasn't easy. Mancks had bad skin and bad teeth and couldn't decide if he should play hostile or dumb.

He finally got up. "I'll see if I can find that key," he said, and walked out.

Ninety minutes later a cop in uniform came in, a big, middle-aged guy with a red nose. "There you are!" he bellowed at me. "Nobody knew where you went."

He unlocked the cuffs and threw them on the table. "You can go," he said.

I rubbed my wrists and stood. "Anybody feel like telling me what it was all about?"

He gave me a big smile. "You got me, buddy. All I know is, you beat the rap, whatever it is. You can go."

I walked back to the hotel. If I hurried I could still make it to Nancy's by six. But as I came up Franklin in front of the hotel, another police cruiser went by. The cop in the passenger seat looked hard at me and turned to speak to his partner.

The car slowed and swung into a gas station at the corner and turned around.

I sighed. I knew what was coming and I knew why, but that didn't make it any easier.

Before the cops got back to me I ducked into the liquor store attached to the hotel and found a telephone.

"It's me," I told Nancy. "I'm having some problems."

"Really," she said, sounding unsurprised.

"Nancy, this is out of my hands. I'm about to get hauled off to jail again."

"My tax dollars at work."

"Can we make it tomorrow night at six instead?"

There was a long silence on the other end. I could see the two cops swaggering up to the glass door, adjusting their hats and nightsticks. "Please, Nancy. I don't have much time, but this is important."

"All right, Billy. Tomorrow night at six." She hung up.

There was a tap on my shoulder. My ride was here.

CHAPTER
TWENTY-EIGHT

This time I was in a holding cell. It wasn't as nice as the interrogation room, but at least I didn't have cuffs. Life is a series of trade-offs.

They kept me until ten o'clock at night, and then they let me go again, still with no explanation.

I didn't really need an explanation. I was getting the message loud and clear.

I needed to be able to move around to get Doyle. Doyle was not going to let me move around.

He had played it cautious, leaving me alive. He didn't know who else might know what I knew. But he could make damn sure I didn't learn anything else.

I made it all the way back to my hotel room this time. I called Ed at home and told him what was going on.

"Figured something like that might happen," he said. "What you gonna do about it?"

"I only have one move. I don't like it much, but it's all there is. Tomorrow morning I'm going to see a high-powered lawyer and lay out the whole thing for him."

Smoke hissed out into the telephone. "What's chances Doyle can get to this lawyer?"

"Pretty good, I'd say. You got a better idea?"

"Nope."

"Well then, wish me luck and watch my back."

"I'll do that, Billy."

Century City sticks up from a surrounding area of low, expensive homes. You can see it from ten miles away on a good day. But there are damned few good days in L.A., especially in August.

I took Olympic Boulevard west. It's usually faster. For twenty minutes I watched the dim fingers of the high-rises growing gradually cleaner in outline. I also watched my rearview mirror, but there were no cops following me this morning.

I pulled into the underground parking lot of one of the buildings just about ten. The sign told me that if I wasn't making about two and a half times minimum wage, I'd be losing money to park here while I worked. L.A. is the only place I know where you can have a job that you can't afford to go to.

Eli Woodstock had an office near the top of the building. It was behind a very plain door that said FINKLE WOODSTOCK & KLEIN. That was it; I guess anyone passing by would know that they had to be lawyers with a name like that. Or maybe anybody who didn't already know wasn't welcome.

I waited about twenty minutes in a small waiting room. For what they had spent decorating it, you could buy a three-bedroom waterfront house in Key West.

Eventually the receptionist, with a cool British accent, informed me that Mr. Woodstock might see me now. She said it like it surprised her—a man like Mr. Woodstock actually seeing something like *me*. She watched me go inside like she was afraid I would stop and pee in the corner.

A woman I knew at one of the big record companies once told me a secret. If you know the system, a person's office tells you exactly, down to the small change, how much they make and how important they are.

The way it works is this: score so many points for a corner office, so many more for each window. A couch with a coffee table gets more points than a chair with an end table. A picture on the wall scores, if it's big and not too modern, and a potted plant counts according to its size.

Eli Woodstock's office was the grand prize jackpot. It was a corner room. Two entire walls were glass. On the other two walls hung four paintings. If they weren't fakes, I had to assume that museum directors would be very polite to this man.

There was a kid leather sofa with a marble coffee table that matched it, and three citrus trees bearing fruit in huge pots.

A short person would get lost in his carpet. Eli Woodstock was tall, even behind his massive slate desk. He still looked like an Episcopalian bishop.

The last time I had seen him, he had been smiling gently, gravely, trying to get my signature on a release for the city. He was not smiling today.

"Mr. Knight," he said, and there was a lot of disapproval in his voice. "Sit down, please."

It was not a request. It was closer to the tone a bailiff uses on a prisoner in court.

I sat in a chair that cost more than my car. He looked at me without blinking for three minutes, his hands steepled in front of him. Then he shook his head.

"Well," he said. "What can I do for you?" He said it in a dry, distant voice, a voice that doubted there was anything I might want him to do that his morals would let him do.

I took a deep breath and told him. I knew it was going to be an uphill battle and that didn't matter. I was used to that.

I laid it all out for him: from Roscoe calling on me in Key West, all the way through my visit to Doyle and my stay in the drunk tank, the visits to the Hollywood bureau. I told it carefully, objectively, without getting emotional or speculating too much. I made one hell of a case.

He let me finish. He made sure I'd told it all to him. He even waited another three minutes when I was done, looking at me over his bridged hands, just in case something else occurred to me.

Then he let me have it.

He shook his head at me for a good half-minute, slowly, elegantly, the gesture filled with upper-class contempt. "Mr. Knight," he said at last, "what is it you expect of me?"

"Aside from the fact that the City might have a problem here, I was hoping you might want to see justice done," I said.

Eli Woodstock laughed. It was a rich, beautiful theatrical laugh. It was a laugh that was all about affecting other people and not at all about enjoyment or happiness. It was supposed to make me feel two inches tall, but it didn't work. I was still well over a foot and a half.

"Justice," he said, with one of those little twists to the word that juries eat up. Now it was a naive dream. *"Justice."* Now it was a curse, a beautiful absolute that I had violated. He shook his head again, a little faster this time.

"What would you consider to be *justice,* Mr. Knight?" He didn't leave any room for me to answer. "Is it your idea of justice to see a dedicated police officer dragged through the mud and possibly damage his career because of your half-baked, groundless, baseless slander? Is it justice to sacrifice Mr. Doyle on the altar of your greed for vengeance? Is that what justice means to you, Mr. Knight?"

I didn't know whether to applaud or throw myself out the window. "What greed for vengeance are we talking about here?" I said politely. "Just so we're all on the same wavelength."

He gave me a knowing smile, almost a smirk. "I think you know what I mean. I think we offered you a more than fair settlement, and you turned it down. For someone in your position to turn down that kind of money? A *fisherman?"* He shook his head, a wise smile on his lips. "I don't think so. I think you must have had something else in mind, even then."

"And this is it?"

"This is it."

I had to think that my hearing was bad. Either that or somebody had slipped me some LSD. "You really believe that, don't you?"

He let the smile widen a little. "Is there a reason I shouldn't believe it?"

"You? No, I guess *you* would have to believe something like that. I guess being what you are, that's all that makes sense."

He held up a hand to cut me off. "Don't think I believe you're a bad person, Mr. Knight. Grief does funny things to some people." He said it in a way that meant, little, mean, dirty, and grubby types who couldn't play tennis. "Nonetheless we can't allow this to go any further."

"You think Doyle killed the McAuleys because of my grief?" I asked him.

"I think you've decided to make a little trouble for the City out

of grief. Understandable, in a way. Which is why I am again authorized to offer you a settlement for your original problem." He gave
me a new smile, an understanding one this time. "Not quite the
original terms, of course."

"And you really think I'll take the money and disappear?"

"You're going to disappear in any case, Mr. Knight. Either back
where you came from or into jail. And yes, I think that if you can
make a little money off all this, you'll be a happy man."

I stood up. "Nothing you can say or do would make me a happy
man, Mr. Woodstock. Just being in the same room with you makes
me want to wash my hands." I turned to go.

"Mr. Knight." His voice lashed at me. I looked back at him. "If
I hear any more about this from you, you are going to find yourself
in court, and then in jail. Is that clear?"

Now I looked at him long and hard. Cops develop resources, and
one of them is the Hard Cop Stare. I gave it to Woodstock, both
barrels. It was easy; I meant it.

I walked over to his desk. I got all the way there without sinking
out of sight into his carpet. When I was there I leaned both knuckles on his desk and put my face as close to his as I could get it.
Across that desk it still wasn't very close.

"I don't know what Doyle told you. I'd guess you're not in it
with him, because that takes a certain amount of warped passion,
and I don't think you're capable of any, warped or otherwise. I
think you're just a garden-variety, self-important slimebag full of
expensive insecurity and you don't really know anything, so you
think money is always the answer."

"Really, Mr. Knight," he started, but I stopped him. He had
already lost a little of the color underneath his expensive tan. I
could almost hear him thinking, *Nobody talks to me this way*.

"Yes, really," I said. "And I'll tell you one more thing. You can
go ahead and plan on seeing me in court. So *you* better find yourself a good lawyer."

He licked his lips, and I left him there.

I rode down to the parking garage, where two cops stood beside
my rented car. "William Knight?" they asked.

CHAPTER
TWENTY-NINE

I was parked in front of Nancy's building by 5:20. I had come straight from the Century City bureau, where once again I had sat in a room with no company until they decided I could go. Still no explanation. I wouldn't have waited for one even if they'd offered it. Carefully observing all the traffic regulations, I drove across town and found a legal parking spot in front of Nancy's building.

I spent thirty-five minutes grinding my teeth and listening to the radio. It seemed like all my doubts about coming to L.A were paying off double. I was getting nowhere with Roscoe's murder. I was actually moving backwards, since all I'd done so far was alert the killer so he'd be ready for the first serious attempt to nail him. That and building up a police record.

And then the whole thing with Nancy. I'd gone into it without a clue about what I was doing and bungled it from the first. If she was still willing to speak to me when I finished explaining, it would be a minor miracle.

The radio droned on about terrible disasters all over the world, while I droned on to myself about all the stupid things I had ever done, just to prove to myself that all this was no fluke. I was back to the first grade, the time I sat on a cactus on a dare, when it was time to go in.

At exactly six o'clock I was knocking on the door to her apartment.

The door swung open.

We just looked at each other for a long moment. I was holding my breath, waiting for her to slam the door in my face. She was holding her breath, too, maybe trying to decide if she was going to slam the door.

Then she let out a long sigh. "Come on in," she said. She held the door wide and I walked past.

I went over to the small sofa. The memories of it made me look up at her. She caught my eye and blushed. "Sit down," she said. "Would you like something to drink?"

"Yes, please," I said. "If you have a beer?"

"Of course," she said, and went into her small kitchen.

I sat. I could feel the sweat starting on my face and on the back of my neck. We had both settled into the stilted, careful formality of two lovers who, having broken up badly, now met by chance. That wasn't the start I needed.

Nancy came back in less than a minute holding a squat bottle of Miller's. "My brother likes this," she said. "I hope it's okay."

"Thanks, it's fine," I said. I wasn't going to taste anything anyway, not until I got through this.

Nancy stood for a moment, her eyes flicking to the empty space beside me on the couch. Then she stepped back and sat primly on the high-backed chair opposite. "Well," she said. "I believe you were going to explain everything?"

It was still freshly organized in my mind from my visit to Woodstock. I started at the beginning. The real beginning this time.

"There's a few things I didn't tell you," I said.

"I'm sure there must be."

"I was an L.A. cop for seven years," I said. "I was married. Had a kid."

It was tougher than I thought. I stopped.

"And now you've decided to go back to your wife," she said, with an I-knew-it-all-along tone of voice.

"Can't," I told her, looking away. "She's dead."

Nancy didn't say anything. I still couldn't look at her.

"They're both dead. My wife and my daughter. They were—killed. Caught up in something connected to my work. That's why I quit, started fishing for a living. To get away, as far away as I could get. I never wanted to come back here again."

"But you came back. Why?"

I looked at Nancy. There were spots of color burning in her cheeks. Her eyes were locked onto me, but I couldn't read her expression.

"A guy came for me. Roscoe McAuley. A cop I knew."

"McAuley—there was a Hector McAuley killed in the riots."

I nodded. "Roscoe's son. Roscoe wanted me to find the killer. I told him no. Then Roscoe got killed, too, and I had to come."

She shook her head. "Hector McAuley was—people are still talking about—"

"I know."

"And you were—that's why you came back to L.A.?"

"Yes."

Nancy looked at me. She chewed on her lip. I wished I could, too. "Have you found anything?"

I looked away again. "I know who did it, and how and why. I can't prove any of it. So I tried to force something. The guy is very well connected, and he was too much for me. I wound up in the drunk tank. Now he's got cops following me, taking me off to jail every two hours. No matter what I say or do now, it's going to look like I'm a crank. The kind who's always finding conspiracies under the bed. So I guess I've crapped out.

"I tried to tell the whole thing to a high-price lawyer the City keeps on retainer. I crapped out there, too. I've pretty much crapped out everywhere, all along the line, and I don't have any idea what I can do now."

"So you're going to quit?"

"Nancy, it isn't that simple."

"Neither is life. But you already quit on that, didn't you?"

"Yes," I said. She got quiet. "Until I met you."

Now she looked away.

"But I've run out of ideas there, too."

She didn't look back at me. Her head was turned to one side. I watched her neck muscles. The red color slowly left her cheeks. I heard a clock tick.

"What is it you want from me, Billy?" She said it so softly I could barely hear her. "I'm not here to be your savior."

"I know that."

"You can't just come barrelling into my life and take it over, that's—I have a lot of other things going on."

"I know that, too."

"Because it was—at first I thought we had something really happening, you know, and then when I thought you were squirreling out on me, I did some thinking."

"Okay."

"And I don't know if I am ready for the kind of relationship you represent, Billy."

"Okay."

"God-*damn* it, Billy!"

Our eyes met.

"Don't just sit there and agree with everything I say. *Talk* to me."

"Nancy—I was starting to care for you, a lot. And that scared me. And made me feel guilty. And I am caught up in something very tough and it's taking the heart out of me. I am at a dead end with both things. I don't have any answers anymore. I don't know if I'm capable of having answers."

There was a long quiet stretched between us. I could see the last of the day's sun slowly pulling its feelers back out the window. The traffic below was muffled but sounded lethal even four floors up.

I couldn't take the quiet anymore. "Anyway, that's what I wanted to tell you. I owed you an explanation. And an apology."

"Oh, stop it."

"I mean it. There might be things I've never talked about before. Maybe I took it for granted that you don't have to talk about them even if you're married to someone, and with you—I'm new at all this, Nancy. I don't always know what I'm doing with you."

"At the moment, we haven't decided if you're doing anything."

"There is that." I saw the beer sitting in front of me, still unopened. Mostly to have something to do, I opened it. I started to take a sip. Miller. Because her brother liked it.

I put the beer down.

"What's the matter?" Nancy asked.

"Nancy, I don't know what to do about us, except to say that I would like it to continue. I don't know how that would work, but I will try as hard as I can at making it work. But about the other thing—"

"The murders, you mean?"

"That's right."

"What about them?"

"What kind of reporter is your brother?"

Dan Hoffman was a dark, very handsome man with eyes that seemed to look right through you, even while he was being patient. He had Nancy's high cheekbones, and when he turned his head so the light caught it I could see the same golden highlights in his hair.

I went through the whole thing for him, the third time today. I was starting to get good at it.

He heard me out, leaning back in his swivel chair, fingers laced behind his head. He was a good listener. Once or twice he leaned forward and made a note on a yellow legal pad.

When I was done he didn't say anything for a while. Then he sat up straight and tapped a pencil on the desk. "Why are you doing this?"

"Because it has to be done. Because there's nobody else who can do it. Because—"

I stopped. Dan had started to hum softly: "The Impossible Dream."

"Sorry," he said. "But your name is going to be in this. And unless people can see right off where you are getting yours, they're going to keep looking. Or make up their own answer. Woodstock was just the first."

"I don't have an angle, Dan."

He looked at me for a while, nodding. Then he looked at his sister.

"How much can I trust him?" he said, as if he was talking about somebody in the next room. She swiveled around to look at me, and the two of them stared like I was an overrated painting.

"I'm not sure," Nancy said. "Pretty much, I think, but I can't be positive."

He looked back at me. "You have to know that I am bound by rules just as strict as those governing the police and prosecutors. I can't print something unless I can prove it."

"I know that," I said. "The point is, I don't have anyplace else to go with this. He's taken away my ability to move."

"So what do you think I can do?"

"I don't know if the murders are provable. Not in a way that will stand up in court, or even get a prosecutor to take it seriously. But I'll be goddamned if I'll walk away from it without sticking Doyle for *something.*"

"Membership in Die Bruders?"

"That's what jumped out at me. It's on the FBI list of subversive organizations and for an assistant chief of police to be a member is illegal."

"Is he a member?"

"I think he's the leader. Maybe you can prove that."

"How?"

"You would know that better than me."

"I'm just a lowly newspaper reporter."

"That's the first time I've heard modesty from one of you guys."

He laughed. It was a good laugh, a lot like his sister's. It didn't do the same things to me, but I could see that it came from the same source.

"All right, Billy," he said, and held out a hand. It was warm, dry, and firm. "I'll see what I can do. But it'll be a lot easier without having to explain why you're in jail all the time. You'd better disappear."

CHAPTER
THIRTY

I drove Nancy back to her apartment, mostly in silence. I felt good about what Dan and I had done. The feeling didn't last long.

When I pulled up in front of her building she turned sideways in the seat to face me.

"I'm not going to ask you up, Billy," she said.

"Oh."

"I don't think that would be right at this point. Because I don't know what I'm looking for from you."

"I know what I'm looking for," I said. "I thought I'd found it."

She looked away and nodded. "That's part of the problem," she said. "I don't think it's the same thing I'm looking for."

"We slept together once. That's pretty early in a relationship to decide all this."

"Meaning we should sleep together again and then decide?" She said it with a mean glint in her eye like she'd caught me trying to sneak a fast one by her.

"That's not what I meant, Nancy."

"Isn't it? Because continuing the relationship at this point means continuing sex, doesn't it? Which is a pretty convenient coincidence for you."

"Sex isn't the only issue here, Nancy."

"I'm very glad to hear that, Billy. Because as far as I'm concerned there isn't going to be any more."

"All right," I said. "Let's talk about the other stuff."

"Damn you, Billy," she said, and now she was crying. "Would you please just let go of me?" And turning away so I would not see her cry, she opened the door of the car and ran into her apartment building.

I watched her go. I felt like a cold dry wind was blowing through my bones. Long after she was inside I sat there, my hands on the steering wheel at ten of two, looking at the door to her building.

Everything was coming unglued. I had found Roscoe's killer and he had beat me up and put me in jail. Now I couldn't even follow up. I had to run for cover.

I had found one small hope for living again, and I had let that slip away, too.

And now I couldn't even go back to my boat, because everything had changed, the careful shell I had built up had been eroded by the dry brown L.A. air.

My hiding place was exposed, and so was the careful picture I had built up of who I was now. There was a recall order for the new, improved Billy Knight. Coming back to L.A. had brought me partway back to life, but that wasn't turning out to be a good thing.

I didn't know where to go, what to do, or even who to be. Every reason I had for living was slipping through my fingers like water.

I went back to the hotel. A police cruiser fell in behind me at Western Avenue and followed me all the way back. I parked in the small lot and waited, but they drove on past.

I went upstairs and packed. The suitcase closed easily. There was much less to put in than I had started with. I wondered if that meant anything. I wondered if the fish were biting, and if Captain Art had any charters for me. And I wondered how it was possible for a reasonably competent human being to screw up everything he touched so completely.

They were all tough questions. I sat on the bed and thought about them. When I couldn't think anymore, I called Ed.

He was at home. He picked up the phone on the third ring.

"It's me," I said. I told him what had happened with Woodstock, the cops, Dan Hoffman. Then I said, "I'm going home."

He let out what sounded like a half-pack of smoke, a long slow breath filled with pain and loss as well as smoke. "You done all you could, Billy," he said at last, like it hurt him to talk at all.

"It wasn't enough."

"It never is, Billy. You just stay careful."

Early the next morning I was on the Hollywood Freeway again for the last time, I hoped.

I hadn't slept much. I had a cold knot in my stomach and another in my throat. All night long I'd rolled around on the small, humpbacked bed, wondering what I could have done differently. I couldn't think of anything.

I never should have come here. I'd known that all along, but I'd come anyway. It didn't make me feel any better to know I'd been right.

I was out of the hotel before the coffee shop opened. I figured that was the only good thing to happen to me in a while. I wasn't hungry anyway.

I took the turn-off downtown onto the Harbor, and then onto the Santa Monica. Traffic was still light. The sun was behind me, throwing gigantic shadows on the road.

I took the Sepulveda Boulevard exit and headed north. It wasn't far. At this hour I even found a place to park.

I walked across the grass to the spot I was looking for. Two small granite markers stood side by side.

"Hello," I said. "I'm sorry."

I tried to think of something else to say and couldn't. That seemed to cover everything anyway. So I just stood.

In the movies, there is always rain falling in L.A. I guess the people who wrote the movies have never been here. Or maybe I was undervaluing them. It might have been wishful thinking. Maybe they felt like me. I could have used the rain, the cold and clean relief of it. But rain does not fall in L.A. Rainy season in Los Angeles is two days every three years.

So there was no rain falling on me, just the wind, the hard hot dry wind that pushes all the razor-sharp yellow air into one corner of the valley and leaves it.

There was no answer to any of my questions, either. There wasn't even anything to say. Just the wind.

I went back to my car.

★   ★   ★

L.A. wouldn't let go of me. I had to wait six hours in the airport before I got a flight. I sat in a cocktail lounge alternating between beer and coffee.

Everyone seemed to be happy about something. A lot of good-looking women seemed to be kissing men in expensive suits. There were more kids in the airport than I remembered seeing in a while.

I read the paper all the way through. It was hard work. Dan Hoffman had a story about a halfway house for battered wives. Darryl Strawberry was not expecting to play any ball this week. I didn't laugh at any of the funnies.

It seemed like several days dragged by before they finally called my flight. I left the paper beside a half-full coffee cup and an empty beer glass. It made a very depressing still life.

I was herded onto a full plane and crushed in between a very large grandmother who smelled like gin and a Cuban businessman who kept elbowing my arm off the armrest.

I know it's supposed to be a lot quicker flying west to east. But it seemed much longer. We made a stop in Dallas where we sat on the ground for over an hour. Nobody moved except the businessman. He elbowed me three times while we sat there.

The grandmother got up and went to the rest room. When she came back the gin smell was stronger. She smiled at me. Her false teeth were so white they looked as if they might glow in the dark.

The plane finally took off again. It was night when we landed in Miami. There were no flights to Key West until the next day. I could camp out in the terminal or take a bus.

It was a hard decision and I didn't know if I had any more hard decisions in me. I sat on a chair, drained.

There were signs all over the airport forbidding smoking in several languages, but there was an ashtray attached to my chair. A man sat next to me and lit up a cigar. He was about five-six, bald, and weighed four hundred pounds. After a moment he was joined by a buddy, slightly taller but just as heavy. He lit up and sat down, too. The row of seats wobbled and tilted.

I decided to take the bus.

We pulled into Key West at 4:38 in the morning. I had dozed

once or twice on the trip, each time jerking awake again, heart hammering, from dreams that were dark and full of pain.

When I got off the bus I felt like my skin was covered with a thick layer of grease. My eyes ached, my head felt large and dull, and that was all a lot better than I felt inside.

The parking lot behind City Hall, where the bus had dumped me, was deserted except for two or three of the citizens who had decided to sleep there. I looked around and blinked for a few minutes, trying to remember where I lived. I felt like I had just landed from another world.

I could feel myself slipping back into that dark sea where nothing mattered. I wanted to fight it, to hang onto something positive. I closed my eyes and tried to think of something good. I couldn't.

I walked up Simonton, across US 1, and got home just after five. The sun was lightening the sky just a little, but it didn't do much for me.

A man was sitting on my front stoop when I got to my house. He was scrawny and bald and wore a greasy nylon parka.

He stood up as I approached. "William Knight?"

"Who are you?"

"Are you William Knight?" he insisted.

I pushed past him and got the key in my lock. "That's right. And you're trespassing."

He looked pleased with himself. "Nope, this here is official business." He stuck a hand inside the soiled jacket and pulled out an envelope. "I'm a process server." He held out the envelope, looking smug.

I took the envelope. "All right, I'm served. Go take a shower."

He stood there watching me open the envelope. I looked up at him. He looked back for a moment. I took a step towards him. He flushed and stumbled backwards. He caught himself and turned to walk away.

I read the documents in the envelope. I was being sued by someone named Peter Schlosser. It didn't make any sense until I remembered Pete, my nightmare charter. He wanted half a million dollars in damages.

Welcome home, Billy.

I went in and fell onto the bed.

CHAPTER
THIRTY-ONE

I woke up late in the afternoon and lay on the bed until dark. After all that had happened, after the way it had ended, there didn't seem to be any point in getting up and doing anything.

Doyle would walk away from it all. He was probably in better shape than before I had started nosing, because now he knew where his weaknesses were. I had failed.

I had failed with Nancy, too. More than failed. A murderer was smug and untouched, and a wonderful woman had been hurt. Nice going, Billy. With an even hand, I had punished the innocent and rewarded the guilty. All I had really accomplished was to push myself back into despair.

I lay there with my eyes open until well past midnight. Then I got up and went into the living room. I stood in the middle of the room for a long time, trying not to think about it. I failed at that, too.

Around two-thirty I turned on the television and that seemed to help.

I was home for two days before Nicky found me. There wasn't much food in the house, but that didn't seem to matter much. I had a couple of cans of soup, and I hadn't really gotten beyond that state when Nicky came in on the third day.

There was an old movie on the TV. I'd seen it a dozen times, but that was okay.

I'd heard rustling outside for a half-hour, and once I thought I'd seen Nicky's chinless, beaked face peering in the window. But it seemed like too much trouble to get up and look. There was a movie on. I was comfortable in the chair. So I ignored the cautious taps and the increasingly energetic pounding on the door until finally he pushed his way in.

"Mate!" he said. His face was lit up with a cautious glow, like a little kid's on Christmas, not sure whether he was getting a new bike or a bundle of twigs.

"Hi, Nicky."

"You're a right sight, you are," he said. There didn't seem to be too much to say to that, and not too much point in looking for something. I watched the movie. After a long moment, Nicky sat in the other chair.

"Well, Billy. How'd it go out there?"

"You were right, Nicky."

" 'Course I was, Billy. Goes without saying. They put the wood on you, eh?"

I frowned. It was hard to concentrate on the movie with him talking like that. "What does that mean?"

"You got lumbered, mate. They put you in jail."

"How did you know?"

He tapped his huge nose. "Smell it on yer. The smell takes a while to wash off. 'Sides, didn't I say they would?"

"I guess so."

"It's all in the stars, laddie. All in the stars."

"Okay."

I sat for a while watching the movie. Nicky sat watching me.

"You going to tell me about it, Billy?" he asked finally.

"Maybe later."

We sat some more. The movie ended. The announcer said a talk show was coming on next. That seemed okay.

"Well, Billy. You ready to get back to work?"

I shrugged. "I don't know." The talk show started.

At the first commercial in the talk show Nicky stood up. He looked worried, but I was watching the commercial. I hadn't seen it before. "Billy," he said. "Listen, old son, I know this has got you down, but you've got to let go of it. Get out of the house, get back to normal."

I glanced at Nicky. "This *is* normal," I said, and went back to watching the show.

He stood there looking down at me for a long spell. "Oh, mate. Oh, Billy," he said at last. He sighed.

"I'll be fine, Nicky."

He didn't say anything for a while. Neither did I.

"Well," he said at last. "I'll see you later, then, all right?"

"Okay, Nicky."

From the corner of my eye I could see him. He stood and watched me for another moment, then shook his head and left.

I watched the show. After that there were some cartoons, then the news.

Nicky came back that night and left me a big pot of stew, but there was a movie on and I didn't get around to it.

In fact there was stuff to watch all night long, and it seemed like such a big effort to get up anyway, so I stayed in my chair and watched most of the night.

The next day was about the same. I thought about getting up and going somewhere, but I couldn't really think of anywhere I wanted to go. I realized what I was doing wasn't good, that there was something wrong with me, but I couldn't think what it was or what to do about it, and anyway there was an awful lot to see on television.

Again in the evening Nicky brought food over. I didn't look at it. He tried to talk for a few minutes, and once or twice I let him. Then he took yesterday's stew and went home.

That night around ten the telephone started ringing. I almost got up to answer it, but there was always something on the television. Around two A.M. it stopped ringing.

The next morning I felt a little hungry for the first time. I went in the kitchen and looked at the food Nicky had brought. It was spaghetti. It was cold. I decided I wasn't hungry.

I went back to the TV just in time to catch a story on "Today." It was breaking this morning in Los Angeles.

Seemed an assistant chief of police was accused of being the leader of a paramilitary racist organization. Civic leaders had already called for his resignation, but Warren Francis Doyle had disappeared in the face of several serious indictments and nobody knew where he was. It was speculated that he had already left the country. A massive manhunt was on for the fugitive.

I got up and got a plate of spaghetti. It tasted pretty good.

"Today" ran the story again. It was a big story. Even Bryant Gumbel tried to look serious. I didn't. In fact, my face felt almost like it was smiling.

When the commercial came on I yawned and turned the TV off.

"Yippee," I said to myself.

I dozed off in my chair. I woke up to an unearthly roar outside my window. I blinked a few times, but the sound didn't go away and I was awake. I got up and looked out the window.

Art was seated on a Harley Davidson 1250 Electroglide, as far as I know the biggest bike Harley ever made. Nicky was perched behind him. Art was revving the motor. I had heard Art owned a Harley. He had supposedly ridden it into town thirty years ago and decided to stay. I had never seen him on it. I had never seen the bike at all.

In fact, the shock of seeing Art anywhere but on the stool in his dockmaster's shack made my jaw sag.

He revved the engine a few more times, kicked down the stand, and climbed off. Nicky bounced off and followed him up to my front door.

I swung the door open. Art stood there gasping like a spent fish.

"Billy," he wheezed. "The hell you doing in here."

I just stood holding the door, still too shocked to speak.

"The hell out of my way, then," he said, and lumbered past me into the house. He barely fit through the doorway. "Got a chair in here?" He answered his own question by sinking deep into my easy chair. The chair groaned and settled several inches lower than it ever had before.

Nicky scuttled in behind Art, hopping anxiously around like a very small puppy following a St. Bernard. "G'day, mate," he murmured and whisked off into the kitchen, looking guilty.

"Billy," Art puffed from deep within the chair. "Nicky says you're watching television." He said the last word with disgust, like he didn't really believe it was possible. He made it sound like somebody had accused me of having sex with farm animals.

"I was," I told him.

"Jesus Christ," he said. "What the hell for? Can't have that shit.

Billy," and he pointed a huge plump finger at me, "got to get the
fuck off your ass and get back to work." He shook his head, sending several chins whirling in opposing directions.

"All right, Art."

"Just like that, huh?" He turned towards Nicky, who was hover-
ing in the kitchen door, and let loose a rattling laugh. "This little
shit weasel was shitting his pants," he said, pointing an enormous,
drooping arm at Nicky.

"He was catatonic, Art, I swear it."

"I'm okay, Nicky. I was just—tired."

"Horseshit."

"Doesn't matter," Art rumbled. "Important thing is to get to
work, make a little money." He winked at me, looking like Santa's
evil brother. "Got a call this morning. Asked for you by name.
Tomorrow morning, brother. You're going fishing."

"Sounds good. Thanks, Art."

"Thanks." He looked insulted. "The fuck is that, thanks.
Gimme a fucking beer, you want to thank me."

I looked at Nicky. "Do I have any beer, Nicky?"

He shook his head sadly. "Not a drop, mate. Not even one of
those horrible weak pathetic American imitation beers."

Art snarled at me. "What kind of dickless dumbo runs out of
beer, time like this, Saturday morning?"

"Nicky," I said.

He cackled, his huge eyes almost out of his head with glee. "I'll
just pop next door and get a few, mate."

Several hours after Nicky and Art left, I was stretched out on the
bed asleep when the phone rang. I fumbled up out of dreamless rest
and grabbed at the receiver beside the bed.

"Hello?" I managed.

There was a familiar hiss of breath down the wire. "Well," said a
smoky voice. "Thought you'd gone fishing or something."

"Ed. What's going on?"

"Tried calling you with this last night, but you weren't answering. Figured you should know, your name's on this story out here.
Doyle gonna know you dropped the dime on him."

"That's good to know," I said. "How'd you guys lose him?"

Ed chuckled. It sounded a little bit more like the old Ed, a little less strained and more amused. "He went and lost his own self. He's under house arrest, discreetly observed by an Officer Bowden, and he just ups and slips off."

"You mean he broke his word?"

"His word," said Ed, and I heard him light a new Kool, "and Officer Bowden's neck."

"Oh," I said. I remembered the terrible speed and strength of those hands. "Where do you think he went?"

"Well, Billy, I can only guess he's gone out of my jurisdiction."

"Good guess."

"But since part of the indictment is federal, I talked some FBI guys into putting a watch on his boat in Texas."

"Good thinking."

"Only half-good, Billy. We got a missing-presumed-dead federal agent on our hands, and that sailboat's gone, too. Got to figure Doyle is taking his self a little vacation."

"Well," I said, "I guess it was too much to hope he'd stand trial."

"Yeah-huh."

"He'll be on his way to Central America by now."

"He could be, Billy. He could be. They got a watch on every port in the Caribbean, all up and down South and Central America. Makes me feel safe." I could almost see that Cheshire grin through the cloud of smoke. "But I'm out of it now, and you are too. One way or another, this is about wrapped up now."

"I guess you're right, Ed," I said.

But Ed was wrong. We both were.

CHAPTER
THIRTY-TWO

Sunday morning at five A.M. I was already motoring slowly out of the channel and under the bridge.

The weather was good, in spite of a hurricane thrashing around in the Caribbean. They thought it might be a big one, and they were calling it Andrew. It was expected to move in on the mainland sometime in the next two days, but I didn't think it would come anywhere near Key West.

Of course, you don't have to be near a hurricane to get some bad storms. Every place within three hundred miles of the eye could be in for bad weather.

But this morning the seas were still calm and I had a charter who wanted a tarpon, no matter what.

My charter was two guys in their mid-thirties, very tan and fit-looking. They said they didn't get seasick; they seemed to think that the idea was a little bit funny. So I opened up the throttle and headed for the Marquesas. If the weather turned bad, we were less than a half-hour's run from shelter.

The two guys, Bill and Bob, didn't say much. They just sat on their seat. Every now and then they would turn their heads slightly to look at something, but other than that they just sat quietly.

They'd been quiet since climbing onto the boat at the dock in the pre-dawn dimness. They'd been there when I arrived, standing beside the slip with a nylon gym bag apiece. They didn't want coffee or anything else from the dockmaster's shack. "Let's not keep the fish waiting," Bill had said. Bob had given him a small "huh" of laughter, like that was a pretty funny thing to say.

The sun was one thumbnail's width up over the horizon when I throttled back in the big lagoon in the center of the Marquesas. "All right, gentlemen," I said. "The tarpon will be coming in the channel and up across the flats to feed. I'll be on the platform over the engine, watching for fish. When I see tarpon, I'll get you close and one of you will cast to it. Any questions?"

They turned four blue, expressionless eyes on me. For the first time I felt a small twitch of alarm somewhere deep in the part of my brain that doesn't need reasons. They just looked. Nothing showed except maybe very faint amusement. "No questions," Bob said at last.

The rising sun was showing a storm front moving by over the Gulf of Mexico. Faint flickers of lightning showed between the dark line of the clouds and the water. "One other thing," I said. "If that storm gets close, we head for shore until it's gone."

"We don't want to get wet?" Bill asked with poker-faced amusement.

I was unlashing my guide pole, an eighteen-foot-long pipe I used for pushing the boat quietly across the flats. I held up one end of the pipe for Bill to see. "It's made of boron," I said. "Boron is an excellent conductor of electricity. If I'm holding onto the pole in a storm, I could get fried."

"We wouldn't want that," said Bill.

"Let's hope the storm stays away," added Bob, and they again looked at each other with secret amusement, like they knew something very funny and weren't supposed to let on.

We fished for two hours. They were both pretty good by then. They picked up the physical skills without any trouble, and neither one of them seemed to have any problem with patience.

One other time I felt that small stirring of alarm. Bob had a tarpon on, a good-sized one. He had fought it up to the boat after a couple of spectacular leaps. I hauled it up for him to see and to photograph if he wanted.

He didn't want any pictures. As I turned away to release the fish, I heard Bill say softly, "If he'd made another run I'd have cut the line. You can't get tired out."

"I'm fine," Bob told him.

Tired out for what? Not my business. I thought it must be another private joke. Still, the way they said it was not very funny, not even to them.

But right then the fish had given a lurch in my hands and I needed all my concentration to hold on to the tarpon until it was revived enough for me to let go. By the time the fish swam away I'd forgotten the remark.

Just about the time the tide started to change and the fishing slowed, a large sailboat glided into the lagoon. It was an Alden fifty-four-footer, a beautiful boat.

"Right on time," Bob said.

They both turned to look at me, heads swiveling as if they were connected. Both faces had the same bland, smug look of disciplined amusement.

"Tide's changing," I said, trying to figure out why the hair on the back of my neck was rising. "We could head out to a wreck that's not too far. Try for some other fish."

"I think we'll stay right here," Bob said, and Bill added a quiet "Heh," as he bent over and zipped open his gym bag.

I was standing on my platform above the motor, the long boron pole in my hands. I could see clearly down into Bill's gym bag. It did not contain the sorts of things I expected—extra shirt, jacket, suntan lotion, snack foods.

What it did contain, among other things, was a Glock 9mm automatic pistol with a large silencer on the end.

Bill removed the pistol without any real hurry and aimed it at my belly button. "Okay, mud-boy," he said. "It's showtime."

As he spoke, Bob was bending to his gym bag. I had a feeling he wasn't going to come out with a candy bar, either.

Mud-boy. A Glock 9mm. The sailboat gliding in on cue.

"That sailboat's gone," Ed had said.

And here it was.

I may not be the smartest guy who ever lived, but I have never felt quite as stupid as I did right then.

Doyle gonna know you dropped the dime on him. And then of course he would come and look for me. Key West is on the way to a lot of really good hide-outs. Especially if you're going by boat.

And if you have a small score to settle, settle it in beautiful Key

West. Enjoy the fabled hospitality of our tropical island paradise while you kill the guy who brought you down.

All this flashed through my mind as I watched Bob bend to his gym bag.

At the moment the odds were me against one guy with a gun. It wasn't going to get any better.

There's a foot control for the small electric motor I sometimes use to move the boat silently. I stepped down on it. The boat gave a very small lurch; not much. Just enough to make Bill lose his balance for a half-second and take his gun off line. When the gun moved, so did I.

I swung the pole as hard as I could. It's a big pole, but pretty light, and it whistled towards Bill's head with surprising speed.

Surprising for Bill, anyway. It caught him right on the ear just as he recovered from the boat's movement. He dropped the gun, stunned.

That was all I needed. I leaped on his partner from my perch five feet above. He was straightening and turning, having heard the gun drop to the deck. I landed on his back and brought him smashing face-first into the hard hull of the boat. Blood squirted from a broken nose. But he didn't move.

Bill moved, though. He had recovered from the whack with the pole. He jumped onto my back and got a chokehold on me.

I drove backward hard with both elbows and felt the right one connect. Bill gave a very satisfying grunt of pain, but he did not let go.

I stood. He clung to me, increasing the pressure on my throat. I was starting to feel it. The world was growing slowly dark and I knew I didn't have much longer before I blacked out.

With my last strength I lunged backwards, smashing Bill's back into the guide's platform.

He gave a kind of crushed gasp and slid off my back.

I managed a deep breath and turned to him. He was lying on the deck, momentarily stunned. I leaned over him, doubling my fists together, and whacked his chin with everything I had in a double haymaker.

Bill's eyes closed.

I turned. Bob hadn't moved. His breathing was regular but shallow. His breath bubbled through the smashed nose.

I took a hank of steel leader from my tackle box and wired their wrists and ankles together. While I worked I thought as hard and as fast as I could.

Doyle was on the sailboat. At any moment he might notice that the wrong guy was still standing. I didn't know how many others might be on the boat with him.

The smart thing to do would be to radio the Coast Guard—but wait. Doyle could overhear on his radio. So what I should do is get away from Doyle and his boat as quickly as possible, and then use the radio. With my superior speed I could easily keep him in sight and outrun the sailboat long enough for help to arrive.

Mind made up and visitors safely wired to their seat, I stepped to the controls and started the engine.

I could see some movement on the deck of the sailboat now. For once, I was just in time. I steered for the channel and opened the throttle wide, putting distance between me and the sailboat.

Over the roar of the engine I heard a flat crack, then three more in rapid succession. They were closely followed by four solid-sounding *ka-thunk!* sounds. The engine coughed, lurched, and stopped.

My engine was trailing four neat plumes of smoke. The boat glided to a stop.

I looked back at the sailboat. About one hundred yards away, it lay still in the water, anchor line taut off the bow.

Even from this distance there was no way to mistake Doyle. He stood beside the mast, rifle cradled casually in his arm. He turned his head and said something, and a moment later an inflatable boat came around from the far side of the sailboat and headed at me.

Three men sat in the boat. One held a hand on the steering arm of a small outboard. The other two, carrying what looked like assault rifles, sat in front of him.

I picked up the Glock from where it lay on the deck. I think I had some idea about sinking the inflatable. But as I raised the pistol there was another sharp crack and the control panel beside me exploded.

I looked at Doyle. He was sighting down the barrel of his rifle. I could feel the crosshairs centered on my chest. I got the idea: he was a very good shot. I put down the gun and waited for the dinghy.

It didn't take long for the inflatable to reach my wounded skiff. One of the storm troopers was crouching in the bow and leaped onto my boat, his aim never wavering from my midsection.

He moved his head in a very fast glance at Bill and Bob, then locked his stare back on me. "Carl," he said, and the other trooper climbed aboard.

"Shit," the second one said. "I told him Otto would fuck it up."

"Tie his hands," the leader said. Carl found the wire leader in my tackle box and did a very good job tying my hands. I could feel them turning blue.

"Untie those two," the first man said. He gave a slight nod of his head at the two clowns I had wired to the seat.

"Fuck-ups," Carl said. But he knelt and twisted the wires off. When he was done he looked up at the first man and said, "Okay."

"Stay with them," he was told. "Move this boat over to the *Battle.*"

"The *Battle?*" So that was the name of Doyle's other sailboat. "Wouldn't the *Retreat* be more like it?" He ignored me.

"How about the *White Flight?*" I asked him.

"Into the boat," he said, waving the gun towards the inflatable.

I shrugged. Whatever Doyle had in mind for me, it would give me a better chance than getting cut in half with a burst from an assault rifle. I got in the boat.

The trip back to the *Battle* was quick. The man with the assault rifle kept it pointed at me. He didn't even blink. I sat between him and the guy at the motor and looked for openings. There weren't any. I couldn't even think of any really cutting remarks.

Doyle stood on the deck watching us. He wore that same patient, understanding smile. As we got closer I thought there might be a little bit of strain to the smile, but that could have been wishful thinking.

"Billy," he said as our inflatable bumped up against the side of the sailboat. There was real happiness in the voice. That didn't make me feel great. "Come aboard."

"Thanks," I said, as if I had a choice. Doyle put one foot on the boarding ladder, reached a hand down and grabbed me by the belt and lifted me aboard, making it look very easy.

When I was on board Doyle leaned over and spoke to the leader of the two in the inflatable. "Where are Otto and Frank?" I guessed he meant Bill and Bob.

The leader shook his head. "They were wired to the seat. I left Carl with them. He'll bring the skiff over."

Doyle nodded. "Well done." He said it to me, too, as if he was pleased that I'd overcome two of his men. And he spread an arm towards the companionway and said, "Come below, Billy."

I stepped down the stairs and into the cabin. It was tall enough to stand in, with room to spare. Doyle had spent a lot of money on the best gear. The navigation station was state of the art, with every imaginable boat-show toy, and a few I didn't even recognize. The cabin was made of half a teak forest, lightly upholstered.

"Well, Billy," Doyle said, coming down the steps to join me. "You put quite a kink in our organization."

I sat on one of the benches. "That's good to know."

He nodded. "Quite a kink. So I hope you'll appreciate what I have to do."

"You mean kill me? No, I don't think I can really appreciate that."

He sat opposite me and lowered his voice. His eyes locked onto mine, and again I couldn't look away. I was holding my breath to hear what he said. I felt like I was about to be let in on big things. It was like talking to the coach, the principal, and the minister all rolled into one.

"That's just a detail," he said.

"Not to me."

"I'm only doing what I have to do as a leader of the movement. It's expected of me to set an example, take revenge. So I have to."

"Was Hector McAuley revenge, too?"

He smiled politely. "No, that was showing off. When there's an obstacle to our goals, I sometimes remove it myself. I like to set an example for my men." He leaned forward confidentially. "And I have to tell you, Billy. It was fun. We come alive in danger, have you noticed? At least I always have. It's a way to measure myself, to try to find my limits.

"I got tremendous *personal* satisfaction from hunting him like that. The area on fire around me, all of them would have killed me in a heartbeat if they'd seen me. His death was necessary," and he sat back again, looking very content, "but by God, I enjoyed it."

"And when Roscoe got on to you, you cut his head off."

The cheerful grin broadened. "Using a straight razor like that—you knew it was a straight razor?"

"I knew."

He chuckled. "And they say our movement has no sense of humor."

"How did you get Roscoe to meet you in that alley?"

He shook his head, amazed and amused. "Incredible, isn't it? A black cop with no street smarts at all. Moss called him and said he wanted to turn state's evidence. But he was afraid for his life and needed to meet where I would never see them together." Doyle chuckled. "He swallowed it. Can you believe that?"

"Hilarious. I hope it's just as funny when you kill me."

He shook his head. "No, Billy, killing you won't be fun."

"Sorry to hear it."

"I owe it to my men, to our organization. You forced my hand. But I don't want to kill a good, strong, righteous white man like you, Billy. You're doing what you think is right, and that's a rare quality today."

"I've noticed."

"But I can't always do what I want to do. The needs of our organization come first."

"Nice to know I'm advancing a cause," I said.

"If I thought I could convert you, I would, Billy."

"I don't think so."

He leaned closer. "You say that automatically, and that's to be expected. You are a product of our times, and our times have prohibited all of us from thinking independently."

He smiled. It was dazzling. "I don't come at this cause from ignorance, Billy. My convictions are a result of years of study, thought, and observation. I was like you once."

"Hard to believe."

"But true. We all start as liberals, because liberalism is a picture of the world as we want to believe it is." He shook his head. "But it isn't, Billy. You know that. It isn't that way at all." He put a hand on my shoulder. "The world is not the way we want to believe it. Look at what happened to you."

He gazed at me, a look filled with compassion and strength. "I read your personnel file, Billy. I know what happened to your family."

He looked. I had nothing to say.

"Would white men have done that, Billy? Good, honest, God-fearing white men? I don't think so."

"Good, honest, God-fearing black men wouldn't either," I said, struggling to break his spell.

"Of course not," Doyle said. "And there are many of them, I'm not denying that. Because the white social order is powerful, and it has converted some, brought some up out of darkness. But the unreachable, the ungovernable, the ones who don't just live at the bottom but drag the rest of us down—there are a lot more of them.

"And they are winning! Against all odds, the weak minority is overcoming the powerful majority, Billy! Something like that doesn't just *happen,* Billy! It's *made* to happen!"

"Sure," I said. "The international Zionist conspiracy."

"That's only part of it," he assured me. "The fact of the matter is, the rest of us *make* it happen. Through intellectual and moral laziness. The greatest sin is the failure to act rightly, and we as a society have committed that sin. We could stop this headlong slide into the gutter, and we don't. Because we are unwilling or unable to look at the problem and call it by name.

"It's a *race* problem, Billy. If you look at this historically, dispassionately, you will notice all our problems started with integration. It was at that precise moment in time when our decline as a society began. Is that a coincidence? Or is it simply the crystallization of the final struggle, the battle lines drawn? If you could *see* it without prejudice, you would see that final struggle for what it is—order and decency and all we represent as a white culture, against the anarchy and ignorance of the black culture."

He was just getting started. I could tell by the way his eyes were focusing on something in the distance instead of me. So I stopped him.

"Thanks," I said. "But I think you better just kill me."

His eyes refocused on me. There was no anger there, no hate, just a friendly regret.

"I want to make sure you understand your choice," he said with one eyebrow raised.

"I understand. If I won't *sieg heil* with you, you're going to drown me in crocodile tears."

There was a faint glint in his eyes. Something was funny. "There's more to it than that," he said. "I told you I'm only killing you for effect. So I have to get mileage out of it, the most bang for my buck." His eyes twinkled. "Learned that in the budget fights at LAPD." He leaned forward, the happiest guy in the world. "What I'm saying is, it's going to be a little bit of a spectacle, Billy. Not pretty, not pleasant. But effective. We videotape it, show it to the troops. An example of what happens to our enemies." He winked. "Public relations. Part of every administrator's workload."

I had no idea what he was talking about. That didn't seem to matter too much. I'd tuned out when his eyes had gotten distant and his face started to flush slightly from sincerity of his ideas.

Doyle was a true believer. He *knew* he was right, so he was sure he could find a way to convince me.

But I was more interested in finding a way out. As he talked I had looked around, hoping desperately for something, anything, besides what I knew was there: three heavily armed, well-trained men guarding the only exit, and between me and the exit a guy with apparently superhuman speed and strength who had already beaten me senseless once.

I didn't see anything helpful. But unless he shot me right now, I thought it had to get better—especially since he was planning to turn my death into some kind of pageant to boost morale.

"Okay, Billy," Doyle was saying. "I had to try. You're a warrior, and I need warriors." He shook his head with a friendly smile. "Besides, it's a shame that this has to happen to you twice."

Before I could figure that one out Doyle stood and took me by the arm. His fingers felt like what Captain Spaulding's grip would have been if the captain had been *really* strong.

"I could have forgiven a lot for a soldier like you," he said, dragging me towards the door of the forward cabin. "Even your moment of weakness with that black slut." He unlocked the door and frog-marched me in. "It's just too bad."

Someone was lying on the bunk inside the cabin. And as Doyle's words sank in and a cold knot rose up in my throat she looked up. "Billy?" she said.

It was Nancy.

"Just too bad," said Doyle happily.

For a moment I couldn't see, couldn't hear. I could only think, *Not again.*

I turned on Doyle as fast as a human being can turn. He was wearing that same friendly grin. I got one good shot into that happy face, a hard right hand with everything I had behind it.

Doyle took a half-step backwards from the force of the punch. I had the satisfaction of seeing his lip split open. Then he clubbed me with a right hand so fast I barely saw it.

I started to fall towards the bunk, but I never got there.

CHAPTER
THIRTY-THREE

I was pretty sure I'd been here before. The throbbing darkness was the same, and the cool hand on my forehead. The voice that was speaking my name softly had been there the last time, too.

"Billy," it said with a warm rum-and-honey tone. "Billy." The hand moved gently across my forehead. "Wake up now, Billy."

I floated up towards the voice—and towards a whole collection of pounding pains.

One of the oddest was the back of my head. It was throbbing, but I could feel that throb in my nose, as if the two places were connected.

My hands were pounding too. They felt like somebody had stuck them in large and awkward mittens.

"Come on, Billy," urged the voice. I swam up; I liked the voice, even though it was up there where everything hurt.

I got an eye open at last. My head was in Nancy Hoffman's lap. It seemed like a good place to be. I was just starting to enjoy it a little when she shook me out of it.

"You've got to get up, Billy. I think this is our only chance."

I thought it was good that we had a chance, but that *only* part bothered me. It was so hard to put it all together. "What . . . ?"

She slapped my face. It stung. That didn't seem right. I shook my head and a few cobwebs fell away. "Why are you here?" I managed.

"I came out of work and they were waiting for me. Just threw me in a car. I think they used chloroform. I woke up once in a small airplane, and then I was on this boat. Doyle thinks he can get back at you and my brother at the same time by killing me."

"The spectacle," I said. Nancy looked at me like she was going to slap me again. "Something Doyle said. He's going to make a circus out of killing us. Show the tape to the brotherhood as a lesson."

She bit her lip. "That doesn't sound like very much fun. I think we better get you on your feet fast. How are your hands?"

I looked at them. They really were too big, puffed up out of shape. I flexed them a little. They worked, but not perfectly.

"They were wired together. I got the wire off, but it may be a while before you get full use back. Can you stand?"

I tried. I managed to sit on the edge of the bunk. The room was heaving violently and I shook my head again to clear it.

But then I realized the room really was pitching. The boat, in what should have been a calm anchorage, was rolling frantically.

I looked at Nancy. "A storm came up," she said. "I heard them talking. They were planning to take us out into the Gulf Stream and drop us over after they kill us."

"That would do it," I said.

"But this storm moved in. The tail end of that hurricane, what is it?"

"Hurricane Andrew," I said. "It's supposed to miss us."

"Well, it's blowing pretty bad here, so they're staying in the lagoon overnight. They've all gone in the dinghy to set an extra anchor."

I sat up straight. "All of them?" It didn't seem possible.

"The two in your boat are dead." That would be Bob and Bill, or whatever their names were. "Doyle killed them and left them in your boat. He wants it to look like there was a fight and all of you died."

That would make sense. When they found my battered boat, it would look better if my charter was on board. Nobody would connect it to Doyle. Still, the brutality of it shook me.

"But there's only one guarding us," Nancy went on. "The rest of them are in the little boat doing the anchor."

I thought about it, which was still a little harder than usual with my head throbbing. But she was right. "It's not going to get any better."

She nodded. "I know that. Now here's what we do."

I looked around. There were two portholes, but they were tiny. Above was a hatch. I pointed. "The hatch is our only way out."

"Will you be quiet a moment? I've been thinking about this. The guard knows the hatch is our only way out, too. Besides, it's locked from the outside."

"Then how—?"

She put a hand on my mouth. "Just hush, Billy. I'm going to start pounding on the hatch. The guard will yell at us to stop. I'll keep pounding. He'll think it's you pounding."

"Why will he think that?"

"Trust me, Billy. I was a tomboy, I hit hard. The guard will open the door. You'll be beside the door. When he comes in you'll knock him out. Can you do that?"

I checked my hands. I wasn't sure I could open a pickle jar with them, but I thought they might work as bludgeons. If the guard was Carl and not the one who didn't blink. "I can do that."

"All right," she said. And then she leaned forward and kissed me, hard, on the mouth. She pulled back again too quickly for me to do anything but stare stupidly. "Let's do it," she said.

I stepped over beside the door and flattened myself against the bulkhead. "Okay," I said.

Nancy stood on the bunk under the hatch and doubled her hands together. "Billy, *no!*" she screamed, winking, and then she slammed her fists against the hatch. "Please, *stop!*" She got into a good, strong rhythm, pounding the hatch. I had to admit, the pounding didn't sound like a slim, beautiful woman's.

"Hey!" the guard called cautiously. "Hey, knock it off." We were in luck; it sounded like Carl.

I cupped a hand to project my voice away from the door and roared something incoherent. Nancy screamed again and pleaded with me to stop, still pounding in a mad rhythm.

"All right," yelled the guard. "You're asking for it."

I heard him scrabbling at the lock. So far so good. I braced myself.

The door swung inward. And then—nothing.

He must be playing it smart, staying a step back from the doorway.

I looked at Nancy. She was frozen where she was, staring past me through the door.

"Get down from there, nigger," Carl hissed. "Where's the guy?"

Nancy shook her head.

"Where is he? I mean it!" Nancy flinched slightly.

"He's—hiding."

"Hiding *where?*"

She pointed down. "In the locker under the bed."

"Get him out."

She stood frozen for a moment, and then I could see her get an idea. I hoped Carl couldn't see it, too. "All right," she said, and got carefully off the bunk onto the deck.

The lockers were under the bunk. You had to lift the cushions off to get them open. That's what Nancy did. She lifted one of the six-foot cushions, turned toward me and, her face hidden from Carl by the cushion, she mouthed, "Now, Billy!" and shoved the cushion towards the doorway.

"Get that out of the way!" Carl shouted. The thing filled the doorway. I slid in behind it and pushed.

The cushion flopped forward onto Carl's assault rifle. In the half-second the barrel was aimed down I was on him.

He snarled and yanked up on the barrel. I moved inside, past the end of the gun, and chopped hard at the bridge of his nose. It wasn't a clean hit or he'd have dropped. He froze for a moment, dazed, and I rammed the heel of my left hand up under his chin and chopped hard at his Adam's apple with my right.

Carl gave a dry gurgle and dropped the rifle, clutched at this throat, and fell to his knees. I had hit him too hard and crushed his throat. He was dying. I hadn't wanted to kill him, but when someone is pointing an assault rifle at you, your options are limited and so is your compassion.

"Billy?" Nancy whispered from the cabin.

"It's okay. Stay there."

Of course she didn't stay. She stuck her head out at once and saw Carl, flopping and drumming his heels on the deck. It made my skin crawl. Nancy hardly blinked.

"Oh," she said. "Are you all right?"

"Fine." My hands were vibrating hard enough to stir cake batter. But my head was clear, probably from the adrenaline rush of combat. And maybe from the nausea of killing somebody. Anyway there wasn't enough time to feel bad right now. "I need a knife."

"Why? He's dying."

I moved through the cabin, searching. "The anchor line."

"Can't you just untie it?"

"The line will end in a length of chain. The chain will be bolted to the boat. I need to cut it. Find a knife."

I cautiously stuck my head up through the companionway and looked for the inflatable dinghy.

It was about a hundred feet away, straight off the bow. Doyle was looking over the side and one man sat beside him. As I watched, the third man surfaced beside them, wearing mask and snorkel.

They were setting the hook solidly by swimming down and ramming it hard into the sandy bottom. That was the safest thing to do in a bad storm. It also gave me an extra minute.

I looked behind. The *Windshadow* bobbed behind the sailboat on a short rode. A plan was forming.

"Billy?" Nancy called softly from below. I ducked under. "I found this in one of the bags," she said, holding up a knife that Crocodile Dundee would have liked.

I took it. "Hand me the rifle, too," I said.

Nancy stepped over Carl, who was all done kicking. There was a stench in the cabin. Carl was all done living, too. His bowels had opened in a very appropriate last gesture of defiance.

It didn't seem to faze Nancy. She picked up the rifle and handed it to me.

"All right," I said. "Come up here. And stay low."

In a moment we were crouched together at the wheel. I pointed to the controls. "This starts the engine. Push the black lever forward, the boat goes forward. Back is reverse, middle is neutral. It's in neutral now. The red one is power. Push forward to go faster."

"I think I can handle that," she said.

"I'm going to cut the anchor lines. The boat will fall off and start to drift that way." I pointed towards the gulf. "On my signal, start the engine, kick it in gear, and steer for that channel marker."

"What about Doyle?"

I patted the rifle. "I'm going to sink his boat. That gives us time to get away. The Coast Guard can come back for him later—he won't get far in this storm. He'll have to hole up on the island."

The wind was rising as I moved forward, and I was lashed by the first hard drops of a rain squall. The taut steel wires of the rigging were squealing. I crouched low, squinting against the wind and rain, and slid forward to the anchor lines.

The lines ran out onto a roller on the bowsprit. But I didn't need to crawl out that far. The lines came up through a metal fitting in the deck. I just had to get that far and cut them there.

I crawled along the deck, rifle in one hand and knife in the other. A sudden blast of thunder almost made me jump overboard. At the inflatable, the man with the mask came up for air again and Doyle said something to him. The man in the water raised a hand, said something, and then went under again.

I got to the two anchor ropes. The first line was holding all the boat's weight at the moment. I pulled carefully and eased the boat ahead, just enough to get two turns around a cleat. That way the boat would not lurch and give me away when I cut the first line.

I cut it. I reached for the second line. The man in the water was climbing into the inflatable. Holding the end in my hand, I cut the second line. I reached for the first and untied it, dropping both lines over the side.

The boat rolled immediately and fell off before the wind. Doyle looked up as the anchor line went slack. And then things started to go wrong.

"Now, Nancy!" I yelled. But nothing happened.

I turned back to Doyle, raising the rifle. But with no anchor to hold it, the sailboat had drifted in a half-circle and now the cabin roof was between me and the inflatable. I couldn't see over it.

"Nancy, start the engine!" I shouted again and scrambled over the top of the cabin.

A shot went past my ear with that flat popping noise you can never mistake for anything else once you've heard it. I hit the deck, inched around the mast, and looked.

The inflatable was fifty feet away and coming in at top speed. Doyle was crouched in the bow, a Glock in his hand. He snapped off another shot and the mast beside me gave a hollow bonging sound.

I had only seconds. I brought up the assault rifle, pulled back the bolt, and squeezed the trigger. I had aimed low, and the water in front of the inflatable boat churned with my shots before they started to connect.

Then the shots hit home into the rubber airbags of the boat. With a sudden lurch, the little boat folded in half and went quickly under, just as I ran out of rounds in my clip. Doyle was thrown forward and disappeared into the water.

I ran for the cockpit. Nancy was grimly grinding away at the starter.

"It's not working," she said, tense but not panicked.

"Doyle must have disabled the engine," I said, diving through the companionway. I handed up another of those damn Glocks that Doyle had so many of. "Watch for them," I told Nancy. "Shoot if you have to."

She gaped at me, but I was already into the engine. With a heavy sea rising, the reefs and mangroves on one side and Doyle on the other, I didn't want to spend one more minute without an engine if I could avoid it.

I found the problem quickly. Somebody—presumably Doyle—had removed the wire that ran from the solenoid to the glow plug. A quick security measure: with the wire pulled the engine might start eventually—if the batteries were strong enough to keep it turning over for a good five minutes.

I connected the wire, and jerked my hand back reflexively as I heard a sharp *pop*. But the sound had come from above. It was followed by three more.

I pulled myself out of the engine compartment so quickly I banged my head, right on the tender spot where Doyle had whacked me. Cursing, rubbing the spot with my hand, I stumbled on deck.

Nancy stood at the rail looking down into the water. "Are you all right?"

She nodded and turned a pale green face toward me. "I—he tried to come on board. So—" And she turned away and threw up over the side of the boat.

I would have liked to comfort her, but there wasn't time. The boat was drifting towards the mangroves. One small, innocent-looking mangrove root can drive a hole through any boat ever built, up to and including a destroyer.

I jumped instead for the controls and hit the starter. I held my breath, but the motor turned over and caught. I rammed it into forward and turned the boat out the channel.

Nancy was still leaning over the rail. She'd held up well, but to shoot somebody at point-blank range had taken her to her limit. There had been three of them in the boat, but I assumed it was Doyle she had shot. It had taken a powerful swimmer to overtake the boat in these seas.

And now he was dead. I couldn't feel bad. I knew Doyle would be turning up in my nightmares for quite a while. The power of his presence, the incredible strength of the man, and that guileless smile as he beat the tar out of me would haunt me.

For the next couple of minutes I was pretty busy. The storm winds were rising, gusting at what I guessed was over fifty knots. Lightning flickered, thunder banged, and the wind screamed in the rigging.

This was a tricky passage, with a lot of unmarked reefs and flats, and if I strayed from the channel I could end up facing a serious storm while aground. As soon as I got clear and Nancy felt good enough to take the wheel, I'd call the Coast Guard. No hurry now.

I'd beaten the odds. I should be dead, but I wasn't. Instead I was sailing away with a beautiful woman and a storm at my back. I'd slain the dragon, won the fair maid. I was going to be all right.

I suddenly felt better than I had in months, more alive, more hopeful.

That's when I heard Nancy call, "Billy! Look out!"

CHAPTER
THIRTY-FOUR

I spun around into a faceful of wind, rain, and lightning.

And Doyle.

Before I could more than blink stupidly, he was up over the transom and on me, swinging his open left hand at my face almost playfully, with that terrible speed and power.

I saw stars and dropped to one knee and in that brief moment he stepped past me and hit Nancy hard on the side of the head with the gun in his right hand. She dropped without a sound and lay on the deck.

As I struggled to stand, Doyle grabbed my collar and lifted me off my feet, holding his pistol in my ear.

"One of the nice things about the Glock," he said in a conversational voice, "is that it's waterproof. Recently most Miami police officers have switched over to it for just that reason." He could have been talking to a friend over lunch instead of standing on the deck of a pitching sailboat in a rising storm with a gun in my ear.

"I get the idea," I said. I looked for some sign of life in Nancy's still form. I didn't see any. A bolt of lightning slammed into one of the nearby islands two hundred yards away. The following thunder almost deafened me. I could barely hear Doyle's polite voice.

"I know you understand, Billy. I have been impressed by your intelligence and tenacity. But now is the time for you to realize you can't win."

"I was about to say the same thing to you, Doyle." There—had Nancy's chest moved slightly in a soft breath? Or was that wishful thinking? Would it happen again? Was I going to lose someone I loved while I stood by helpless?

Doyle smiled, that soft, fond-uncle smile again. "But I *can* win, Billy. And I will."

"Alone? In a hurricane? With the Coast Guard looking for you?"

He nodded. "Yes." To him it was that simple. And maybe he was right.

"I don't think so," I said, but it was hard to sound convinced. He still held me off the ground, apparently without effort. In the brief struggle he had turned me. I was now looking forward and he was facing the stern, where the *Windshadow* still bobbed in our wake.

There—Nancy moved, a small breath, I was almost sure of it.

"I think so," Doyle was saying. "This boat is rigged for single-handed sailing. I could solo it around the world if I wanted."

My eyes flicked from Nancy to the bow and my heart thumped with a small spark of hope.

The boat was headed straight for a shoal.

Keep him talking . . . just a moment longer . . .

"You can't sail through a manhunt. Every port in the Caribbean, Central and South America will be looking for you. You'll never slip through."

His gentle smile widened. He was a very fond grownup, proud of a child's cleverness. "Of course not, Billy. That's why I'm sailing to South Africa."

I blinked. Why not? If he was half as good as he seemed to think, if he had a little luck and missed the big storms, a boat like this could make South Africa easily. And he would certainly find friends there.

He nodded again. "I can see you agree. It's not a problem, really, is it?" The lightning and thunder blasted again. The rain blew at us in blinding sheets. Doyle sighed regretfully. "There's really only one problem left, and that's you, Billy. I'm afraid I can't wait to drop you into the Gulf Stream, so—"

The loudest sound I ever heard, far louder to me than the thunder, was Doyle working the slide on his pistol with it still in my ear.

"I really am sorry about this, you know," he said. I thought I could hear his finger contracting on the trigger. And then—

There was a terrible, crusty grinding sound and the boat slammed to a stop, hard aground on the shoal.

Doyle lurched, dropped me, and fell to his knees. I landed on my feet, knees braced. Moving as quickly as I ever had in my life, I took a half-step and kicked into Doyle's face as hard as I could.

He straightened. Blood spurted from his nose. Through the blood he smiled at me. I kicked again.

Doyle caught my foot and threw me backwards. I hit the frame of the companionway and lost my breath.

As Doyle stood I rushed him. My shoulder caught him in the sternum and he grunted, but then he had those terrible hands on my neck.

I slammed my head forward with all my strength. My forehead smashed into his already broken nose. I did it again, and again.

Doyle grunted and threw me down, hard. He raised a foot to stomp down on me and I rolled in the crowded cockpit, just enough to make him miss. The deck rang as his foot slammed down.

I clawed my way up the steering wheel to my feet. Doyle paused, looking at me. Lightning flashed behind him, outlining him in fire. The blood ran across his mouth and his fair hair stood out, giving him an eerie corona.

Very deliberately, Doyle placed his gun on the seat. Then he stepped forward.

Okay, he was saying. He'd give himself a little challenge. Test his limits. That's all I was to him, a light workout before dinner.

It was not even arrogant. It was a statement of how things were. If he got those hands on me again, I knew it would be over. I had to stay away, find some way to even the odds.

My thoughts flickered to the *Windshadow*. I had a couple of good knives on board, and some other tools that could do damage. For that matter, even a sturdy fishing pole could cut him up.

So as Doyle crouched and moved in on me, I jumped for the transom. One hand on the edge, I vaulted over the side into my battered skiff.

Quicker than I would have thought possible, Doyle followed,

and the skiff lurched under his weight as I scrabbled for my tackle
box.

The sailboat's engine was still grinding away, kicking up a small
surge of water and sand, which had pushed the *Windshadow* up onto
the shoal in about a foot and a half of water. Even though the
sailboat was hard aground, it was deep enough for the skiff, and we
bobbed and pitched as we scrambled for position.

I had one hand on my tackle box when Doyle jumped. I stumbled back just ahead of him, falling backward over something that
shouldn't have been there.

My hand closed on the obstacle—my guide's pole. Carl had not
secured it properly. It was lying loose on the deck, one end of its
eighteen-foot boron length sticking over the transom beside the
ruined engine.

I jumped up, holding the pole. Doyle grinned and waited for my
move. It was a savage grin this time, the blood from his nose turning his teeth dark.

I swung. Doyle ducked easily and the pole whistled past him. I
brought it around again in a backhand as fast as I could, but he was
ready.

He caught the pole and got both hands onto it. Grunting
slightly, he lifted and my feet left the deck. Before I could let go he
flipped me straight up into the air.

I was ten feet up, over the water. I let go. As I fell towards the
shallow shoal water, Doyle swung the pole and smacked me in the
head, hard.

I landed on my back and went under. It was only eighteen inches
to the bottom and I scrabbled sideways hard and fast to get away
from the grinding propeller of the sailboat. But before I could make
it to the surface the pole came down on my chest and pinned me to
the bottom.

I looked up through the wavering haze of the water and saw
Doyle standing far above me like some nightmare giant, rippling as
the water churned. He was backlit by flashes of lightning as the
storm moved closer.

I fought to get clear but he leaned forward, putting all his weight
on the pole until I felt sure it would burst through my ribs and pin
me to the bottom.

I knew I was fading fast. I had maybe one last chance. Doyle weighed about two twenty-five. The pole was no more than ten pounds. I could bench-press two fifty, three or four times on a good day. Simple. I told my hands to swim over and grab the pole just above where it was grinding my chest into dim gravel. My hands fluttered, a pale imitation of a breaststroke. *Come on,* I told them, mildly annoyed. *This is for all the marbles.*

The lightning flickered around nightmare Doyle. He was leaning harder now, probably bored and wanting it to end so he could pull the wings off some other fly.

My hands were very close to the pole now, but they were telling me they didn't much feel like gripping. I was losing consciousness, fighting to keep the blackness back—

But why fight, really? One small part of me was screaming not to give in, but the rest wasn't listening, was telling me to relax, let it go.

After all, wasn't it better this way? Wasn't it better to admit I had totally screwed up my life and just let it go, move to the back of the line, start over again? Besides, if there really was anything at all to this afterlife stuff, I'd get to see Jennifer and Melissa again. They'd be waiting for me, just the far side of the beautiful blue light.

I thought I could see the blue light now. It was flickering around Doyle. I raised up my arms to move closer to the blue light. *I'm coming, Jenny.* My arms drifted slowly away from the pole. I opened my mouth to let in a long deep breath of beautiful, life-taking water.

The weight lifted off my chest and I frowned. *That's funny,* I thought. I focused on the flickering figure far above me, the dim outline of Doyle-as-God. He was raising the pole straight up. He held it like a spear, ready to slice down through the water and end me once and for all, and I thought, *okay.* This solves everything. The pole started down.

And the world ended.

Lightning slammed into the pole. There was a tremendous explosion that I could hear even a foot and a half under the water, and Doyle disappeared. For one unbearably bright moment I saw him outlined in fire, and then he was gone.

I was thrown up out of the water, jolted back into choking, retching consciousness.

Up into life.

CHAPTER
THIRTY-FIVE

I stood in the shallow water with the storm howling around me for a full minute before I could make my body move towards the boarding ladder up into the sailboat. Small pieces of charred, blackened something littered the surface of the water nearby. I couldn't tell if it was Doyle or boat pole and I didn't want to know. I sloshed through to the boarding ladder.

I didn't think there was strength enough left in my hands for them to tremble, but that's what they did as I reached to feel for Nancy's pulse.

She had one. She was breathing. I killed the engine, moved Nancy below to a bunk. I found a spare anchor in a locker and managed to drop it off the bow. It would at least keep us from drifting away into worse trouble. It was all I could manage.

I dogged the hatch and fell down beside Nancy.

There was nothing left in me. I felt as weak as a baby. The boat shook in the storm, but I couldn't have done anything no matter how bad it got.

It didn't get much worse. The blast of lightning that had wiped away Doyle had been the peak of the storm. We rocked and lurched for another hour and then things began to get noticeably better.

I checked on Nancy one more time. Her breathing was regular, her pulse strong and steady. By then I couldn't keep my eyes open any longer, even if it meant that the boat would sink.

Just before I closed my eyes, completely drained of all energy and feeling, the last crash of thunder blasted in the distance and the pitch of the wind in the rigging dropped an octave.

I fell into sleep.

Art had grumbled. He'd called me a dick-brained butt-sucker. Said it was very bad for business to bring the charter back dead. I said at least I'd brought them back, and he'd grumbled some more, but it was just for appearances. He was impressed.

Nicky had hopped around with relieved anxiety, alternating between rubbing his face and giving me huge bawdy winks as he looked at Nancy. "Good one, mate," he'd said, looking her over with approval. "A keeper."

I told him I thought so, too, but that it wasn't up to me.

Nancy had a mild concussion and the hospital kept her overnight. I had three broken ribs and a number of sprains, cuts, and bruises. They didn't keep me, and Nicky drove me home in my car.

The storm had given Key West a thorough cleaning and knocked down a couple of old trees, but that was all. It was nothing compared to the beating Miami had taken, as we were learning from the news.

Many of the trees were stripped of leaves. Odd chunks of flotsam showed on the shore: chunks of wood, half a small boat, a five-foot shark, a bookcase, most of a piano, three cushions that didn't match. There was a strange, brand-new feeling to the world, as if everything before yesterday had been erased.

There was a sensation of hopefulness in the air. Driving through the strangely clean streets, people actually waved, spoke to one another, acted as though we were all in this together. The contrast to normal Key West was eerie.

I went back to the hospital on Stock Island the next morning to check on Nancy. She was sitting up in bed when I got there, chatting happily with one of the interns, a handsome black man from Jamaica. He grinned and sauntered off when I got there.

I sat beside Nancy. She was wearing one of those open-backed hospital gowns, and somehow she made it look glamorous. I wanted to take her hand but I felt oddly shy all of a sudden, as if the last few hours had wiped out what we had been through and left us the same people who had said goodbye in front of her apartment.

"Well," I said, "you look—" And I stopped because what tried to come out was *edible,* or *stunning,* and to have that trail off into something like *better* didn't seem right.

She seemed to understand. She gave me her second-best smile and said, "I am. They say the danger is past and I can leave today. Get back to my life."

She said it in a funny way and I twisted my head to see her face a little better. She gave a half-shake. "I don't think I want to get back to my life, Billy."

"Whose life would you like?"

She frowned. "I'm serious."

"So am I, Nancy." I took her hand. She didn't yank it away. "This is Key West. It has special magical properties. People come here all the time and live somebody else's life."

She smiled. "And whose life do you think I should take?"

"You can have mine."

The words were out before I knew I was saying them. Nancy turned her head sharply and stared at me. All the blood Doyle hadn't spilled out of me slammed into my face.

Nancy smiled. It was a little better than the number-two smile this time, with a touch of the devil in it. "I don't think so," she said. "I couldn't take all that getting hit on the head."

She had taken it as a joke, and maybe that was better. But now that it was out there, I felt I had to say it anyway. "Listen, Nancy—"

She squeezed my hand. "I know, Billy. But we both have some thinking to do. And some talking."

"I guess I know that. But I want you to know how I feel."

"I *do* know. And I'm not saying no to that, either. I'm just—" She shrugged and took her hand away. "I still don't know if it's possible for us to be together. If we want the same things."

"I don't know, either. But I'd like to try."

She turned to the window, where the morning sun was coming in off the bright green of the trees and the blue of the sky and the water outside the window. For a moment she seemed lost in the view. "Welcome to paradise," she whispered.

"Nancy, they would probably hire you here at the hospital. I asked."

"I know," she said. "I asked, too."

I took her hand again, and she gave mine a good solid squeeze.

I thought about what we had been through, and I thought about Doyle—how he'd come so close to killing us both, and how it was maybe only luck that he hadn't.

And I thought of all that had gone before, the trip back to my past. And the ghosts who lived there. I did not want to live with ghosts anymore. I wanted to live in the now, and I wanted that now to have Nancy in it.

And she might not be able to say yet whether she wanted that, too, but she was thinking about it. And as she turned back to me she was giving me her number-one smile.

I looked at that dazzling smile and felt alive, because for the first time in two years I had hope, and if hope was all there was, it was still better than living with ghosts.

"Penny for your thoughts?" she said.

I just shook my head and kissed her hand.

Sometimes hope is enough.